S0-BAI-039

Cumberland County

By John P. Schroeder

PARADIGM PRESS - 2000

 For more information contact Paradigm Press, PO Box 123, Ashland, Wisconsin 54806.

E-mail: pdpglov@win.bright.net

Visit us on the Web: http://www.booktraveler.com

Cover design by Jared Glovsky

Editing by Jared Glovsky and Lois Glovsky

Printed by Morris Publishing, Kearney, Nebraska

First printing

ISBN: 1-889924-05-9
Library of Congress Catalog Card Number: 00-90366

Book 3 in the *`Historic Preservation Series'*

Chapter One

A measure of life left the animal with each jump, the deep snow and fatal wound draining its great strength. Pain and fear could no longer motivate it. It struggled forward on instinct alone.

Not far behind, the two boys followed. The larger boy was leaving his brother behind. With a wave of his arm he shouted, "C'mon Whiley!"

The cold wind blowing across the field burned his face and caused his eyes to tear. Through blurred vision he saw the deer entering the woods on the opposite side of the field. The tracks told him the animal's jumps were shorter now. The color of the blood was deep and it was chunky.

Frank reached the other side of the field quickly and looked back. Whiley was still coming.

He made his way into the thicket, where the tall pines had spread their branches and caught most of the snow. The going was easier now. In the shallow drifts he saw where the deer had staggered. Frank marveled at the animal's ability to keep going. For a moment he even pitied it, but he shook those thoughts from his mind and concentrated on being the hunter.

Slowly he moved, stopping every few minutes to look and to listen. As silently as a ghost he stalked the animal. Crouched down, he brushed aside a low-hanging branch and was rewarded with snow down the back of his neck.

"Damn!" he muttered to himself. Everywhere the snow hung heavy on the branches, and though it made the going easier, it cut his visibility. He stooped down to look underneath. No good, the trunks were thick and dense. There was nothing he could do but follow the tracks and stay quiet.

Ahead he could see light, which told him there was a clearing. He felt it now...the surging feeling that he was close. His heart raced with excitement. Without even thinking he cocked his rifle. It proved unnecessary however, for moments later, there in the small clearing, lay the deer. Frank advanced cautiously. The beast's sightless eyes and stiff, protruding tongue told him it was over.

Exhaustion overwhelmed Frank. He stuck the rifle butt into the snow and dropped to his haunches. Despite the cold, trickles of perspiration ran down his sideburns. He took off his cap and wiped his brow with his jacket sleeve.

He looked up to see Whiley half running and half walking, clumsily navigating his way through the trees, ducking under the branches. He dropped down on all fours beside Frank and sucked in deep breaths of cold, fresh air, too winded to speak. Minutes passed before either boy moved. Finally Frank pulled himself to his feet using his rifle. At seventeen, he already stood well over six feet tall. He was a big rawboned, good-looking boy with shocks of coal-black hair.

"Let's get him out," he said. Whiley nodded and pushed himself up. Together they stood and looked down at the buck.

"He's a beauty, ain't he Whiley?" Frank remarked.

"He *was,*" said the younger brother.

"What do you mean, he was?"

Whiley looked at Frank. "Life was his beauty. Without it he's just a piece of meat."

Frank shook his head. "I don't know why you bother coming with me, Whiley, feeling the way you do."

"I come with you because you're my brother. Brothers are supposed to help each other."

Frank grinned and slapped Whiley on the shoulder. "Okay, little brother," he said, "so help then!" Together they dressed out the deer and started to drag it to Hemlock's shack.

Old Hemlock stood by the door of his cabin. *The boys should be back soon,* he thought. Hemlock was nearly eighty years old and had spent most of them in Cumberland County, Michigan. He was a round little man with twinkling eyes and a gray beard that always held evidence of chewing tobacco around his mouth. His face had a leathery look about it, a gift that brutal Michigan winters had bestowed upon him little by little over the years.

He spotted Whiley emerging from the woods behind his shack. The boy looked around and disappeared again. A moment later, both boys came into view, dragging the deer. Hemlock hurried to help. The three of them ran with the deer the short distance to Hemlock's slaughter shed. They hung the animal without difficulty, walked out and shut the door behind them.

Hemlock smiled broadly. "Come on in, fellas. Got hot water on the stove."

The three of them entered the one-room shack that the old man called home. He hurried to the old wood stove that served for both cooking and heating. A table and two chairs were situated near the stove. In the corner was an old brass bed covered high with ancient quilts. Traps were piled in another corner - traps that were used less and less each year now - and the room was saturated with the smell of cooking grease. A large basin filled with hot water was placed on the table. Frank and Whiley took off their coats and shirts, rolled up the sleeves of their long johns, and began to scrub the deer's blood off their hands and arms. Hemlock sat down in a chair and watched the two boys.

Never saw two brothers who look so different, he thought. *Frank's big - like his daddy. Now Whiley, he's like his mother. Got her blue eyes and delicate features. Looks like a person whose feelings get hurt easy.*

Deep down the old man loved Frank and Whiley like they were his own, though he would never allow himself to show it.

"Clean enough," said Frank, drying himself.

"Make sure," said the old man. "Don't want your Pa getting suspicious. You know how he feels about killing God's forest creatures."

This prompted a feeling of guilt to sweep over Whiley. "We better get going," he said to Frank.

"Okay, in a minute," Frank answered. He turned to the old man and said, "I left the gun over in the corner." He dug into his pocket and produced three remaining shells. He handed them to Hemlock.

"Only used one?" Hemlock asked.

"Two," said Frank.

"I thought I only loaded four in the gun," Hemlock said, shaking his head. "Can't keep anything straight anymore!" He sighed. "That's the curse of growing old, I guess. Soon as I get the meat butchered, I'll be by with your share."

"Come early in the evening, before supper. When Pa is still in the barn," Frank said as they left the shack.

Outside, Whiley took a deep breath of air. Frank laughed and said, "You're going to die in that shack if you don't breathe!"

"Don't that greasy smell bother you?" Whiley asked.

"Hell, no!" Frank lied, as the two boys started home.

John Burns was an absolute giant of a man, standing six-foot-seven, with broad shoulders and enormous bones. He was the most imposing figure in Cumberland County. He walked slowly from the barn, just as a light snow began to fall, and looked to see if the boys were coming. Down the long road that led to the farm, he could see two figures approaching. He turned and walked to the porch. He was careful to scrape the bottoms and sides of his boots before entering the house, using a metal manure scraper that hung beside the front door. Inside, he removed his boots before going too far. Agnes Burns would not allow footwear used in the barn to enter her house.

Agnes was just putting supper on the table. The two Burns girls were helping her. She was a delicate, attractive woman with light hair, dancing blue eyes and an engaging smile that had turned all the boys' heads years ago. Her two daughters,

Rachel and Caroline, showed evidence of doing the same one day. Caroline was 15 and fit between Frank and Whiley. Rachel was 13, the youngest. Out of all the Burns children, only Frank resembled his father.

"The boys are coming down the road," John Burns reported.

"I thought they might be late," Agnes replied, "they were going to split some wood for Hemlock."

John Burns nodded. "We'll wait."

The food was on the table and everyone was seated when the back porch door opened and slammed. They heard the shuffle of boots coming off and coats being dusted of snow and hung. Frank and Whiley hurriedly washed and took their places at the dinner table.

When they were seated they received a stern look from their father, but he said nothing. A stern look was all it took from John Burns to let his feelings be known. All bowed their heads. Grace was said, and the meal began.

That night as they lay in the darkness of their bedroom, Whiley asked, "Frank, do you think there's a heaven for animals?"

"What do you mean?"

"You know, when cats and dogs die, or any animal, do they go to heaven like people?"

Frank thought about the deer. "I don't know," he replied. "I hope so."

"So do I," said Whiley, closing his eyes. In minutes they were both asleep, while outside a silent, steady snow blanketed Cumberland County.

Chapter Two

Otis Beecher rose from his bed at five o'clock, as he always did. He dressed, stoked his fire and ate his breakfast. He had lived in the back of his general store for 12 years - since his wife died.

After eating, he walked into the store.

"Another day," he said aloud, with a sigh. And worse yet, a Sunday. Nothing much *ever* happened in Fairchild, Michigan, and even *less* happened on a Sunday. Otis Beecher did not like Sundays, since the passing of his beloved Betsy. Things were too quiet on Sunday, too dull, and that allowed her memory to slip in and give him pain. He didn't *have* to open the shop on Sundays, but he needed to keep busy. It was the only way to forget.

He walked behind the counter, grabbed an old lantern and lit it. He unlocked the front door of the store and stepped out into the cold, pre-dawn darkness. It had snowed overnight, quite a bit. *Feels a little warmer than it's been,* he thought, as he hung the lantern on the wooden peg beside the door.

Turning to go back inside, something caught his eye in the alley beside the building. It was a dark hump in the otherwise pristine white snow. Unable to make it out, he took the lantern from the peg, holding it in front of him, and walked over to where the alley met the main street. He examined the dark hump closely, and his eyes widened. There, in the soft light of the lantern, half buried in snow, was a man. Quite dead, by the looks of him.

"Holy Christ!" Otis Beecher cried.

Chapter Three

Carmin Jones stood in the snow, looking down at Doc Spencer, who was examining the body. Fairchild, Michigan's tall police chief had gray hair, a gray mustache and heavy, bushy eyebrows, which were furrowed as he watched Doc work.

Charley Lambert, Carmin's assistant, stood beside him. Charley was a short and stocky man, who looked like he could take care of himself, come what may. The sun had begun to rise in the east.

Carmin broke the silence. "Well Doc, what have we got?"

Without looking up Doc answered, "A body."

Carmin clenched his teeth and closed his eyes. "I know that," he said.

"Then what the hell did you ask me for!" the Doc snapped, still examining the body.

Difficult old bastard, Carmin thought, rolling his eyes.

Doc stood up and said, "It's Millard Hoffman, the swamper down at Ryman's saloon."

"I know that *too,"* said Carmin, nodding elaborately. "You figure he had a few too many, passed out and froze to death?"

"I'll know better after we thaw him out and I can examine him closer."

Charley Lambert spoke for the first time. "You think something's funny, Doc?"

"Yes, I think something's funny Charley. But I don't think any of us are going to be laughing about it."

"Okay Doc," said Carmin, "we'll get him up to your office."

Though it was still early and barely light yet, a crowd had gathered outside Otis Beecher's general store. *Hell,* thought Carmin. *Only seven in the morning and already the day is ruined!*

Carmin Jones had a funny feeling in his stomach, and such feelings were not often wrong.

Chapter Four

John Burns and the boys had finished the morning chores and the boys were already in the house getting ready for church. John walked out of the barn to hook up the sleigh, smiling to himself. He always looked forward to the sleigh rides to church. A little cold for the women usually, but not too bad today. It was cloudy and dark, but warm, temperatures nearly above freezing.

He owned three horses; two big work horses and the mare. She was his sleigh and buggy horse, used only for transportation. The sleigh had three seats, each one big enough for two people. It was slight of build, an easy pull for the mare. He drove to the front of the house, tied the horse and went in to wash and change into his church clothes.

His family was nearly ready to go. Frank and Whiley sat in the parlor. Whiley, a proud member of the church choir, said, "We're going to sing some new songs today." His face was beaming.

"Oh boy," said Frank, twirling a finger.

The girls were chattering in the kitchen. The loudest was Rachael, who said, "When we get to the church yard this morning, if that Tommy Collins' face is dirty and his mother spits in her hanky and wipes it again, I'm going to throw up!"

"Rachael!" her mother cried, shaking her head.

"Let's go!" said John Burns, emerging from the bedroom in his Sunday best and grabbing his coat. They all filed out.

Frank and his father sat in the front of the sleigh, Whiley and his mother next, and the girls in back. Mrs. Burns handed the girls a blanket, which they placed over their laps and wrapped around their legs. She and Whiley did the same. Frank and his father chose not to use their blanket.

"Hey Frank," said Whiley, grinning, "you and Pa are good for something after all!"

Frank looked back. "What?"

"Windbreaker."

Mrs. Burns looked at her younger son and smiled. Agnes loved all her children dearly, but she had a tender, secret place in her heart for Whiley. Frank was like his father, and the girls were just that: girls. *Naturally* she would relate to them. But she also related to Whiley in the same manner, and she loved him for it. He truly was her baby.

The church yard was buzzing with talk about the death of Millard Hoffman. John Burns couldn't remember the man, but felt a sense of loss anyway. The topic of conversation between the men soon changed to the weather, stock, and who was going to plant what come next spring, but always came back to Millard.

The church bell ran and everyone filed in. The preacher, Stuart Evans, changed his sermon from the evil of greed to the evil of alcohol, not wanting to miss a golden opportunity. He culminated in a rousing flourish about wasting one's life and ending up frozen in a snowbank.

Then came singing and Whiley took his place with the choir. They sang two songs and then Whiley sang a solo.

My God, thought Frank, listening intently to his brother's steady voice, *he really can sing.* There was a hint of envy in his heart. When he finished, Whiley came back and sat down next to Frank. He smiled and Frank grinned back and rolled his eyes. Whiley turned away, embarrassed.

After the service, the men gathered in small groups for some small talk. This went on for nearly half an hour. During this time the women spoke amongst themselves and the children ran throughout the church restlessly, at intervals asking the parents when it would be time to go.

Getting into the sleigh, John Burns commented benignly on the dark clouds that had gathered around Fairchild. He didn't then know just how dark it was going to get.

Chapter Five

Sunday afternoon found Carmin Jones and Charley Lambert walking up the stairs to Doc Spencer's office.

"What did Doc say?" Charley asked.

"Only that he had to see us," said Carmin. "Doc don't care much for socializing, so it must be important."

Charley nodded. "Millard Hoffman was trouble when he was alive; hope he ain't going to be trouble now that he's dead."

"We'll see," said Carmin.

They reached the top of the stairs and knocked. "Funny he don't have a downstairs office," Charley commented.

Carmin shrugged and rolled his eyes. "Maybe he gets his kicks from watching old people struggle up the stairs. Probably brightens his day."

"Come on! He ain't *that* bad," said Charley.

Before Carmin could answer the door scraped open and Doc motioned them in with a jerk of his head. The men sat down on a long couch in Doc's waiting room. Carmin fixed his eyes on Doc and said, "Well?"

"Died of a broken neck," said Doc, getting right to the point.

"Well then, he got drunk, fell down and broke his neck," said Charley. "That's simple enough."

"Not quite," said Doc. "How in the hell does a man fall down in an alley, into a thick, soft pile of snow and break his neck?"

"It could happen," replied Carmin. "There's lots of ice out there too."

"You really believe that?"

Carmin didn't answer that. He didn't know *what* to believe and would not have shared it with the Doc anyway.

Doc continued. "He's got a nasty bruise on the side of his neck," he said, "like someone hit him a good one, and I mean a *good* one!"

Carmin cleared his throat. "Got any idea what he was hit with? *If* he was hit, that is."

"Nope, it could have been most anything," said Doc. "Even a fist. Wasn't much to old Millard, you know."

"Uh huh. Where is the body now?"

"Down at the Clark funeral parlor. What the hell you think, I keep them piled up *here?"* the crusty old surgeon replied sharply.

Carmin almost replied, *"They're the only ones that could tolerate you!",* but he refused to be dragged into an argument, which is what Doc seemed to be after. Instead he turned to Charley and said, "We better go have a talk with Moses Clark."

Doc watched the two men leave. He had gotten under Carmin's skin and that always gave him pleasure.

Outside on the snowy street Charley fell in beside Carmin. He knew the Chief was deep in thought, so he said nothing. He looked down the main street of Fairchild, Michigan. Not much activity. Only the saloons were open. Otis Beecher's general store - and the few other businesses that bothered to open on Sunday - were always closed by noon. The false fronts on the weary, wooden buildings made them appear taller than they really were. It was just another illusion, like so much in Fairchild. Seventeen hundred people lived within the actual limits of the small town. It was serviced by rail and was the shopping center for all the surrounding farmers; supplies, feed, material, hardware, lumber...it even had a small foundry. The people of Fairchild were good people and hard working, but the town had - like many other towns - a quiet discontentment among its ranks, and dreams of growing larger, reaching beyond its current limits. Charley knew it was only a dream. Fairchild was a good farming community, but it would never be anything more than a good farming community. Even now, some of the younger people were leaving for Detroit, where Henry Ford was building the Model T. That was where the jobs were.

And that suited Charley just fine. He and Carmin were the only law in town. Not much ever happened in Fairchild, and Charley and Carmin could handle whatever came up. Yep, Charley Lambert liked things just the way they were.

"I don't know about this," Carmin said suddenly, interrupting Charley's thoughts.

"Huh?"

"I don't like it. Doc's right, something's wrong."

"Ah Chief, Millard just got drunk and fell."

Carmin shrugged. "We'll see," he said.

They arrived at Moses Clark's funeral home. As they entered the marble catafalque with its background of maroon velvet curtains trimmed with gold cords and tassels, Charley felt depressed. It didn't bother him to handle dead bodies in the woods or in their homes or wherever they might be found, but once they got to the funeral parlor they scared the hell out of him. There was something dreadfully unnatural about the pageantry that accompanied someone's death: an extravagantly decorated funeral parlor, equally luxurious coffins (for some, anyway). He knew that it was all meant to comfort the grieving, but it bothered Charley. Death was death, plain and simple. And no amount of red and gold trim could change that. In Charley's opinion, it only made the concept of death worse.

Carmin said, "Moses? You in here?"

"Be right out," answered a voice from a room off to the side.

"Never mind, I'll come back there," shouted Carmin. He turned to his partner. Aware of Charley's feelings, he said, "You want to wait here?"

"Yes," answered Charlie gratefully. Carmin disappeared into the room. Charley sat down on a maroon chaise lounge and waited, fidgeting, for what seemed forever. When the Chief and the mortician emerged from the room, Charley stood abruptly to greet them.

"Hi Charley!" said Moses. "How's everything?"

"Fine, Moses, fine," Charley replied. "We about ready to head out, Chief?" he asked Carmin, with a little embarrassment. But he couldn't help it. Moses Clark was friendly enough, but Charley could not get over what he did for a living.

Carmin turned to Moses and said, "Well, thanks for everything. You've been a big help."

This was a lie, but Carmin had lived long enough to know it didn't pay to ruffle anyone's feathers (even a little bit) in a small town. *Especially* "pillars" of the community like Moses Clark. Word got around quickly in Fairchild.

"By the way," he added, "turn in the bill for the funeral. I'm sure Cumberland County will have to pay for it."

"No relatives?" asked Moses.

"None that we know of. If any turn up, we'll let you know. Come on, Charley. Thanks again Moses!" The undertaker nodded and watched the two men leave.

Out on the street Charley asked, "Where to now?" He was thankful to be out of there and was ready to start doing his job again, which was, basically, to follow Carmin wherever he went. They headed back up the street in the direction they'd come.

"Ryman's Saloon," said the Chief.

"Still ain't satisfied?"

He wanted to tell Charley that he hadn't gotten anything out of Moses but a recitation of his dull undertaker duties, nothing to shed any light on the case anyway. But he settled for, "We'll see."

Light snow had begun to fall as they entered Ryman's Saloon. Ryman's was the busiest and largest saloon in Fairchild.

The long mahogany bar could accommodate a good share of thirty patrons and the six tables could take care of any overflow. The tables were empty now, but the bar was packed from one end to the other as the two officers made their way to it. Carmin let the bars open up on Sunday in Fairchild. It was his own decision. Carmin thought, for the most part, that taverns kept people *out* of trouble, by giving them something to do. A lot of people disagreed vehemently, but it was his belief that boredom, more than anything else, was what caused people to commit crime and get into trouble. The State boys hadn't ever said anything about it to him, and the county sheriff didn't care one way or another.

George Ryman, the owner, was behind the bar. When he saw the two elbowing their way up, he came over to them.

"Hello George," said Carmin. "I 'spose you've heard about Millard."

The bar owner leaned forward. "Uh-huh," he answered.

Carmin said, "What can you tell us?"

"Not much," said George Ryman. "Still can't believe it. He was here last night till about eleven o'clock." He straightened and said, "You boys want anything to drink?"

Carmin shook his head, answering for both of them. Charley's spirits fell. He could have used a drink.

"Just information," said the Chief.

George Ryman shrugged. "Well," he said, "like I said, I can't tell you much. Why? Is something wrong?"

"No, no, we just always check these things out."

"Oh," said George, relieved.

"Who was around when Millard left last night?"

"Why?"

"Because," said Carmin, "maybe someone left with him."

"No, he left alone. It was just the usual bunch here last night."

"No strangers?"

"Nope."

"Did Millard have a lot of money on him?"

"Millard? Hell! He *never* had any money! He was broke from payday to payday. In fact, I had to charge him a bottle last night when he left. Supposed to take it out of next week's pay. Guess I'm out that, now."

"He did some work for you, didn't he, George?"

George nodded. "Yeah, did some cleaning around the bar, some tending now and then."

"When did you pay him?" asked Carmin.

"On Wednesdays. That's when his rent was due at the Old Capitol Motel. If I'd payed him on Fridays, it would have been gone by Wednesday and he would be sleeping in the snow."

"Millard ever mention any relatives?" Carmin asked.

"He mentioned a sister once, but I got the impression that she was longtime dead."

Carmin nodded slowly. "Okay. Nothing unusual happened last night, did it?"

"Nope."

"Thanks George. See you around."

Carmin and Charley left Ryman's Saloon.

The Old Capitol Motel was old and run down. It was one of the first buildings raised in Fairchild in the mid-19th century. The lobby was filled with old furniture and haggard-looking plants and ferns. Old man Kelser was behind the worn front desk.

"We want to take a look at Millard Hoffman's room," said Carmin. "Where is it?"

The old man pushed himself further over the desk and looked inquiringly at the two men, his hand cupping his ear.

"Could you tell us where Millard's room is!" Carmin yelled, growing impatient with the old man and the investigation in general.

"One floor up," Kelser finally said, his mouth smacking as he talked. He had only a few teeth left. "Room 107. Need a passkey?"

"No, Millard had a key on him. I got it from Moses."

"What say?" said Kelser.

Carmin kept his cool. Kelser was getting up there in years, way up there, and had turned a little senile and a *lot* hard of hearing. Carmin waved the key in front of the old man and he and Charley climbed the stairs.

Room 107 was like a biography of Millard's life; dismal and nearly barren. There was a hastily made bed, a dresser with a large yellowed mirror and a bed stand with a pitcher of old water and a basin. The only other piece of furniture was a rocking chair against the opposite wall in the corner. A white-enameled, cast iron radiator supplied ample (overbearing) heat and two dirty windows allowed light to shine dimly into the room.

On the dresser lay two objects; a pair of reading glasses and a comb. Carmin opened the top drawer, revealing a collection of socks and a straight razor. The rest of the drawers produced only old clothing. Charley watched over Carmin's shoulder as he knelt down and inspected each drawer thoroughly. Carmin closed the last drawer and stood up.

"Let's check the closet, Charley."

The closet showed only a battered suitcase and a trunk. Charley opened the suitcase. It was empty. Together, they pulled out the trunk. Inside were more clothes and three envelopes, all blank. Two of them had photographs in them. Neither man recognized anyone in the pictures.

"Family, you think?" Charley asked.

"I don't know," said Carmin. "Could be. They're probably all dead, judging by the age of these pictures."

The third envelope was larger than the first two and contained six separate letters and an ad torn from a newspaper, advertising a mail-order truss for people suffering from hernias. Carmin discarded the advertisement and began to read the letters. They were all worn and dog-eared, looking as though they'd been read many times over. All were without addresses. Four were signed, *`Love, Matilda'*, and the other two said simply, *`Your friend, Tom'*. They told Carmin nothing. He replaced them in the big envelope and dropped it back in the trunk. He closed it and pushed it back into the closet with Charley's help.

"Charley," he said, walking to the window, "let's talk."

Charley knew what this meant and sat down in the rocking chair. When the Chief said *'Let's talk'*, he knew he was in for a lot of listening.

"First," Carmin began, "we've got Millard Hoffman dead in a snowbank with a broken neck, which we're not sure how he got. He may or may *not* have fallen down. I doubt it, personally. It would have had to have been one hell of a fall. The fresh snow took care of any tracks there may have been. We have no witnesses. Millard had no money - everyone knows that - so robbery was no reason for doing him in." He looked at his partner rocking in the chair. "*If* someone did him in."

"So what's the problem?" Charley asked. "It was just an accident. You're letting what old Doc said influence you too much. He just likes to get you riled up, and you know that."

"Where's the bottle?" Carmin asked.

"Huh?" said Charley. "What bottle?"

"The whiskey bottle Millard got from George before he left Ryman's Saloon."

Charley shrugged. "Maybe he drank it."

"Millard? Hell! Three beers and he could barely stand up! He was all burned out, Charley. That bottle of whiskey would have lasted him a week or two."

"Maybe he dropped it, or someone helped him drink it."

"Who?" the Chief said.

Charley shrugged elaborately. "I don't know! It could be buried in the snow right next to where we found him, for all we know! A lot of snow fell last night!"

Carmin shook his head. "No, no, not the way people were tramping around there. Somebody would have stepped on it or kicked it up."

Charley thought Carmin was making more out of it all than was necessary, but he would never say so. "So what are we doing to do?" he asked.

"Nothing officially," Carmin answered. "But we're going to keep our eyes and our ears open."

"What about Doc?"

"What about him?"

"He could start talking, getting other people all riled up."

Carmin shook his head. "Naw, Doc won't say nothing. He'll sign the cause of death as a broken neck - accidental - and that will be that. He don't give a damn anyway."

"What are we going to put in our report?" Charley asked.

"We're going to put, *'Death by misadventure',*" said Carmin.

"Ah," said Charley, rolling his eyes and standing up.

Carmin locked up the room and the two men descended the stairs. In the lobby of the Old Capitol Hotel Carmin said, "You go ahead home, Charley. I'm going to turn in the key and have a word with Kelser."

"Good luck," said Charley, glad to be set free. Carmin watched him walk through the lobby and out the front door of the hotel.

As Carmin approached the desk, the old man noticed him and stood up attentively. Leaning forward he placed his long, bony fingers on the registry and pushed it forward. Carmin dropped the key on the desk and said, "You can take Millard's things out of the room and store them for a couple of weeks. If no one shows up for them, you can do whatever you want with them."

Kelser leaned even further over the desk and said, "What say?"

Carmin blinked, then he sighed and said, "I said just as soon as Moses gets Millard all dressed up and looking good, we'll bring him over here and put him back in his room." He turned and exited the hotel.

Old man Kelser looked bewildered, then enlightenment swept over his face and he picked up the key.

"That's fine," he said hesitantly, "that's fine." He nodded his head in agreement and placed the room key back on its assigned hook, then sat down to watch the Sunday pass away as so many before.

Chapter Six

It was late Wednesday afternoon when Hemlock came to call at the Burns house. He had pulled his toboggan a mile and a half through the woods and across the field. Hemlock rarely, if ever, used the road. It was rough going, and he was winded. Ten years ago it would have been no chore at all. Even five years ago. But now age was beginning to creep up on him, stiffening his joints and making him less tolerant of the cold. He sighed heavily and knocked on the door.

Agnes answered. "Well hello Hemlock. Come in."

"Hello Agnes," said the old man. "I brought over some venison. Kind of payment for the boys cutting my wood."

"That's very kind of you," said Agnes, "but you know how John feels."

"Oh Agnes," he replied, "the animal is already dead and not eating it ain't gonna bring it back to life."

They went through this banter every time Hemlock brought over venison and it always ended the same way.

"Oh all right," said Agnes, smiling. "I suppose we really could use the extra meat."

Hemlock carried the meat into the cold step-out porch just off the kitchen, setting it down beside a small pile of firewood. He walked back into the kitchen. The two Burns daughters, Rachel and Caroline, were helping their mother prepare dinner. Hemlock's nose twitched as he sniffed the aroma.

"One of you girls consider coming over and cooking for me?" he teased.

"They might not mind the cooking," said Agnes, "but they sure don't like doing dishes."

Hemlock shrugged and smiled. "That's okay," he said, "when ol' Hemlock gets done eating, I just throw the dishes out the back door!" The girls laughed at this.

"Come and sit with me in the parlor," said Agnes. "You're staying for supper, of course."

There was not another house in all of Cumberland County that Hemlock would consider taking food at, other than the Burns house, and there he considered it an honor. "Thank you Agnes," he said. "That's very kind of you."

John Burns and the boys finished chores and came into the house. They talked of trivial things with Hemlock until it was time to sit down to dinner.

Throughout dinner Hemlock ate slovenly, smacking his lips and rolling his eyes in a ridiculous manner, making the girls giggle. Frank and Whiley both smiled, but lowered their heads slightly to conceal it in the presence of their father. Even Agnes laughed out loud once. John Burns usually did not allow such foolishness at his dinner table, but had long since given up trying to maintain a sense of quiet when Hemlock was there. He looked about the table with disapproval, but did not say anything.

After supper, the women cleared the table and set to washing the dishes. John sent Frank and Whiley on some chores in the barn. He then invited Hemlock back into the parlor. The two men sat down, bathed in the last light of evening.

"I brought over some meat," Hemlock began.

"I figured that when I saw the toboggan," said John.

"Well," said the old man, rubbing the back of his neck, "the boys stop by and do a turn for me now and then, so I figure I owe you."

"What kind of turn do they do for you?" John asked.

"Split wood. Pile it. That kind of thing."

"Since when do you need someone to do that for you?"

"I ain't gettin' any younger, you know, John."

"How long have the boys been killing your meat for you?"

The direct question caught Hemlock by surprise. He knew it was no use lying any further, and perhaps it was unwise as well. John Burns was generally a gentle man, but he was a large man. And a serious one.

"About as long as I been bringing your share over," he said as casually as possible. "Maybe a year and a half." John Burns was silent, so Hemlock asked, "How long have you known?"

"Around a year and a half," John answered.

"You want to discuss it further?" asked Hemlock.

"No."

"You gonna stop them, John?"

"No."

Hemlock was curious to know what had caused John's change of heart, but he dared not risk it. Now that the truth was out, Hemlock felt embarrassed for his part in the deception.

"It's the times, John," he said. "The boys ought to know how to shoot. Ought to be able to fend for themselves, if need be." He thought a moment and added, "Protect themselves too."

John Burns said, "Times are going to get worse. I can feel it. War's coming."

"You believe that?" asked Hemlock. He could just barely see the man's face in the darkness of the parlor; reserved, stoic.

"It's coming, and I'm afraid the boys will be dragged into it."

Hemlock shrugged and said, "Maybe not. Might all blow over. Might never reach this country."

"I don't believe that," said John, "and neither do you. We *both* read the papers."

"Time will tell, John," said Hemlock, "and speaking of time, I better get started home."

Standing on the steps in front of his house, John Burns saw Hemlock off, watching the old man cross over the field slowly, pulling his toboggan with what seemed like great effort. He disappeared into the stand of pines on the far side, just as a wind picked up. John's eyes scanned the farm and the land around it. The skies had cleared out. A thin white strip in the west was the only light. Stars were appearing overhead. Other than the faint voices of Frank and Whiley in the barn all was peaceful. It seemed the whole world was at peace.

John Burns put his family - and their well-being - before all else. He wondered how a war going on across an entire ocean could possibly touch him - or someone he loved - here, yet he felt sure it could, and would. If Divine Providence had allowed him to look into the future, he would have seen the danger to him and his family was not across an ocean, but right there in Cumberland County, beneath the calm currently spread out over the crisp, still landscape.

In the barn, the boys lay on their backs in the loft, laughing uncontrollably, speaking of things that boys will speak of only when the rest of the world cannot hear them.

Chapter Seven

The winter of 1915 passed slowly, but it finally gave way to spring. To the people of Fairchild (weary from another Michigan winter) spring meant promise. To Doc Spencer, spring meant mud. It also meant wet feet and being caught with the wrong clothes on when the wind switched from south to north, turning an otherwise beautiful spring day quite cold.

But mostly, it meant mud.

He cursed under his breath as he teetered on the plywood board stretched across the muddy alley between his building and the hardware store. The board was raised by two bricks on each side and looked dangerously close to snapping in the middle, right where Doc had paused and was struggling to keep his balance. He was using his bag much as a highwire walker would use his pole to balance himself. But Doc was not going to be able to balance himself forever, and he knew it. Just as the board was beginning to bounce, threatening to shake him off into the deep, thick mud of the alley, Doc saw Frank Burns walking past him on the sidewalk.

"Hey!" Doc called to him. "You come here, boy!"

Frank stopped, looked, and saw it was Doc Spencer calling to him. He walked into the alley and pressed his foot down on the board, to stop it from wobbling and shaking.

"Not on the board, you damn fool! It's barely holding *me!"* the Doc exclaimed. "You got boots on! Walk out here and take my hand!"

Like a lot of other people in Fairchild, Frank thought about telling Doc what he could do with his idea and his manner, but he controlled himself. He sighed loudly, rolled up his pants legs, tucked them into his boots, and waded out into the mud and water, which came up almost to the top of his boots. He took Doc's hand and lead him safely to the hardware store side of the alley.

Doc said, "Thanks. Burns, ain't it?"

"Yes sir," said Frank.

"Thought so. You still in school?"

"Yes sir," said the boy. "Be done in June."

"How old are you?"

"I turned eighteen in March," answered Frank.

"Know anything about automobiles?"

"No, sir."

"Well, I'll be taking mine out when this damn mud dries up. You come by and help clean it up and you'll earn a little spending money."

"Yes sir," said Frank enthusiastically. He knew of only two automobiles in Fairchild. One was Doc's. The other belonged to Melvin Johnson, the mailman.

"I'll let you know when," said Doc, waving goodbye. He walked on, leaving Frank standing there.

Across the street, Carmin Jones had been watching Doc's dilemma since the old man first stepped onto the board, hoping to see him take a head-first plunge into the mud. But Frank's happening by had dashed his hopes.

"Shit," he thought, and walked away.

That night Frank decided to visit Hemlock. He had heard his father say that Hemlock was mechanically minded and any advice he could get might help with Doc's automobile, when the time came.

He crossed the field, went through the stand of pine trees, caught the road on the other side, and walked the mile and a half to Hemlock's cabin. There was no way to avoid the mud, and his boots felt like they weighed ten pounds apiece by the time he arrived. But Frank didn't care too much. It was a lovely evening. He could hear the first of the spring peepers in the woods, and there was a wet, pleasant warmth to the air. A full moon rose in the east as the sun set, casting purple light all around.

"What brings you over tonight?" Hemlock asked with surprise when he opened the door.

Frank explained his conversation with Doc and asked for any help Hemlock might be able to give him.

"Well," said Hemlock, scratching his head, "I never worked on one myself, but I got a general idea of how they operate. Sit down and I'll explain what I know about them."

For the next two hours Hemlock explained the workings of the combustible machine, even going so far as to draw pictures on an old sketch pad. When he finished, Frank marveled at his knowledge. It was amazing what Hemlock knew from just having looked at one years ago, when it was widely known around town that the old man had trouble remembering everyday occurrences.

With the lesson over, Hemlock changed the conversation. "How's your father doing?" he asked.

"He's just fine," said Frank. "You know Pa: strong as a horse and twice as willing."

"Oh yes," said Hemlock, "I remember your Pa way back when he was just a little older than you and sowing his wild oats."

Frank looked astonished. "Pa? Sowing his wild oats? I don't believe it!"

Hemlock chuckled. "One time, your pa was as rough as they come and proved it to a lot of good men. May be hard to imagine for you and your brother, but it's true."

The old man had Frank's full attention now.

"Tell me about it," Frank said.

Hemlock's eyes seemed to be looking back through the years as he spoke. "This one time," he said, "I remember best was about thirty years ago. It was a beautiful night in September, with a big full moon, kind of like tonight. The kind of night just made for young folks, the kind of night that gets them all goggle-eyed." He looked at Frank and smiled.

"I fancied a lady at the time," he said. Frank's eyes widened with surprise. "Yes," Hemlock laughed, "believe it or not, boy!"

Frank's face turned red. "I'm sorry," he stammered, "I just...you don't seem, that is, I wouldn't have thought *you'd* be interested in something like a harvest dance." Frank, and everyone in town, knew Hemlock generally didn't want much to do with people.

"Nowadays, yes," said the old man, "but back then I was all goggle-eyed myself. I was invited to the harvest dance by the lady, her name was Martha. It was the only time I ever went to such a function." He paused, and his face darkened for just a second, then he continued.

"Anyways, we were all down at the old Washington School for the annual harvest dance. The music was playin' and the folks was all about on the dance floor. Your father stood head and shoulders above the other dancers. He was waltzing with his sweet little Agnes Kemper...your ma, that is. They were a *sight!* He held her real soft and gentle; like a flower he was afraid he might crush. The way he looked at her and the way she smiled at him it was clear your pa was leaving all his rivals behind. Your ma had a sparkle in her eyes that told the world her decision: he was the one.

"All of a sudden, another young man approached. I had seen him and Agnes together on another occasion. Well, the three of them began talking and I could see Agnes was worried. Everyone in the school was watching them now. You could almost feel the tension building. Even the music had stopped. Your father and the man were talking loud, standing face to face. Your Pa didn't look so big next to the other man. Agnes was standing there with her hand over her mouth, tears in her eyes, really scared, you know? Your pa's face was flushed with anger. The other man motioned toward the door and your father nodded his head. They walked outside and in twenty seconds there wasn't nobody left in the schoolhouse. Everyone had followed your pa and the man outside."

Hemlock stared straight ahead, remembering. "It was incredible," he continued, shaking his head slowly, "they just stood there toe to toe, hitting each other with terrible blows. Neither was trying to defend himself. They was just trying to whup the other at all costs." Frank listened in amazed silence. "I thought one was going to kill the other for sure. Then the other man began to give ground and your pa just waded right into him."

Hemlock's eyes glanced at Frank. "We should have stopped it, I guess," he said. *"Someone* should have. But we was all too afraid. Imagine two fellas your pa's size going at it! Ashamed, we all just watched nervously. Then, like some unspoken truce had been called, your pa stopped and lowered his arms. Then the other man stopped and let down his guard as well. They both just stared at each other a moment. Then in a flash of lightning - no kidding...like a flash of lightning! - your pa swung long and hard. It was so fast I couldn't tell whether the man tilted his head back or your father simply misjudged, but the blow missed the man's jaw and caught him flush in the throat. The man went down like a rag doll. I thought your pa had killed him, and I think your *pa* thought he had killed him too. That was the only time I ever saw John Burns looked scairt. After a while they got the man to sit up, but he couldn't talk. Didn't speak a word for a week after that, and when he did it wasn't natural. There was this odd crackling to his voice from then on. Your father did something to the man's talker."

Frank was speechless, hearing this about his father. He knew his father was strong, and could carry his own in anything, but never would have imagined John Burns being aggressive.

Hemlock continued. "That was the last time your pa ever let himself get angry enough to fight. His size and demeanor don't often put him in a position to *have* to fight, but I don't think he's ever fought since that night." Hemlock sighed deeply and added, "And your ma must have forgiven him because they was married and along come you kids."

"What happened to the other man?" Frank said.

"Oh, he stayed around for a while. But he started drinking pretty heavy. Kinda wore out his welcome, and he moved on. I think he cared a lot for your mother. The last I heard he was up north, around Birchwood. Met a woman there and got married.

Talk is, she had a son, but she died in childbirth. The son now lives with him."

"He never comes back?" asked Frank.

"Oh sure, he pops up now and then. In fact," the old man said, then he stopped. He seemed to be considering going on with the story, but decided not to. Instead he said, "I never thought it would end there, not with the bad blood between them. But I guess it did. At least, I hope it has. Still..." Again he stopped and thought silently.

The boy waited, but Hemlock had closed his mouth and he knew the old man would say no more.

Frank Burns walked home soon after, under April's pink moon, and would never view his father - or the world - in quite the same way again.

Chapter Eight

Every morning after chores, John Burns hitched up the mare and drove the four miles into Fairchild to take his children to school. After school he picked them up again. This had been his practice, day in and day out, ever since they were little.

On this beautiful April morning, Whiley seemed concerned. He and Frank were waiting for their father in front of the house.

Whiley turned to his older brother and said, "You're gonna be out of school pretty soon. Are you gonna leave home?"

"Hadn't really thought about it," Frank answered. He knew his father was counting on him to stay and help out on the farm, at least for a while. But he also knew the decision was his to make. His parents would not pressure him. He thought for a moment and said, "I guess I'll stay around for a while."

"Good!" said Whiley, relieved.

That noon at school a boy Frank knew walked up to him.

"Hi Barney," said Frank cordially.

"Hey Frank," said Barney. "I saw Doc Spencer in town this morning. He told me to tell you to stop by this Saturday."

"What for?" Frank asked, though he knew what for.

Barney Payne shrugged. "He didn't say." With that, the boy walked away.

The thought of helping Doc with his automobile excited Frank. It would be a long week to wait.

Chapter Nine

Carmin Jones sat in his office playing with a pencil, twirling it over and over in his fingers and staring at the wall. The itch that had started with Millard Hoffman's death was turning into a rash. He had not learned anything yet, and he knew waiting around for *something* was going to accomplish *nothing.* Everyone in town just accepted that Millard Hoffman had gotten drunk, slipped, fell, froze and died. Carmin couldn't accept that. He didn't know why, but he couldn't.

He decided the best course of action to take was to investigate Millard's alleged sister, who may or may not be dead. A letter down to Lansing might turn up something. He would feel like a fool asking for information on someone he knew absolutely nothing about, or if she even existed. But all other roads were dead ends. He resolved to write the letter. The only hope he had was that the *Matilda* who had written letters to Millard - which Carmin had found in Millard's room at the Old Capitol Motel - was indeed his sister. At least he was making an effort.

He took out some paper and wrote the letter. After half an hour of writing and twenty minutes of rewriting, he was satisfied that he did not sound too *much* like a fool, though disdain and ridicule were inevitable. His encounters with the boys down south *usually* brought only disdain and ridicule, and what he was asking for now would only fan the flames of their contempt.

Christ, he thought, shaking his head, *they're sure going to love me down there now.*

But it was the best he could do, and besides, it was their job - as fellow government and law enforcement officials - to help him.

He sealed the envelope and started for the door. Right when he got there it swung open and Charley came in with a smile on his face.

"Hey Chief!" said Charley. "Goin' somewhere?"

"Down to the post office," replied Carmin. "Hang around 'til I get back."

"Right Chief!" said Charley. He walked around the desk and sat in the chair Carmin had vacated. Without another word, Carmin left the office, closing the door behind him.

Charley wondered what was up. The Chief had looked grim. But then, the Chief *usually* looked grim. Oh well, it was a beautiful day, and Charley felt good.

"Hell with it," he said aloud, propping his feet up on the desk and pulling his hat down over his eyes.

Chapter Ten

The week dragged by, just as Frank Burns had expected it to. On Saturday morning, he was up early. He told his father he was going over to Doc's place. Whiley pleaded to go into town with Frank. John Burns would have just as soon had *both* boys stay home and help him around the farm, but Whiley persisted. John looked at Frank, who shrugged and said, "It doesn't matter to me."

"All right," said John, "be better to have you two out of my hair today."

"Yay!" said Whiley.

The sun was shining bright and the temperature was warm as they walked into Fairchild, having caught a ride in with Chester White, a farmer who lived down the road from the Burns. Whiley was full of questions about how Frank had gotten the job helping Doc prepare his automobile for summer.

"He knows a good mechanic when he sees one," said Frank boastfully, choosing not to tell Whiley that he had attained his enviable position simply by helping Doc over the mud.

They arrived at Doc Spencer's building and climbed the stairs to his office. Doc met them at the door and said to Frank, "I see ya brought some help, did ya?"

"Nah," said Frank. "Whiley's going to meet some friends. He just stopped by to look at the flivver." Frank had heard some boys in school referring to a car as a flivver, and this was the first opportunity he had to use the term.

"Oh, I see," said Doc. "She's out back, boys. Go take a good look at her. I'll be down shortly."

Behind the building, the two boys looked at the Ford with wonder. Whiley, in particular, was fascinated, looking at it like it was some strange, exotic animal he'd never seen up close before. Frank walked up and quite possibly became the first person in the history of the automobile to kick a tire. They stood on the driver's side running board and peeked in. They walked around it and eyed it from all angles. Both boys decided it was a dandy, to say the least, even all covered with dust from winter storage.

When they had absorbed it fully and the inspection was over Whiley said he as going down Main Street and would meet Frank later to go home.

Alone, Frank continued the inspection, from a *"mechanic's point of view."* He got down on his knees and peered underneath. Yup, there was a bottom. He stood up, wondering what his first job with the machine would be.

He didn't have to wonder long. Doc appeared with two buckets of soapy water and a handful of rags.

"You wash her up good," said Doc, "inside and out. If you need more water, come and get it." He left the master mechanic looking disappointedly at the soap and water.

Well, thought Frank, *from humble beginnings...*

Five buckets of water and an hour and a half later, he had scrubbed every speck of dirt and dust from the outside of the auto. Satisfied, he opened the door and climbed in to clean the inside. He was busy scrubbing and rinsing the steering wheel when suddenly he stopped. Slowly he lay the rag down on the seat. He turned and looked all around cautiously. Convinced no one was watching, he sat straight up in the seat with the steering wheel in both hands, turning it slowly to the right. Satisfied, he turned it slowly to the left.

Upstairs, Doc happened to pass by the window of his office that looked out behind the building. He stopped, turned and peered out. His eyes widened. He could see the tires of his Model T turning to the left and then to the right, back and forth. Scratching his head he bent lower in an effort to see who was inside the car. He could just barely make out Frank's boots and pants. He opened the window, stuck his head out and said, "Frank!"

Frank jumped, hitting his head on the ceiling of the car. Sheepishly, he looked up at the window to where Doc was peering out. "If you don't quit driving around," Doc yelled, "you're gonna wear out my front wheels!"

Mortified, Frank resumed his cleaning duties.

An hour later, Doc stood beside him, inspecting the car. He nodded his head with approval at the job Frank had done.

"Looks pretty good," he conceded. Indeed, the black Ford glittered like the day it had been built. "Pretty good. What do I owe ya?"

Frank shrugged. Doc handed him two dollars, which was an exorbitant amount.

"Thank you," Frank muttered, unable to hide his disappointment.

"What's the matter, not enough?" said Doc indignantly.

"No sir, it's fine. I just, well, I kinda thought we were gonna do some work on it."

"Don't need no work," said Doc flatly. "But I tell you what. Next time I work on it, I'll let ya know and you can come over and help me, okay?"

"Yes sir," said Frank, his face brightening.

"And every Saturday you can come over and wash it for me."

"Yes sir!" said Frank, enthusiastic at the possibility of more money.

They said goodbye and Frank walked down Main Street, his good humor restored. He looked up and down the street for Whiley, planning to buy something for both of them at the confectionery. It was a glorious day. The weather was fine, he had two dollars, and he felt good.

Ahead, something was going on. There was a crowd of people in a big ring. They were all excited and shouting. Frank walked idly to the ring and looked over their shoulders. In the center was a large boy whom Frank knew only as Dumont. Frank knew he worked for room and board over at Chester White's farm and he had seen him about town now and then.

Dumont was standing behind another boy that Frank couldn't see. He was shaking the smaller boy viciously by the collar. With a violent thrust he threw him to his hands and knees. The boy looked up at Dumont, tears of fear and embarrassment in his eyes. The boy was Whiley.

Rage boiled up in Frank. He pushed his way into the circle. By now Dumont had placed his boot on Whiley's rear end and push him down on his stomach.

Frank said coldly, "Dumont, you touch him again, I'll break you in half."

A titter of relief and approval came over the crowd. Dumont turned to Frank. He knew who Frank Burns was and his sheer size cautioned Dumont. He stared and measured the intruder before him.

Suddenly another voice - a gravely voice - from outside the ring of onlookers said, "You lay a hand on my boy and you'll answer to me!"

Frank turned to face his new adversary. Pushing his way into the ring was a big, barrel-chested man with a heavy black beard. His eyes were just as black and wide. He was not quite as tall as Frank Burns' father (falling short by only an inch or two), but he was just as big around, and just as imposing. Frank knew this was a dangerous man.

"Well?" said the man, in that low, gravely voice. "Do we have a problem here?"

Frank knew he was overmatched. He wasn't afraid, but he also wasn't stupid. And the point was not how much he could take, but rather getting Whiley to safety. That had to be his main concern.

The crowd was buzzing in anticipation. This was the kind of situation Frenchy Dumont loved: the chance to slap around a young pup. He delighted in an opportunity like this. He had strength and experience on this young kid. And this young kid was very big. If he came after Frenchy, no one in town could criticize him for responding.

He stepped toward the kid. Someone in the crowd said, "Who is that?" in a low whisper. It was quiet so everyone heard the question.

"That's Frenchy Dumont."

"Who's the kid?"

"Frank Burns."

Frenchy stopped in mid-step and stared at Frank. The kid had looked familiar before, but now it was obvious. Of course! This was John Burns' son he was dealing with!

The name infuriated him. Frenchy Dumont had beaten up many a man in his day. Some were helpless and some were damn good. His reputation was well known and he feared no one. No one, that is, except John Burns. *He* was the one man Dumont feared - and hated - most in the world. He had heard that John Burns had changed, that he had settled down into farm life and wasn't the wild man he used to be. But he knew that Burns would never stand for anyone beating up his kid. The thought of having John Burns on his tail made him shudder. He made his decision quickly.

"Steve," he croaked to the boy who had pushed Whiley to the ground, "get back to the farm."

Obediently the boy said, "Yes, Pa."

Frenchy stared at Frank for a moment, amazed by how much he resembled his father, then walked away. The crowd broke up, half relieved and half disappointed. Frank turned to Whiley, who was still on his knees. He helped his younger brother up. Whiley wiped his eyes dry with the sleeve of his shirt and looked at the knees of his pants. They were soiled and torn.

"What am I going to tell Mother?" he said, weeping helplessly.

"Tell her they got soiled and dirty helping me with Doc's car," said Frank. "How did this happen anyhow?"

"We were just standing on the street," said Whiley, hyperventilating with tears, "Billy Mitchell, Tommy and me, when along came Steve Dumont. He started pushing us around. He's *always* like that."

"Uh-huh," said Frank as they made their way down Main Street. They passed Ryman's Saloon. Steve Dumont was nowhere to be seen, but his father Frenchy Dumont was standing outside the saloon, glaring at them. Whiley walked close to Frank as they passed, clinging to his arm. No words were spoken but Frenchy never took his eyes off the two boys as they moved up the street. He walked into Ryman's Saloon and ordered whiskey. He was in a black mood, as black as his beard. He felt he had lost all face in front of a lot of people, and all because of that damn kid and his damn father!

All his life Frenchy Dumont had blamed other people for his own misfortune. He hadn't expected to come back to Fairchild. He hated the damn place. It held nothing but bad memories for him. But he wanted to get his son boarded out. Steven was sixteen now and Frenchy had brought him to Fairchild to put to work on someone's farm. Chester White took him in quickly. This pleased Frenchy. He was now free to move about as he pleased; the kid was on his own.

Frenchy smiled and drank his whiskey. At least he had settled *one* account while he was in Fairchild. He would have liked to have settled another - one that had been bothering him for a long time - but he didn't have the guts.

He had spent the winter in Fairchild (mainly to make sure Steven was secure on Chester White's farm and wouldn't end up returning to him) and he was running out of money. He had drank most of it up and was forced to consider going to work. *Where to go,* he thought. *I guess it don't matter...just away from here. There's gonna be trouble if I stay here. Goddamn, I'll* make *trouble!*

The old rage swarmed over him and he drank hard that afternoon. In three hours he was blind drunk, barely able to hold himself up on the bar. Thoughts of messy revenge crawled through his muddled brain again. After so many years, the thoughts still took hold of him. He tried to resist them but they were persistent, and they wore him down with anger and hate.

"Someday, someday," he muttered, his eyes bloodshot and half-shut, swaying back and forth on the bar.

George Ryman watched Frenchy carefully and quietly. He knew Dumont had drunk more than his share and had had enough, by the looks of him. Ryman didn't allow unruliness in his bar and had been known to handle his own against many men, but he was careful - oh so careful - how he handled Frenchy Dumont.

Eventually, and luckily, Frenchy left on his own, crashing through the doors of Ryman's Saloon, out onto Main Street with an angry, untamed swagger.

Chapter Eleven

All week long the man with the coal-black beard and piercing eyes dominated Frank's thoughts. Even in school, Frank found it difficult to think of anything else, certainly not his studies. He wanted to ask his father if he knew this man, but that might lead to questions and questions about the man would naturally lead to Whiley's part in the affair. They had told their mother that Whiley soiled and tore his pants while helping Frank with Doc's car. If the truth came out, not only would their lie be exposed, but also Whiley would be crushed if it were known that he had been bullied and humiliated. Frank sensed that Whiley was just recently becoming aware of himself, aware that he had inherited his mother's soft features and delicate build, rather than the physical strength that Frank had received from their father. Frank wasn't sure, but he thought Whiley was bothered by this. Frank couldn't imagine why. Steven Dumont had been the one in the wrong, as all bullies are. And Whiley could sing, really sing beautifully.

None of that mattered though. Whiley would be terribly embarrassed, and worried about what their father would think. John Burns had always told his sons to be strong, to never back down. The fact that Steve Dumont was three times the size of Whiley would not matter to John Burns, he would expect Whiley to have stood his ground. So Frank kept quiet about the entire ordeal.

Frank figured that the girls, Rachel and Caroline, had heard about the incident in school, but so far neither had made any mention of it. Then on Thursday night his mother and father took Whiley to the minister's house in town to discuss some new hymns to be used in choir on Sunday. Frank took this opportunity to approach the girls on the subject.

It was after supper. Frank peered out the front door to make sure the carriage was still heading down the road toward town with his father, mother and Whiley in tow. Then he walked into the kitchen, where the girls were busy cleaning the dishes. Frank sat down at the kitchen table. Slowly he traced a pattern on the oilcloth with his thumbnail. The girls were busy washing and seemed to take no notice of him.

He thought about how best to broach the subject, then said finally, "What's the latest gossip at school?"

Both Rachel and Caroline turned and looked at him with surprise.

"What do you mean?" asked Caroline.

Frank shrugged, frustrated with how clumsily he'd handled the question. "I don't know, what's new?"

"Isabel Montgomery's got lice," said Rachel, smiling at the thought of it. She and Isabel had never been friends.

"Where did she get them?" asked Frank, trying to look and sound casual.

"Who knows!" said Rachel. "But they're gross!"

Caroline smiled, lowered her head and turned back to the dishes. Then Rachel did the same. Frank was left sitting there, which he did until they were finished, in silence.

"Will you *please* play some checkers with me?" asked Rachel, clinging to her older sister.

"All right," said Caroline. "You go into the parlor and get the board all set up. I'll be right out."

Rachel ran out of the room excitedly.

When she was in the parlor, Caroline looked at Frank and said, "I gather by your earlier question that you're wondering if Rachel or I know about last Saturday in town."

Frank nodded silently.

"Yes," she said. "I know. Camille Broton and Geraldine Roles were both there. They saw it all, and told me about it."

"You didn't say anything to Mother, did you?" asked Frank.

"No," said Caroline. "Nor did I mention it to Rachel. I don't think she knows, either, or she would have told me. I figured if you and Whiley wanted anyone to know, you would tell them yourselves."

"I don't think it would accomplish anything to tell anyone," said Frank. "But it sure was a funny thing."

"I don't think it's very funny," said Caroline.

"I mean it was strange."

"Well," Caroline said, smiling, "I don't know about *that* either, but I know it was wonderful of one brother to come to the aid of another." She walked toward him, leaned down in a graceful swoosh, and kissed him lightly on the cheek. Then just as gracefully she moved out of the room. Caroline was like their mother; sweet and graceful.

Frank smiled. His cheeks flushed red. "Yeah, yeah," he said aloud, though he was alone in the kitchen.

Feeling proud of himself.

Chapter Twelve

Hemlock lifted a small log on the sawbuck. It was a beautiful, warm day in May. The warm weather came early that year in Fairchild, and it stuck around. There had been little or no precipitation all spring.

Panting and sweating from exertion, Hemlock said to himself, "Gonna be a hot, hot summer."

As the teeth of the saw ripped into the wood, Hemlock's mind drifted...probably more than it should have. Hemlock did whatever work he had to do diligently, but methodically, and once he got working for a while his mind was usually no longer where his body was.

He usually thought about his life, attempting to relive the memories in his mind. He had lived long and - generally speaking - happily. He knew the end of his life was out there, waiting. Perhaps not soon (he had showed no signs of ill-health yet...just slowed down a bit), but eventually...five years, ten years tops. He couldn't see living (or wanting to live) much past ten more years. That would put him in his nineties. *That's when the mind starts to go,* he thought.

As he cut he stared across the field that surrounded his shack and thought wryly, *And I sure as hell ain't got nothing much* but *my memories. If I lose those, well...*

He continued to cut wood. Soon his mind had drifted completely, back to *another* field, another spring day, more than 50 years before.

Cumberland County

The date was April 6th, 1863. America was in the throes of the Civil War. Long lines of men in blue trudged along despondently. Defeat was in their eyes and the smell of death - the *smell* of death - hung over all of them.

Among them was a young private, hardly more than a boy. His name was Peter Christian. He was an infantryman in the Army of the Potomac. The war had begun for him with his enlistment in Illinois. He had left Michigan for Chicago, where he went after fortune, as many young men do. But fortune is an elusive thing, and soon - with the urging of a new-found friend - the idea of joining the Union Army seemed romantic.

Can't find fortune, Peter Christian thought. *Adventure's not a bad substitution.*

Together he and his friend enlisted. Peter was found fit, but his friend was tubercular and was rejected. Peter found himself thrust into the Army completely alone.

He took his training and soon it became evident he was a good soldier, a *perfect* soldier. He was physically capable of performing any order, but more importantly he *took* orders without question or complaint.

After training, though, boredom - something Peter never thought he'd experience in the Army - set in. Peter was a quiet fellow and had made few friends in training.

One of them said, "Christian, you ain't gonna be bored for long!" And he was right.

After his defeat at Fredericksburg, Union General Burnside resigned. President Lincoln appointed a new leader. The man he chose to lead the Army of the Potomac was General Joe Hooker. Men and supplies were amassed for the designated army. Peter Christian was assigned to the infantry, thus, he was destined to become one of the men to follow *Fighting Joe* into one of the most brazen offenses of the Civil War.

Upon arriving in Virginia with his fellow replacements, the enormity of it all - of what he was now involved with - shocked him. There were soldiers, horses, doctors and cannons everywhere. For the first time in his life, Peter felt inadequate; most of the men were veterans of the battle of Fredericksburg.

They were despondent men; downtrodden men; men who had suffered bitter defeat. When Peter arrived, morale was at rock bottom. He tried desperately to fit in with his new comrades. He spoke with anyone who would talk to him. But every man seemed to be locked inside himself, ambling sightlessly across the dull, muddy ground. Few were interested in anything he had to say, and those who were spoke very little in return. Only a sergeant named Potter even attempted lively conversation.

This was not the romantic, exciting life he had envisioned. He saw nothing but gloom and suffering...real, all encompassing *suffering,* both physical and mental. All around there were men without spirit, without arms and legs, or without minds. Peter quickly grew lonely and despondent too. Even the weather was foul. Everything seemed wrong. This went on for weeks. Then, when things seemed to be at their lowest ebb, it all changed quickly.

Hooker, now in firm command, began to replace officers with men who still had a proud, fighting spirit. Medical supplies finally arrived, and the wounded started to receive better treatment. Suddenly, seemingly overnight, there was no more idleness. On days when the weather permitted, the troops who were still fit to fight trained, while new infantry arrived every day. Fighting Joe Hooker was stirring the Army of the Potomac, which - for two years - was the workhorse of the Union Army. Attitudes changed and spirits returned. Men even started joking again. Best of all, with the tension lifted, Peter was accepted. Men who had not spoken five words to him since his arrival now talked freely. He became friends with a private named Cody Thompson. This comforted him greatly. Though everyone knew that the positive changes were in preparation for yet another battle, nevertheless life in the Union Army was becoming tolerable, sometimes even enjoyable.

The new officers boasted freely and loudly now about what was going to happen to those devils in gray when they got their hands on them. There was almost a carnival atmosphere, one of great anticipation.

And the feeling was well founded. Across the Rappahannock River, the Confederate Army was destitute. General Lee could not even feed his horses, let alone his men. Supplied by one small railroad, they were short of everything but determination. And that, as had once been the case with the Army of the Potomac, was dwindling.

Cody Thompson was a bright young man. He was talkative, and spoke most often about his home in Philadelphia. He told Peter of the many opportunities for fortune that would exist there when the war was over. Peter smiled and listened politely. He had sought fortune in Chicago, had failed, and now did not have the same enthusiasm as his new friend. Nevertheless, they both agreed that they would head to Philadelphia together when all of this was over. Partners to the end.

One night it was deathly quiet and dark. There was no sound, and yet every man was convinced he could "hear" the enemy across the river.

In a tiny whisper that sounded like a shriek in the quiet, Cody asked, "Peter?"

"Yeah," Peter answered just as quietly.

"You afraid?"

"No," said Peter. "Just a little nervous, I think. But when the battle starts I ain't gonna hesitate."

"Well, don't be nervous," said Cody. "According to headquarters, it's gonna be an easy take. We got more men, more ammunition, more supplies...more *everything!* The Rebs don't have a chance. I'd like to march over that river right *now* and flush 'em out!"

Peter took a deep breath and said, "Just the same, we ought to stick together."

"Well that's what partners do, right?"

From a distance, Sergeant Potter listened to their conversation. He couldn't see them too clearly, but he knew they had just shook hands, as *partners* do. They made plans for after the war with no thought that one or both of them may not *need* to have a plan when it was all over.

They're going into battle for the first time, he thought. *And if they both get out, neither one is going to be the same person.*

On the morning of April 26th, 1863, Peter and Cody were summoned to Potter's tent. He was a short, stout, powerful man with a bald head, who was more physically capable than he looked, and had been in the war from the very beginning.

Peter and Cody stood before him. The sergeant looked at the two boys and said, "General Hooker has ordered out Stoneman's Cavalry. It doesn't matter where they're going. The only thing that matters is that it's beginning." The two soldiers looked at each other. "I want you to understand what's expected of you. Most of the men in this infantry have been in battle before. You two haven't. That's why I'm speaking to you alone. We got a hundred and thirty thousand men out there, but when the fighting starts, you're gonna feel pretty much alone. I want the two of you to stick together, just as you promised to each other." With this, the two young soldiers glanced at each other with looks of puzzlement. Potter continued. "And *remember,"* he said, "the piece of ground you're standing on is yours to defend. The piece Johnny Reb is standing on is yours to take. Am I understood?"

"Yes sir," they answered in unison.

Potter nodded. "Protect yourself, and each other. That's all. Dismissed."

Outside Potter's tent, Peter looked out across the swollen Rappahannock River and wondered what the enemy on the other side was thinking. Probably exactly what *he* was: You follow orders. You defend what's yours. You take what's theirs. There is no room in a soldier's mind for anything else.

Prolonged cannon fire shook the stillness of April 29th. The previous day men worked quickly to assemble pontoon bridges across the Rappahannock. Now the march was on. Peter and Cody marched silently alongside each other. Sergeant Potter kept an eye on them whenever he could. Across the south bank, death awaited the unwary. For the first time, Peter's stomach felt hollow. He was scared. The feeling of adventure and courage deserted him.

"Keep moving, keep moving," said Sergeant Potter to the men, continuously.

Advance troops had already crossed and secured the bridgehead. Peter looked at Cody, Cody looked at Peter, and they both tightened their grips on their rifles as they walked steadily over the bridge. All the way over, they expected fire but none came. Suddenly they were on the south side of the river and it was still quiet.

"Maybe staff is right and the Rebs have run," said Cody quietly, looking around.

"Maybe," said Peter.

Sergeant Potter shouted, "Form a skirmish line into the underbrush!"

Peter and Cody assumed their positions along the line and dropped to their bellies into the wet, muddy underbrush.

Behind them infantry and artillery poured across the river. They were ordered to face east and already men ahead of them were marching out. The sky continued to darken as Potter ordered the men east into the late afternoon.

Peter wondered why they had not encountered resistance. Then, as if in reply, gunfire sounded ahead. Sweat beaded on his forehead and the tension he had first felt upon arriving in Virginia returned to him. His heart pounded. Darkness came early and so did more rain; a steady, driving downpour. The order was given to halt. Someone stepped in beside Cody and Peter. They both flinched.

In the darkness they heard Potter say, "How are you doing?"

"All right," said Peter. "Where are we going?"

"Chancellorsville," said the sergeant. "We're meeting the cavalry there."

"I never heard of it. How big a town is it?"

"Well, it ain't exactly a town. It's a farm house with a few buildings. Hooker just put an X on the map and called it Chancellorsville, as I hear tell it."

"Oh," said Peter, not really understanding and not soothed by Potter's explanation.

They stopped for the night and the next morning they marched on. Now and then they heard rifle skirmishes but it was always distant. Peter and Cody stayed together. The bond between them seemed to strengthen with each passing moment, though few words were spoken.

"I wonder what the Rebs are doing," said Peter, looking around nervously.

"God, I wish I knew," replied Cody.

The two soldiers didn't know it, but several miles ahead the Rebs were busy digging in.

That evening, Peter and Cody felt the tension mount not only within themselves, but all the men around them as well. To take their mind off it, they talked about their hometowns. Cody described to Peter the hustle and bustle, the energy and opportunity, of Philadelphia. Peter told Cody about the deep, peaceful woods and streams of Michigan.

The next morning they advanced across the Fredericksburg Turnpike, past the Fairview Cemetery. A mile past the cemetery the battle began. Peter and Cody met the enemy for the first time. They both fired in small skirmishes.

Then news of the disaster ahead of them began to trickle in.

The morning of May 3rd, Peter and Cody found themselves in the front lines. The battle was frenzied now. Explosions, gunfire, shouting and screaming echoed all around them. Peter fired round after round. By his side, Cody did the same. Fires were burning everywhere. Rebel after rebel fell, still they kept coming. Everywhere men were screaming and dying. Smoke from the fires burned their lungs and brought tears to their eyes as they coughed. It also made it difficult to see. They were deep in the trenches, neither side giving ground. Peter's rifle became hot and burned his hands. His face was black with smoke.

The battle lasted all morning. Miraculously, Peter and Cody remained untouched. Sergeant Potter jumped down beside them, his hand badly sliced and bleeding down his arm.

"You boys all right?" he shouted.

"Yes sir," they answered.

"Good! Now get ready! We're going to retreat to Mineral Spring Road!"

"What!" said Peter, astonished. He couldn't believe what he was hearing. "But we've stopped them!"

"We've lost Hazel Grove!" said Potter. "The Rebs' guns are looking down our throats. Chancellorsville's in flames. Even Hooker is wounded. The guns at the cemetery are gonna cover us as long as they can. Now cover *yourselves* and retreat, damn it! They're in front of us *and* in back of us!"

With that he was gone.

Men were moving back all around them now. Some on horses, some on foot, some dragging themselves along the ground, screaming for someone to help them. Confused and discouraged, Peter and Cody pulled back with the rest.

That night they slept in the woods. The following day brought more skirmishes in the thicket and more bad news. The once mighty army had broken into several patches of men. Trying to regain order and control, Hooker - who was humiliated and blaming everyone around him for the disaster - ordered a general retreat back across the Rappahannock River. Most of the men were more than willing to retreat to safety. Peter accepted the fact of the retreat, but Cody resisted.

"They're outnumbered!" he said bitterly. "We stopped them! We did our part!"

"You're damn right we did," said Peter, tugging on his friend's arm. "We should have kept going, but we didn't. Now we better retreat or we'll be left behind. An order's an order!"

And the order was, specifically, *"Fall back, position yourself, then fall back again!"* They did so, Confederate snipers nipping at their heels all the while.

"Why don't they charge right into us?" asked Cody, as he and Peter rushed to find safety.

"I don't think they got the men or the ammunition to mount a full-scale attack," Peter answered. "They're just playin' with us now."

At mid-day word came to stop, rest and eat. Rations were short. Sergeant Potter reappeared, giving instructions again. He stopped by the two young soldiers and said, "Be careful now. This could be a dangerous time. A man could get careless and those snipers are just as deadly as a full-scale attack. Just as soon kill you as take you prisoner! In fact, they're worse, because you don't see them. Stay low!"

Then he disappeared.

Peter was confused and frightened, but he had begun to feel confident that they would survive. Lying behind an enormous fallen tree he turned to Cody. It was late in the day and very quiet except for the occasional sniper shot.

He saw the look of anxiety and fear on his friend's face. "Tell me again about Philadelphia," he said.

Cody smiled weakly, his unusually white teeth glistening against his completely black, smoke-charred face. He did not speak right away.

"Come Cody," said Peter, nudging him, "what are we going to do in Philadelphia?"

"There are lots of opportunities," Cody began finally, "good food, pretty girls." His face brightened, thinking about it. You're gonna love it there Peter. I know these two girls that..."

"Wait," Peter said suddenly. "Listen."

Cody became alert. "What, I don't hear anything."

"That's just it," said Peter. "There hasn't been a sniper shot in over five minutes."

They looked around. The sentry didn't seem concerned and no one else was paying attention. Evening supper was on. Some men were sleeping, others just sitting and staring, but no one seemed alarmed.

Cody and Peter stood up and looked to the south, across forty yards of open field to the woods, through which they had retreated. Suddenly a flock of birds took wing on the other end of the field. The two soldiers watched closely. Then, faintly, there came a soft drumming sound, growing louder slowly.

"What the hell is that?" asked Peter, his eyes widening.

Cody shook his head slowly and listened more intently. Then his eyes widened. He turned and screamed, "Cavalry!"

They came like gray demons on horseback, screaming the Rebel yell as they raced across the field. Out of the woods they poured. The men in blue, caught completely by surprise, screamed as they died. Peter and Cody fired as fast as they could, but their effort had little effect. They were standing, shooting into the thundering herd when the bullet caught Peter's cheek, spinning him around as he lost consciousness.

When he stirred, he was first aware of a searing, wet pain on the right side of his face. Slowly he raised his hand and touched his cheek. It felt like a furrow had been plowed across it, the skin ripped into high ridges. He examined his hand through squinting eyes. It was bloody. Around him, he could hear the moaning and crying of dying men.

Cody, he thought, pulling himself to his knees. Beside him lay his friend. Crimson covered the breast of his blue coat. Hysterically, Peter tore open the coat and shirt, exposing the gaping wound.

"Oh my God," he cried, trembling.

Cody's eyes fluttered. "Peter?" he asked weakly.

"I'm here."

Cody coughed and blood trickled from the corner of his mouth. "Oh, Peter," he said.

"Don't try to talk. We've got to find help."

Cody's eyes saw nothing. His bloody chest heaved and convulsed with each hoarse breath. "Peter, pray with me," he said.

"I will," said Peter, helplessly.

Together they began, *"Our Father, Who art in Heaven..."* Halfway through the prayer Peter was praying alone. Just like that. No drama, no fanfare, no resonant last words. Cody Thompson was dead, when an hour before he'd been alive and talking about Philadelphia with every confidence that he would return to his beloved city.

Peter lifted Cody's head to his chest. Hugging him, he rocked slowly back and forth, weeping bitterly, the tears burning his torn cheek, for a long time. Soon he realized that it was unwise to stay where he was. Reluctantly he laid Cody's head down. It was quiet now, an eerie quiet. All the wounded had either died or lapsed into unconsciousness. The gunfire had stopped, or it was very distant.

He picked up his rifle, turned to go, and found himself staring into the barrel of a revolver, pointed right between his eyes. Holding the revolver was a Confederate officer sitting atop a large gray.

Peter was stunned. He had not heard the man or his horse approach...not so much as a whisper. For a moment he thought he might be imagining the soldier. But that was impossible. His imagination would never have created such a pitiful-looking soldier. The officer was painfully thin, his face shrunken to grotesque proportions. As he held the revolver at arm's length from atop his equally unhealthy horse, he scratched himself continuously all over his body. Indeed, his neck, hands and arms were open and bloody, not with gun wounds but with sores. This was hardly the image of the "gray devil" Peter Christian had in his mind.

Peter glimpsed helplessly at the rifle in his hand. He knew to try and raise it meant certain death. *Oh my God, it's all over,* he thought. Instead of raising his rifle, in pure fear, he closed his eyes and turned his head to the side with a grimace, waiting for the killing shot.

It did not come. After a minute, Peter opened his eyes again, thinking maybe he *had* imagined the wretched Confederate officer on horseback.

But no, he was still there, atop his wretched horse, pointing the revolver right at him. His sunken eyes had turned sad.

Then the officer spoke. "Aw hell. Drop it and git."

Though he would reflect on that moment countless times for the rest of his days, at the time he didn't think or hesitate at all. He dropped his rifle and began to run, run hard. He had run thirty yards (expecting to be plugged from behind the whole time) when in his haste he stumbled. He was back on his feet instantaneously.

He looked back only once. Neither the officer nor the horse had moved. The officer had holstered his gun and was watching him.

He ran hard for a long time, still entertaining the frightening thought that the officer had merely set him loose so as to hunt him down slowly. But it did not turn out that way. Finally he could run no more, so he rested, then picked his way through the woods slowly and carefully, stepping over thousands of dead Rebel and Union soldiers. He scavenged a rifle from a dead Union soldier. He was determined that when he caught up with what was left of his infantry, *if* he caught up with them, he would not be without a rifle. He slept in the woods warily.

The next day he continued. Three times that afternoon he hid in the thicket when horsemen approached. He watched as the rebel soldiers, in small groups, returned from the raid jubilant from their victory. Some were leading large groups of Yankee prisoners. The briar bushes tore his uniform and ravaged his skin, but he did not care. He felt he was going to make it if he could put up with the discomfort and the sadness for just a little longer. It seemed he walked for a dozen hours (though it had only been five) when finally he saw the columns of blue ahead of him. It was sunset when he crossed the pontoon bridge across the Rappahannock River to safety. It seemed like several years had passed since he had crossed it going the other way.

His wounds were treated and Peter Christian was reunited with what was left of his unit. There he learned that Sergeant Potter had been killed. This compounded his sense of loss and sorrow.

The next several weeks were difficult for Peter. When he thought of Sergeant Potter and his friend Cody, a bitter hatred consumed him. But then he'd think about the sad eyes of the Confederate officer who had spared his life - *literally* spared his life - and his hatred ebbed. This brought a profound sense of guilt, a feeling that he had betrayed his old comrades by surviving and being unable to maintain his fighting spirit.

Life was intolerable for Peter then. Lonely once again, friendless and burdened with guilt, Peter labored under the tremendous weight of his conscience. It was only time, healer of *all* wounds, that finally allowed Peter Christian to put it to rest.

His cheek healed, but his face was left with a long, ugly scar. This bothered him, until a German officer told him it was truly a badge of courage. In Germany, a young soldier would be proud of such a wound. *The women find such things dashing,* he'd said.

Peter did not know if he believed this or not, but it made it easier to accept.

A year passed before the Army of the Potomac marched at full strength again. This time, it was Richmond, but he saw little action. Before he could go to the field again, his enlistment ended and a grateful Peter Christian left the Union army.

Returning to Chicago, Peter took a job with a railroad company and quickly fell in love with a beautiful girl named Ann Day. Ann returned his affection three-fold, but her parents - appalled by Peter's facial appearance - discouraged their daughter, effectively. She apologized profusely to the brokenhearted young man, but she could not be swayed.

Disillusioned, and a little bitter, Peter returned to Michigan. Several years later in life, love came to Peter again, one more time. Her name was Martha Kare. She was slender, kind and comforting. But Peter painfully discovered that what *German* women may have found *"dashing",* American women did not. And though Martha showed him kindness in every way (they became close friends), Peter was forced to accept that she would never love him. Eventually he watched her marry another man and leave Fairchild forever. Their correspondence after that was fleeting, and then not at all. Humility would prevent him from ever seeking love again. His confidence gone, Peter Christian was doomed to a life of loneliness and solitude, which he had never come to enjoy, only accept. He was never unfriendly or discourteous to the people of Fairchild over the years, just anti-social; saying as little as possible, only when necessary. Thus, few ever got to know the man. Few ever realized that the beauty of Peter Christian lay on the inside. Few in town knew a man named Peter Christian. They knew only "Hemlock", the strange hermit who lived in a shack in the woods, who came into town as little as possible, who - over the years - became the subject of many a frightening tall tale among Fairchild's young people.

The last piece of wood fell from the sawbuck. He threw it on the pile with the rest, and wiped beads of sweat from his brow, panting. He thought of Frank, and Whiley, and all the young men in the future who might be called to serve their country once again, in the war that was currently raging across an ocean or another in the future. He was a simple man, but he knew enough about the nature of mankind to know that there would always be war, in one form or another.

His hand went to his face. Beneath his beard he fingered the long, hairless, ridged scar that lay hidden there and had for the last sixty years.

Chapter Thirteen

Every two weeks, on a Saturday, Agnes Burns did her shopping in Fairchild. Like he did with his children during the school week, John Burns devotedly dropped off his wife and his daughters in town in the morning, and picked them up in the afternoon. It was always an exciting day, especially for Rachel and Caroline. It was simply a matter of supplying the household with necessities for Agnes, but for the girls it was their time to check out new things; fashions, gossip, trinkets. There was never any time to look around in the stores after school, and farm life did not offer them a great deal of opportunity to socialize, to be *girls.* So it was with tremendous, chattering anticipation that Rachel and Caroline arrived in Fairchild every other Saturday morning with their mother.

Whiley, still humiliated and nervous from the ordeal the Saturday before, chose to stay home and help his father around the farm. Frank came into town with the girls, hopped off the buggy and headed straight for Doc's place, where he would administer soap and water to the grit and grime that once again stained Doc's machine.

"See you this afternoon!" he cried as he raced off, leaving his mother and sisters on the Main Street.

Because of the girls' impatience, Mrs. Burns found it was most expedient to visit the millinery stores first. The girls' demands were never excessive. In fact, generally, the shopping spree consisted merely of trying on a hat, modeling a coat, gaping and gasping with wonder at the latest fashions and staring with wide eyes at the beautiful jewelry. There was very little buying.

Agnes allowed the girls a fair amount of time for this - usually most of the morning - and then they went on to make the necessary purchases. As usual, Camille Broton joined the group. She was Caroline's classmate and best friend. The three girls laughed and gossiped as they followed Mrs. Burns down the street.

By now it was 12:30 and there were still groceries to be purchased. Kelly's General Store was Agnes' choice for food. There John would meet them, load the groceries into the buggy, and from there it was home again. The girls, anxious to talk, begged to stay outside on the corner while Agnes finished the shopping. She conceded, leaving the three girls to chattering and laughing.

Clifton Williams, a blacksmith in Fairchild and a wound-up ex-boxer who was always willing to bring even a minor dispute to fisticuffs with *other* men, moved away from Frenchy Dumont slowly. He walked to the far side of Ryman's Saloon. It was only noon and already the burly Frenchman was in his cups. Clifton knew Frenchy's disposition and deemed it prudent to put as much space between him and Frenchy as possible.

George Ryman had had just about enough of Frenchy in the past few months. Every day - *every* day - he would stagger in, drink himself blind and start trouble. And every day George Ryman was forced to bravely (and carefully) ask Frenchy to leave. He usually did, but each time the Frenchman was more troublesome and each time he was not as quick to leave. George feared eventually there would be an ugly confrontation.

Frenchy Dumont was particularly nasty that morning. George watched him carefully. *So help me Christ,* he thought, shaking his head. *If he starts something he's out of here for good!*

Frenchy gulped down a shot of whiskey, chased it with a beer and belched loudly. Then he dug into the pockets of his soiled pants and produced some crumpled bills.

"Fill 'em up!" he said loudly. Clifton Williams and the other patrons of Ryman's Saloon watched nervously, making sure never to make eye contact with the man.

George walked over, filled his whiskey and his schooner of beer and said, "Last round for you, Frenchy."

"What?" Frenchy replied, his voice raspy and slurred.

"Time to head home," said George, "get some rest."

"I ain't tired!"

"You've been hitting it heavy," George insisted. "Oughtta give yourself a break."

"You tryin' to tell me what to do?" said Frenchy, his eyes narrowing angrily.

"Yes," said George flatly, maintaining his eye contact. "Drink up and head out."

With those words he slowly reached below the bar and produced a hard, maple club, carved like a baseball bat, only wider. He held it at his side, tapping it against his leg.

Frenchy took his shot and drank the entirety of his beer in one drink. He slammed the schooner down on the bar and eyed the club. He knew that with the aid of *Billy* (George's pet name for the weapon), the bar owner was no one to monkey with. And unlike a lot of men who readily brandished weapons, Frenchy knew George Ryman wouldn't hesitate a moment to actually use it.

He turned and headed out. He waited until he was by the table nearest the door. He reached down, grabbed one of the chairs and threw it. It bounced across the floor, coming to rest against the bar. Frenchy Dumont kicked open the door of Ryman's Saloon and walked out onto Main Street.

When he was gone, the whole bar sighed a nervous sigh of relief.

Outside, the bright sunlight of early afternoon made Frenchy's eyes hurt. *George may be right,* he thought. *I need to rest.*

He headed for his favorite spot to sit for a while. On the next block, in the alley alongside a variety store, was a large rain barrel. Beside the barrel was an enormous wooden crate, which had been sitting there for ages. There was just enough room between the two objects for a nice, comfortable fit. And the building made the area nice and shady. He was also well-hidden from passerby's on the sidewalk.

With a contented sigh, Frenchy Dumont sat down on the ground between the crate and the barrel, leaning up against the variety store building. He clasped his enormous hands over his chest and stretched his legs out to nap. Only his boots were visible poking out from between the rain barrel and the crate, and then only if one were looking closely. It was a nice, private spot, and a nice warm day to be in the shade of the alley. He closed his eyes.

He was almost asleep when a noise disturbed him. Aggravated, he lifted his head up.

"What the hell?" he mumbled, listening carefully. It was laughter he was hearing...the laughter of a young woman. He sat up and peeked around the rain barrel to see where the laughter was coming from. He squinted, his eyes trying to focus.

"Agnes," he said in his drunken stupor. His blood fired up as the laughter continued. "Are you laughing at me?" he said. "Don't do that. Don't laugh at me Agnes!"

He became filled with self-pity. There was some talking, then more laughter, this time explosive and jubilant. It was his Agnes...*she* was laughing at him, mocking him. And that John Burns was there as well, the man who had disgraced him and damaged him.

Frenchy's eyes widened in rage. Scooping up the nearest rock off the alley, he jumped up and heaved it. Unable to stand from his drunkenness, he stumbled back, which took some strength out of the throw. It was a large rock and it flew in a high arch. A scream jolted Frenchy into the realization of what he had done.

He ducked back down, hoping no one had seen him do...whatever it was that he had done. He wasn't sure. The rock had hit someone, he knew that much. In a panic he bolted down the alley faster than he had ever moved. He came out in the field behind the variety store. Across it were the woods. He started across the field at full speed. Escape was his only thought.

They'll lock me up, he thought. *Nobody wants me around here as it is! This'll be it...that Carmin Jones or Charley what's-his-name will come and I'll be trapped!*

"Get out of Fairchild! Get out of Fairchild," he said aloud as he disappeared into the woods. He thought about his boy, Steven, for a moment, but Steven was on his own now. He'd *have* to be on his own.

There was a 1:30 train out of Fairchild. He had just enough time to get his things out of the old abandoned shed he'd been sleeping in (since old lady Lindstrom put him out), and get back to town. Once on the train, he could make up his mind where to go. Somewhere far away.

Caroline saw the stone coming out of the corner of her eye, but it was the last thing she would have expected so she didn't think to duck. It struck her on the forehead, knocking her unconscious. Rachel Burns was the one who screamed, dropping to her knees beside her stricken sister.

"Get my mother!" Rachel beseeched Camille Broton. Camille ran quickly to fetch Mrs. Burns, crying with fear.

Caroline was conscious when Camille and Agnes arrived a few minutes later. An ugly blue welt had already begun to swell on Caroline's forehead, but there was only a little blood. Someone from the gathering crowd suggested taking the girl to Doc Spencer. Agnes agreed.

"Please," she said, "someone help me take her there!"

A husky young man stepped forward and together he and Agnes helped Caroline to her feet. Caroline held onto her mother tightly and was silent.

Frank was working industriously on Doc's car when a voice came from the window.

"Frank!" Doc cried, "get up here now!"

Frank set down his soapy rags and ran upstairs to Doc's office. He was surprised to see people there, and shocked to see his mother and sister. Rachel was still crying. He knew something was wrong. He walked over and hugged his mother.

"It's Caroline," said Agnes, "she's been hurt."

"How?" he said, numbed.

"It's her head. She's been struck by something."

"What?" said Frank.

"I don't know, I don't know," said Agnes, tears welling up in her eyes.

Then the door of Doc Spencer's office flew open and John Burns entered, Whiley at his side. Agnes flew into his arms.

"I was at Kelley's Grocery," he said, "waiting. They told me what happened."

Now that her husband was there Agnes no longer felt she had to be strong. Her composure left her and she wept into his shoulder. John Burns held her and spoke softly. Frank couldn't hear what his father was saying, but the words seemed to comfort his mother. He saw her nod her head in agreement. Soon she was serious, but calm. The tears were gone.

The door to the dispensary opened and Doc emerged. He closed the door behind him.

"Is she all right?" said Agnes in a low whisper.

"She's fine," said Doc. There was a gentleness in his voice that came out only at times like this. "She's resting now with a cold compress on her forehead."

Overwhelming relief showed on the face of everyone in Doc's office that afternoon, especially the Burns family. Doc Spencer added, "It's just a little cut, no stitches are necessary. What happened?"

Rachel was calm and able to talk, now that she knew Caroline would be all right. "Someone threw a rock at her!" she said. "A big rock. We were on the street, me, Camille and Caroline, and out of nowhere comes this big rock! We didn't even see it!"

"Who could have done such a thing?" Agnes demanded.

"I know! It was Steve Dumont's father," blurted out Camille. "I saw him! At least, I think it was him. He's a big man, with a terrible black beard, like a pirate!"

"Dumont," said John Burns angrily. He turned and burst through the door.

"John!" cried Agnes, but she was too late. He was already down the stairs and out on Main Street. Frank moved to follow him but Agnes promptly stepped in the way. Frank looked at her angrily, but he had no choice but to stay where he was.

His long strides carried him swiftly down the street. John Burns knew where to look for Dumont. *Ryman's Saloon,* he thought. The fury in him was building, but he was also afraid. Afraid of the fact that if he caught Dumont, he would kill him...in no uncertain terms. This was a personal issue that went back thirty years, ever since the night of that harvest dance. After that night he had vowed never to become so angry as to resort to violence. There was one extenuating circumstance to that rule, and it was Frenchy Dumont's return. John Burns had warned Frenchy to leave town and stay away, or he would kill him. Now, thirty years later, he *would* kill Dumont for what he had done, if he could find him. John Burns, gentlemen farmer, was capable of hate. And he hated Frenchy Dumont.

Inside Ryman's Saloon, gaiety prevailed. The crowd came alive once Frenchy had left the premises. The conversation was loud as the men drank the tonic that made them laugh, sing and tell extravagant lies to one another.

The door of the saloon flew open and the conversation died quickly. Everyone expected Frenchy to be there. There was a general titter of surprise when everyone saw it was John Burns.

He walked right up to the bar and said to George Ryman, "Where's Dumont?"

"Not here," said the bar owner, wiping his hands on his white apron.

"Where can I find him?"

"He was in this morning," said George, "pretty drunk. Might be sleeping it off in his room."

"Where's that?"

"What's going on John?" asked George.

"Where is his room!"

"Lindstrom's Boarding House," said George. He didn't want to be the one who had enabled one man to kill another, but

John Burns was a serious man, and would not have been after Dumont if it weren't something terrible.

John knew where Lindstrom's Boarding house was. He turned and walked out of the saloon. He walked to the boarding house. It was a large, well-kept Victorian home with flowers growing all along the front porch. Two elderly men were sitting in chairs on the porch smoking pipes.

"Afternoon," said John calmly.

The two men waved at him silently, smoking their pipes.

"I wonder if you could go in and tell Dumont a friend of his is outside."

It was lame, but it was all he could think of. He couldn't walk into the house and tear it apart. The destruction would have been awesome. And that would be hurting Esther Lindstrom; a kindly woman who had helped many decent people who had nowhere else to go. No, he had to get Dumont outside.

The old men didn't say anything, and John knew they were afraid.

He tried a different approach. "Would you ask Miss Lindstrom to come out, please?"

One of the old men jumped up and hurried to the door of the house. He disappeared inside. Three minutes later Esther Lindstrom appeared on the porch. The old man returned to his chair.

"Hello John," said Esther. She was a heavy-set woman with gray hair and a jolly face.

"Afternoon Esther," said John, tipping his hat. "Dumont here?"

"He's gone," said the old lady.

"Gone," said John, "gone where?"

"Heaven only knows," said Esther. "And only the devil cares. Ain't seen him in a week. Took off in the middle of the night without paying me for a week's worth of rent."

"And you're sure you don't know where?"

"If he hadn't left," she answered, "I would have had to put him out anyway. Wasn't too bad at first, but lately...why I just couldn't put up with him any longer. Dirty, drunken heathen!"

Frustration filled John Burns. "Thank you," he said calmly and turned away.

He formed his own manhunt then, and an hour later it was apparent Frenchy Dumont was nowhere in Fairchild, Michigan.

Frank was alone in Doc's office, waiting for his father. He kept trying to piece together what had happened and why. He was beginning to form a theory. That night, he would talk to Hemlock and get some answers.

He heard someone come trudging up the steps outside Doc's office. It was someone big, and for a moment Frank's heart raced, thinking it was the man with the black beard. But it was his father.

"He's gone," he said. "Must have left town right after it happened.

"Doc took everyone home in his car," said Frank.

"Let's go then," said his father.

The ride home was silent and seemingly endless. Frank didn't ask any questions and his father volunteered no answers.

Chapter Fourteen

It was a quiet dinner that evening at the Burns house. Anger surged in Frank every time he looked across the table at Caroline's swollen forehead. He vowed that neither Dumont nor anyone else would hurt his family again...not if he could help it.

After supper he announced that he was going for a walk. No one objected, nor gave much indication that he was heard. All were in the parlor; Whiley and Rachel playing checkers, Agnes and Caroline both reading, and John Burns in his favorite chair, sitting with his head tilted back and his eyes closed. Looking at this scene Frank felt - for the first time in his life - a wave of restlessness come over him, though he didn't recognize the significance of it at the time.

Frank had taken to using the trails through the woods rather than the road (as Hemlock did) whenever he could. It was shorter and a more interesting walk. Crossing the field he thought intently about this man named *Frenchy* Dumont, who was Steve Dumont's father. In only a week's time Frank had nearly come to fisticuffs with him, the man had thrown a rock at his sister and risked damaging her seriously, and his father had, Frank sensed, sought to kill him when he stormed out of Doc's office that afternoon. A week ago Frank didn't even know Steve Dumont *had* a father, and now there he was, pushing his way into all of their lives so violently. He hoped Hemlock could provide some answers.

The dim light of the lantern shone through the dirty windows of Hemlock's shack. Frank's knock brought an immediate response from the old man.

"Come on in," said Hemlock, opening the door wide and allowing Frank to enter. He was glad to see Frank, glad to be spared another night alone. Frank noticed a tired look in the man's eyes.

"Thought I'd come visit for a while," he said.

"Glad ya did," said Hemlock. "Wanna play some checkers?"

"Sure, why not."

"Good," said Hemlock. He had bought the checkerboard years ago, thinking that it might be good to have in *case* he had company one night. But over the years Hemlock didn't have any company, as he grew more and more alienated from the town. Many nights (especially during the winter, when there wasn't much to do and nowhere to go) he sat at the table alone, moving both sides of the board, even going so far as to talk to himself. It was a treat for him to be able to play with someone *else.* Hemlock had a deep affection for Frank. He liked both the Burns boys, but lately Frank had been spending some evenings with him, just keeping him company. And Frank treated Hemlock not as the mysterious old hermit of Cumberland County, but as a man with stories to tell, knowledge to dispense. Hemlock was very grateful for that.

They talked of many things that night, playing game after game of checkers. Frank mentioned his coming graduation.

"Oh yeah," said Hemlock, as if it were news to him. He shook his head, looked at the boy who was quickly becoming a man, and said, "I remember watching Agnes change your soiled drawers when you was a kid. When you was smaller than *Whiley!"*

Frank lowered his eyes, smiled and blushed. There was a moment of silence, in which they heard a coyote yap in the woods near the shack. Then Hemlock said, "You gonna leave Fairchild afterwards?"

"No, I think I'll help Pa for a while around the farm."

The old man's face brightened. "I was hoping you'd stay for a while. Sometimes leaving home can lead to bad experiences."

"Well you don't have to leave home to have bad experiences," said Frank.

"What do you mean?"

"Hemlock, do you recall telling me a few weeks back about a fight Pa had with another man over Mother?"

Hemlock leaned back in his chair, rubbing his bald head, concern showing on his face. "Yes," he said.

"Who was that man? You never mentioned his name."

"His name is Alex Dumont," said Hemlock.

"Frenchy Dumont?"

"Yes."

Frank's suspicions had been right. He told Hemlock of the incidents involving both Whiley and Caroline, and then told him about his father's manhunt through Fairchild that afternoon.

Hemlock shook his head gravely and said, "I'm glad Caroline's all right, and I'm glad your pa didn't find him. He would have killed him." He thought and added, "I've always been afraid of something like this happening. Both Frenchy and your pa are stubborn men, and both are big men, and both can be violent men. Every time Frenchy has come back, over the years, I've worried that something was going to happen. This is the *farthest* it's gone that I can remember." Hemlock shuddered. "I hope he don't *ever* come back now!"

"I hope so too," said Frank.

And yet there was a part of him that wished Frenchy Dumont *would* return so that he, or his father, or *someone,* could settle this affair once and for all.

Chapter Fifteen

Earlier in the evening, before supper, Doc Spencer deposited the Burns family at their farm. He gave simple instructions to Agnes on how best to care for Caroline, then he left. His drive back into Fairchild was spent deep in thought. Twilight was falling on the small hamlet as he drove down the main street. He had passed John and Frank Burns on the road going the other way, but had only waved. The meeting of Burns and Dumont was preying on his mind. Rather than head home, he decided to pay a visit to the police chief.

The light in Carmin's office was on, so Doc entered. Carmin looked up from his desk with surprise. Doc thought he looked tired. Indeed, the chief rubbed his eyes and said, "Oh, hello Doc. What can I do for you?"

"Just need a little information," said Doc. "What happened between Burns and Dumont?"

Carmin tilted his head. "Between who and who?"

"You know," said Doc frustrated, "over the Burns girl!"

"I don't know anything," said Carmin shrugging. "I've been out at Lost Lake all day helping the sheriff's department. Charley's still out there. Some damn fool fisherman went out in a canoe and got himself drowned. We've been dragging the lake all day with hooks. Still hadn't found him when I left."

Doc sat down in the chair facing Carmin's desk and told of the day's events, leaving out no detail.

When he finished, Carmin let out a deep sigh. "Christ," he said.

"What are you going to do with Dumont when you get him?" Doc asked.

"Well, that's up to Judge Baker," said Carmin. "But Dumont's probably clear to Pennsylvania by now. And throwing a rock is not exactly a hanging offense."

Doc looked at him sternly. "A little lower and that girl could have lost an eye."

"But she didn't," said Carmin. "We have no reason to believe he did it intentionally to harm her. Dumont's a fool. He was probably drunk and didn't realize what he was doing. Which, as far as I'm concerned, describes his entire life."

"Bah!" said Doc. Carmin shrugged again. Doc jumped up. He reached the door and turned around to fire his parting shot. "If you held an elective office, I might be tempted to vote against you!"

Although Carmin didn't show it in front of Doc, the situation concerned him. He had seen similar incidents - family grudges - explode into real violence. He locked up his office and headed down to Ryman's Saloon. He didn't relish facing a drunken Frenchy Dumont, but he had no choice. It was his job to keep the peace.

He stood in the door of Ryman's Saloon. It was packed wall to wall. Carmin scanned the crowd and ascertained that Frenchy was not among it. He spotted George Ryman sitting at a table. He was eating from a tray of cheese and crackers and washing it down with an enormous schooner of beer. Carmin procured himself a schooner of beer from the bar and sat down next to Ryman.

George looked at him and smiled. "Hi ya, Chief!"

Carmin extended his glass slightly, nodded, then took a sip. He set the beer down on the table gently. "Dumont around?" he asked.

"Frenchy? Naw, I hear he left town in a hell of a hurry today!"

"Hear anything else?"

"Only that he got his ass one step ahead of John Burns," said Ryman, drinking heavily from his schooner. "Too bad ol' Burns didn't catch up with him and give him something to take along! Like a broken nose!"

"I take it you don't care for Frenchy too much either," said Carmin, smiling. The saloon was crowded, smoky and very loud. Carmin was having difficulty being heard.

Ryman gave a look of disgust. "That son of a bitch!" he said.

"Well, I think we've seen the last of him," said Carmin.

After that the two men fell to talking of other things. Every once in a while, George Ryman found someone else to tend the bar while he became a *patron.* And when he did he was a great man, a great talker. Carmin found himself having a good time talking with Ryman about everything, and yet nothing at all. But there was business to attend to. He finished his beer and rose to leave.

"Hey!" said the saloon owner. "Where ya' going!"

"Got work to do George," said Carmin. "See you around."

"Ya sure," said George disappointedly. Then as an afterthought he said, "Say Chief, you ever hear from any of Millard Hoffman's relatives?"

"Don't know that he had any, why?"

"Oh, we were talking about him the other day," said George plaintively. "Kind of miss him, ya know? Despite his drinkin', he was a good old fella."

"Nope, didn't hear anything yet, George." Carmin didn't mention the letter he had written to Lansing.

"I 'spose it don't matter anyway," said George.

"What's that?" asked Carmin, perking up. He hadn't heard back from Lansing yet and the thought of finding out something on his own about the six-month-old Millard Hoffman case was enticing.

"Well, one of the boys said Millard told him that he had worked as a mason up in Birchwood at one time."

"Birchwood, huh?"

"That's what he said." George Ryman shrugged. "Just thought I'd pass it along. Might not mean anything."

"Thanks," Carmin said, "I appreciate it."

Out on the street Carmin rolled the events of the day over in his mind. John Burns and Frenchy Dumont dominated his thoughts. He shook his head, thinking about the 20-year grudge held between the two mammoth men.

Foolish, he thought. *Just plain foolish!*

He took a long walk on that warm night in May. There were lots of stars and it was too hot to sleep anyway. He walked from one end of town to the other, then along all the side streets. There were lots of people out, enjoying the weather as well. Everyone he saw said, *"Hi ya, Chief!"* or *"Evening Carmin!"*

He felt good, in a variety of ways. The walk untangled his mind at the end of what had been a very stressful day. Between John Burns, Frenchy Dumont, Millard Hoffman and the fisherman on Lost Lake (or at the *bottom* of Lost Lake), he thought his own life wasn't in such bad shape. He was confident Frenchy Dumont was gone for good. Eventually he would hear from Lansing. Maybe they had even found the fisherman by now. Then all would be normal again, nice and quiet.

The way he and Charley liked it.

At midnight Agnes Burns was staring out her bedroom window. In the yard below, her husband stood in the warm moonlight. His stirring had awakened her. She pretended to be asleep, listening as he quietly dressed and left the room.

She knew where he was going. Whenever he was troubled, he always retreated to what he referred to as his thinking spot; a small, grass-covered knoll just in front of the fence line, by the road.

And there he now stood, with an unobstructed view of the road, the field on the other side, and the thick pine forest beyond that. The moonlight sprinkled silver dust over the land, making everything dimly visible. Every once in a while a lone cloud would drift in front of it. There would be a moment of darkness and then an unfolding of the natural gray light as the cloud passed.

John Burns was a hard, serious man, but he had a deep appreciation for the beauty of the natural world, which, it seemed, only Agnes knew about.

Beautiful night, he thought, looking across the road. *Perfect for all the night hunters.*

An owl breezed by him silently and lit in a nearby tree. John watched it intently. *Beware field mouse,* his thoughts continued, *death sails on the silent wings of the night.*

Another lone cloud passed in front of the moon and all was dark. John looked up and wondered if the field mouse thinks an owl overhead is a just a passing cloud, before it feels the pressure, the stinging, painful pressure on its neck as it is lifted off the ground.

It is a violent world, thought John, a little sadly. All the animals hunted and protected themselves in violent ways. Man was no different. Thus, the violence of Frenchy Dumont (and the thought of confronting it) did not bother John. That was part of the natural order of things.

But Man *was* different in one way. For the creatures of the woods, violence was a method of survival. It was never gratuitous, never anything other than a means to an end. Man had one characteristic that no other animal on Earth would ever experience: A need for revenge if wronged. In the field, the other mice did not rebel against the owl when their brother was lifted off to his death. Their lives went insignificantly on. Revenge and cruelty were traits of humanity alone. And it was not good to find oneself at the receiving end of it.

John thought about the bitter revenge that had churned in Dumont after all those years. Would he come back and attempt even further harm? *No,* John decided. *That would be too risky. Dumont would not dare come back to Fairchild after what had happened. He's a coward.*

But revenge does not require rational thought. In fact, revenge fortifies itself on *irrational* thought. Standing there in the moonlight, John Burns could not have dreamed how close to insanity Alex Dumont was, even now. And it was going to get worse.

Chapter Sixteen

Silas Klinger sat at his desk reading the letter from Cumberland County. As he read he clicked his tongue repeatedly, his left foot twitching. When he finished he set the letter down, sat back in his chair and let out a horse-like sigh. Rubbing a palm over his bald head, he looked at the bright sunshine coming through the one window of his office at the Public Records building. It cast a bright gold rectangle across his desk and on the floor beyond. A dust storm was raging in the box of light.

Klinger sighed again, this time with more of a flourish. It was a beautiful day in Lansing, a perfect day to knock off early. Someone *always* managed to spoil it with damn fool requests!

Abruptly he rose, snatched the letter from his desk and walked over to his assistant's desk in the opposite corner of the room.

"Hey Arnold," Klinger said, "let me tell you a story."

Arnold looked up. "Yes sir?"

"It's about a little boy in a faraway village called Fairchild, in Cumberland County, Michigan. Now this little boy fell off a chicken coop when he was very young, and landed upside down on his head, scrambling his brain like an egg." He lifted his pointer finger up. "And that *very* little boy, whom *no one* thought would accomplish more in his life than being named the town's resident simpleton, grew up and became the *police chief!*"

"So what are you trying to tell me?" said Arnold, tilting his head inquisitively.

"That there is hope for *you!"* said Klinger. He exploded in laughter, his eyes open wide, his mouth gaping, his whole body shaking.

Arnold Hayes, his serious-minded assistant, still didn't get it. Klinger snorted and dropped the letter on his desk. Arnold lifted his glasses up to his face, picked up the letter and read it.

When he finished he said, "So, what are we going to do?"

Silas Klinger snatched the letter away in a violent motion. Carefully he began to fold it. When he was finished, he inspected it carefully. There was no question; it was one of his *finest* works.

Taking aim, he launched the paper airplane to a perfect bulls-eye in Arnold's wastepaper basket.

"What are we going to do?" Klinger said. "Well Arnold, you just saw me *do it!"*

Arnold laughed weakly, repulsed by his boss' lack of professionalism, but forced to go along with it supportively, for the sake of his job.

Klinger started back toward his desk, but then he paused and without turning back to Arnold said, "I did what *I'm* going to do. Now here's what *you* are going to do. Send a letter back to Chief What's-his-name. Tell him we have neither the time nor the manpower to fill his request. Use all that formal letter talk so that he - like everyone else - will think his government is something more than the idle, fool operation it is. Tell him if he wishes to journey to Lansing, we would be more than happy to open our records to him. He can go through them at his leisure." He turned around and smiled in a disturbed way. "Tell him if he can sort them all out, put the records into some sort of *order,* they're all his! That will keep him busy till, oh, about 1950 or so!"

"Yes sir," said Arnold, with a blank expression on his face.

He watched Silas Klinger walk back to his desk, throw himself down into his chair and start staring again, as he had been all day, until the mail arrived. Arnold Hayes was becoming increasingly aware that things were not quite right with his boss.

There was a great tension building in him. Silas had never married. Didn't seem to socialize much. Only had his job. His government desk job, which he hated.

Arnold Hayes didn't know it then, but he would be violently introduced to the full scope of Silas Klinger's personal issues two months later, when Silas showed up at work one morning with a shotgun and a blank expression all his own.

But for now Arnold obediently pulled out a piece of letterhead, loaded his typewriter, and began responding to Chief *"What's-His-Name"*, wondering if he should start looking for employment somewhere else.

Chapter Seventeen

"Beautiful, isn't it?" asked Morgan Wells.

John Burns nodded in agreement, gazing at the gold pocket watch twisting slowly on the chain.

"Yes sir," said the farmer, "it certainly is."

Burns had entered the jewelry store and had asked Morgan Wells - point blank - to see the finest watch he had. Morgan had hesitated, not from skepticism but from surprise. He knew John Burns was a frugal man, who had no need or desire for such extravagances.

"The *finest,"* said Morgan.

Frank nodded slowly. "Yes sir, the finest."

The spinning timepiece was the result of that request.

"With proper care it will last you a lifetime," commented Morgan.

Forty dollars, thought John uneasily. *How will I explain that to Agnes?*

"Yes sir," said Morgan, pressing the sale now that he was sure John was actually interested in the piece, "it's a watch you'll be proud of."

"It's not for me."

"Oh," said Morgan, "really."

"No, it's for my boy. He's graduating from high school."

Morgan Wells became alarmed. He had to think fast. Would a man *actually* spend that much money on his son? He thought not. He prepared to shift tactics.

John Burns thought deeply about it. Frank would be the first in a long line of Burns men to graduate from high school. That was something fantastic as far as John was concerned.

But Frank was also the first of four children. The other three children were equally as bright and were sure to graduate soon themselves. He would certainly have to spend at *least* as much on them when it was time for their graduations.

"Perhaps you would like to see something a little less expensive," said Morgan, feeling the sale slipping through his fingers.

"No," said John, "this will be fine."

"An excellent choice!" said Morgan, relieved and excited. When he first acquired the timepiece he never thought he would be able to sell it in Fairchild. Taking a silk handkerchief from his breast pocket he smiled and wiped his brow.

"I hadn't counted on spending quite that much," said John. "I'll have to pay part now and the rest when I pick up the watch."

"Certainly, certainly," said Morgan.

John dug into his pocket and produced a roll of bills bound tightly with a rubber band. He counted out twenty-two one dollar bills. Wells wrote out a receipt, *"Paid on account."*

John looked at the rubber band, then at his remaining money, and sighed. He pocketed the bills, leaving the rubber band on the counter and turned to leave.

"Be back next week," he said as he exited.

He walked down the main street, worried about his purchase and proud of his purchase at the same time. A block down a familiar face surprised him. It was Hemlock. The old man was rarely seen in town. He had his thumbs hooked through the strap of his packsack, adjusting the weight on his back as he walked along. A smile lit his face when he saw John Burns.

"Hello!" he said. "Bad enough I gotta come into town. Nice to see a friendly face!"

"What brings you into town?" asked John.

"Beans," replied the old man. He spit a wad of chewing tobacco onto the sidewalk. "Just about out of canned goods out at the shack. How's Caroline?"

"She's okay. No serious damage," said John.

Hemlock noticed a tone of anger in John's voice. He frowned and said, "You take care, John. That Dumont is a dangerous man."

"He's gone," said John. "He won't show his face around here anymore."

Hemlock only grunted.

"You headed home?" John asked him.

"Yep."

"Come along, I'll drop you off."

"Much obliged," said Hemlock happily. He was not looking forward to having to walk home with a packsack loaded down with canned goods.

The horses and hayrack were in front of Tony's Meat Palace, the local butchery. Hemlock raised his eyebrows when he saw the empty wooden pens in the rack.

"Selling some stock for butchering?" asked the old man.

"Just a couple pigs and some chickens," said John. *Gonna be selling some more, too,* he thought. *What am I going to tell Agnes?*

Hemlock slung his burden of canned goods and placed them on the open rack. Burns jumped up and offered his hand. The old man took it and he was pulled up easily. All the way to the shack, the two men laughed and talked of trivial things.

When John continued down the road and Hemlock was alone, he stood by the door of his shack, a terrible feeling of loneliness overtaking him. He hoped Frank would come to call that night. He enjoyed their visits. Talking with John during the ride home he realized that he, like his son, was an enjoyable man who had interesting things to say.

Hemlock never thought it would happen, but he was beginning to regret his years of isolation, and it was tearing him up inside. He had loved Cody like a brother and Cody had died. He had given his heart to two women and two women had rejected him. To the shy and emotional Peter Christian, this proved to be fatal.

But now, talking to fine men like John and Frank Burns, Hemlock was beginning to see things in a different way. He was starting to not view the world, or people, in such a cynical light. And the thought of the years that had been wasted was starting to tear him apart inside.

Chapter Eighteen

The hallways of Fairchild High School were lined with the pictures of American presidents. Frank passed them every day, but had never really studied them. Today he paused, examining their serious, intelligent faces. All week he had been stopping and taking in different scenes from around the school, viewing them in a way he never had before. A certain level of anxiety had risen within him as the day of his graduation drew nearer, and Frank could not explain it. It wasn't nostalgia, per se. Unlike Whiley and the girls, Frank had no real friends in school, no *close* friends. He was a loner. He never attended a dance, sporting event, or any other school function. The other students looked upon him as a big, good-natured boy who did his work, was pleasant enough, but didn't have much to say to anyone other than his family. Only once was Frank thrust into the "spotlight" (to where the other kids were talking about him, much to his chagrin), and that involved the *Medwick Theory,* early in his senior year.

Harry Medwick graduated from college with a degree in teaching and an unprecedented record as a heavyweight boxing champion; undefeated three years in a row. He was arrogant, fancying himself an urban sophisticate. He was also a socialist, who believed the surest way to prepare for and achieve greatness was not through chasing money and foolhardy dreams, but through discipline, sacrifice and punishment. This was the basis for the

Medwick Theory, and Harry Medwick applied it to the classroom with a fervor. Heaven help the student that acted up in *his* classroom. He was six-foot-two, all muscle and big bones, and he lulled those around him into a false sense of security with his soft voice and gentle demeanor, which kept the lighted fuse within him hidden.

His first teaching position was 11th grade history in a small town in Ohio, just outside of Cleveland. He spent his first day there appraising his new class in silence. He mentally noted the students he thought would be disruptive to his class, forming a sort of enemies list. In that particular class at that particular time there were many. The very next day he began to rectify the situation.

He did this in three ways: a slam against the wall, a vice-like grip behind the neck (accompanied by rigorous shaking), and in extreme cases (any kid who *dared* attempt to undermine his absolute authority in the classroom more than once) grabbing the front of a shirt and slapping the face hard two or three times in rapid succession, before the kid knew what hit him. He took care to always use an open hand, but a couple of open-handed slaps from Harry Medwick was sufficient enough to ring the bell of even the largest, most "disruptive" student.

After one month, Harry Medwick's 11th grade History class was the best-behaved class in the school. Medwick had effectively browbeat the children into quiet submission. This allowed him to heap a load of *silent* study material on them while he sat idly at his desk, dreaming of other things, things outside the world of that schoolhouse. Those who flunked a Medwick test took great pains never to flunk another, as the man was also talented in the art of humiliation. The names of all flunkies were drawn up on a poster board in big dark letters and hung at the front of the class. On Friday Harry Medwick would go through the list in front of the entire class and ask each individual student to explain why he had let the others down by failing, encouraging taunting from the flunky's peers.

This system worked well for Harry. He got the maximum from his students with the minimum amount of work on his part in the first month of each school year, and the rest of the year was easy sledding.

For three years, Harry Medwick practiced his *theory* in Ohio, and no parents, teachers or staff-members complained. Then disaster fell upon him, over a boy named Melvin Cutter. It could be argued that Melvin deserved the slapping he got more than anyone Harry had ever disciplined. Melvin was a spoiled, obnoxious boy, but he was also the son of one of the town's most influential businessmen. Melvin told his father and his father stormed upon the school administration with raging indignation. Harry was summoned, and after a boisterous session with school officials in which Harry attempted to explain the *Medwick Theory* and the importance of discipline (with no shame or hesitation), he was unanimously dismissed.

Though he did not mention *this* to the school officials, Harry felt the *Medwick Theory* gave credibility to his socialist ideology as well. He had observed in his three years of teaching that it was usually the rich children, spoiled and jaded, from affluent, money-hungry families, who were the most troublesome. The poor ones, those from farm or laborer families, were generally quick to obey.

Still, he was out a job. He cursed himself for being such a careless fool, and vowed never to make the same indiscretion again. After that there was a new variable in the *Medwick Theory,* and it involved the family status of the student in question. Children of powerful, influential, or just plain rich families would be given slack. To a point.

The following autumn - the autumn of 1914 - he accepted a position at Fairchild High School.

Standing on the wooden platform of the train depot, he glanced at the white sign with black lettering: ***Fairchild.*** He set his suitcase down, pulled out a handkerchief from his pocket and wiped his forehead. The late summer heat was oppressive. His coat hung on his arm, his collar was open and his tie was loosened. Through thin, round spectacles he eyed the dusty road before him, which stretched for several hundred yards. Beyond that stood

Fairchild, his new home, a mere collection of run-down buildings, a sore on an otherwise lovely landscape.

He felt despair to the very depths of his soul. It was even *worse* than he imagined. He cursed under his breath as self-pity overwhelmed him. He was used to urban living. Hailing from the very New York City itself, he had thought the *last* town had been isolated. Looking down the road into Fairchild, he now longed for the "cosmopolitan" town in Ohio he'd left behind.

How could this have happened, he thought with a groan. He was totally unprepared for what he saw before him. He knew from the correspondence when he accepted the position that Fairchild was small and located in Upper Michigan, but he'd needed a job desperately and managed to convince himself that it couldn't be any *worse* than Grangeville, Ohio.

Hell, he'd thought, *I could learn to hunt and fish. Become wise in the ways of nature. And it's a job. It's not permanent...or it doesn't* have *to be.*

The train ride told a different story, however. He'd been told that Fairchild was a farming community, but the countryside he saw drifting by slowly from his train seat was woods; dense, all-encompassing...a wall of thicket towering up and over the train tracks as he chugged along, afternoon sunlight flashing through the trees onto his face.

Now, it was confirmed. Fairchild was not a *bustling* farm community (with an urban Mecca close by to escape to on the weekends), but a *poor, isolated* farm community that had yet to find the 20th century. Despair and bitterness began to swarm in on Harry Medwick.

I can always leave, he thought anxiously. Yes, that was a good idea. Keep heading west, perhaps, to Chicago. He could find a job there.

He looked around, spotted the stationmaster and walked to him.

"Good afternoon sir," the stationmaster said. "Welcome to Fairchild, Michigan. Anyone meeting you?"

Harry had been about to speak when the stationmaster spoke up first. Now Harry paused and winced. *Don't have much money,* he thought anxiously. *I could* get *to Chicago, but won't have much to go on from there. Nowhere to stay, nothing to eat...and no job. No job. No money.*

"No, I don't think so," he said, sighing dejectedly. He dug into his pocket and produced a letter. He unfolded it, scanned it over a moment and looked up at the stationmaster. He was an older man with a face that spoke of proper, happy small-town ignorance. He had probably lived his entire life - some fifty years or so - in that very town, doing that very job.

"Can you tell me where Murry's boarding house is?"

"Oh yes, sir," said the stationmaster, looking past Harry and pointing. "Follow the road straight into town. Go through town. It's the last building on the right before there's no more town!" He smiled in a silly way, like he thought that was funny.

Harry nodded politely and said, "Thanks." He pointed to his steamer trunk. "Okay if I leave that here till I can come out and pick it up. I don't feel like carrying it into town now."

"Suit yourself," said the stationmaster.

Harry left his trunk in the stationmaster's quarters, picked up his suitcase and started walking into town, cursing the bad luck that had brought him here. But it wasn't bad luck. Though his arrogant (and at the same time flailing and insecure) mind would *never* allow him to admit it, it was simply a lack of teaching jobs and very poor references that brought Harry Medwick to Fairchild.

Augie Johnson taught 8th and 9th grade mathematics in Fairchild. He was a conservative man, quiet and not inclined to socialize any more than necessary. He was of medium height, slight of build, with hips that seemed too wide and always made his shoulders appear to be pinched at his neck. To make matters worse he wore thick glasses and had begun to lose his hair. But located just behind his glasses was a mind of vast intellect, which few people (judging, unfortunately by his physical appearance) appreciated. It was a mind that would have carried a stronger, more forceful man to unlimited success.

Physically, his wife seemed a perfect match for Augie. She was a small, plain woman with dull features. Mentally, however, she was his very antithesis. Unlike Augie, she was dull of *mind* as well, chattering on endlessly and boisterously about trivial things. *Not even trivial,* Augie often thought at the dinner table, watching her. *Less than trivial. "Trivial" speaks of something unimportant but interesting. Her talk is neither important* nor *interesting! It's asinine!*

Still, Augie Johnson loved her, for reasons he could not quite explain. He felt a great comfort with her. She wasn't unintelligent, in other words she wasn't a *fool*, she was simply not on the same level as Augie and never would be. Most importantly, she didn't *want* to be. Perhaps that was part of what Augie loved about her. She did not pretend to be something she wasn't, and did not hide what she was.

Besides, she was his wife...a devoted wife, and Augie was a devoted man.

For three days she had urged her husband to pay a visit to the new teacher staying at Murry's boarding house.

"School will be starting next week!" she told Augie. "Go make him feel welcome! Invite him to dinner!"

It was unfortunate that Margie Johnson was uninteresting, because she loved having company and loved cooking dinner. And she was a good cook, just a lousy conversationalist. "Come on!" she insisted, when Augie expressed his reservations. "Be *neighborly* for God's sake!"

Augie gave in. He never looked forward to company, but he *was* interested in meeting the new teacher. He'd heard he was a young one from out east. That afternoon he went to the boarding house and introduced himself to the young man. They chatted aimlessly for a moment, then the invitation was made. Medwick accepted. He would dine with the Johnson family the following evening.

Delighted that the young teacher had accepted the invitation, and excited by Augie's report that the man seemed *"friendly enough"*, Margie outdid herself, preparing roast chicken, corn on the cob, mashed potatoes, gravy, rutabaga, pickles, home-made bread, biscuits, apple pie, blueberry pie and coffee - enough of each to satisfy an entire infantry division.

Although inwardly bored with these people, Medwick never let it show. It would be unwise to alienate someone in town before even setting foot in his classroom. Besides, the meal *was* delicious, and he was charming and worldly throughout, taking delight in slinging extravagant tales of his "travels" right over the head of the little woman and watching her feign comprehension. She was titillated, giggling like a schoolgirl at Medwick's every word. Augie's intelligence and instinct ran deeper than his wife's of course, and by the end of dinner he had decided to himself that he did not like Harry Medwick.

"So charming, so charming," said Margie Johnson when the young teacher had left. "And so handsome."

That night he and his wife made love for the first time in many months. It was Margie, much to Augie's surprise and shock, who initiated it. Augie wondered why, but did not decline.

Two days later, Augie deposited a package at the post office for shipment and was hurrying home. As he passed Ryman's Saloon a strong hand seized his arm. He turned and looked into the eyes of Harry Medwick.

"Hi ya Augie!" Medwick said loudly. "Glad I caught ya! I've been meaning to thank ya for the *wonderful* meal the other night!"

Augie, shocked by this behavior coming from a teacher, nodded and said, "You're quite welcome, Harry."

"Say, 'spose I show my appreciation by treatin' you for a coupla drinks!"

Augie could smell the alcohol on Medwick's breath, vaporous and foul. Medwick had obviously been drinking all day. *Odd,* he thought. *I would not have pegged him as a drinking man.*

And he was right. Medwick *never* drank. Physical fitness was his lifeblood. "Physically fit for the revolution!" he often said to himself. He had always taken care of himself. Indulgence in alcohol - indulgence in *anything* - was a sign of weakness. Self-pity and loneliness had *started* taking him to Ryman's Saloon, however, and were now taking him there earlier and earlier each day.

"I'm weak, you know," he said, his face close to Augie's, his eyes glazed. "I'm turning weak. Let me buy ya a drink!"

"Thanks for the offer," said Augie, "but I really must be getting home."

"Bah!" said Harry, spraying Augie's face with saliva. "It's early! You got time!"

He grabbed Augie by the arm with a strong hand, and pulled the mathematics teacher into the saloon.

Resigned to his fate, and so damn polite he did not want to get angry with Harry because he sensed the new teacher must be terribly unhappy, he sat down with Medwick at an empty table.

"Beer?" Medwick asked.

"Fine," said Augie.

Medwick stumbled to the bar, ordered, and returned with two large schooners. The two men got to talking and it soon became apparent to Augie that Medwick's unhappiness was due to loneliness. Medwick told the same stories he had told during dinner at Augie's house; about traveling the around the world, art museums, avoiding bourgeois society. Only now he spoke without the pretense and in a pitiful, melancholy tone. Augie softened a little.

"Tell me Harry," he said, "how is it that you happened to come to Fairchild?"

Harry looked at the simple man at the table with him. He hesitated, considering, then decided he could trust him. He looked around, leaned over, and whispered with slightly slurred speech, "It's the Medwick Theory."

"The *who* theory?" said Augie.

"The Medwick Theory," said Harry impatiently, "you know! Me! I'm Harry Medwick!"

While Augie ran his finger around and around the top of his schooner, Harry told him everything; his politics, his days in college, his success as a boxer, and his time at the school in Ohio. He also explained the *Medwick Theory* to Augie in great detail, and further how it had gotten him into trouble.

"An undicsiplined society is a *weak* society!" said Medwick. "People don't understand that. They think I'm harsh.

I'm not harsh. I'm giving kids the greatest tool they will get in their lives: a sense of order, DISCIPLINE! History, mathematics, good verbal skills, they're all important, but without the ability to apply these skills effectively and forcefully, they're USELESS!"

When he finished, Augie was astonished, not only by what he heard but also by the fact that Harry had told him.

"I'm afraid you won't be able to do any of that *here,"* he remarked.

"Oh, I won't," said Medwick quietly. "I do not intend to make the same mistake twice. But you must agree with me on the matter of discipline, don't you?" Augie said nothing. Medwick nudged his arm and said, "Don't you?"

"Certainly," said Augie. "But there are different methods."

"Damn right there are!" Medwick said with a flourish. "And the one *I've* devised assures the maximum effect with the minimum risk of defiance and the minimum amount of effort!"

Augie said nothing.

Medwick took a sip of beer and added, "And lately I've *perfected* the theory."

"Oh?" said Augie. "How so?"

"It's really quite simple," Harry said smugly. "I should have thought of it before. When I first got started, I would pick out *all* the troublemakers, every last one of them. Then I figured I should, for the sake of my job, cut the rich kids in town some slack. I didn't want to incur another angry, obnoxious, capitalistic father! Now I think I was wrong *both* times. What you do, is simply take the biggest kid - the *biggest* kid - the one all the other kids step aside for, rich or poor it doesn't matter, and shake him up. Not violently. Just some shaking, a little intimidation. *Push* him as far as you can! That will put the fear of GOD in the rest!" Harry flashed a smile of satisfaction. "Discipline and *strength!* Get it?"

Augie stared at him. There was a hint of cruelty in Medwick's eyes. *He's not a teacher,* thought Augie, staring at him. *He's a revolutionary, a dictator!*

"Very interesting," Augie said. He grabbed his schooner, gulped the rest of his beer and set it back down. "Well, I must be going. It's past suppertime. Thank you for the beer."

"Sure thing Augie," said Medwick. "Just remember, us teachers gotta stick together."

That will be the day, thought Augie, hurrying for the door. He decided he would keep an eye on Harry Medwick.

School began the next week. Harry sat at his desk, watching his new class closely. Already he had put a name with a face for about three-fourths of the students. The size of the class surprised him - nearly forty kids. He had not expected nearly that size in a small town like Fairchild. The influx, he decided, came from the many farms that peppered the area outside of the city proper. *They certainly believe in big family labor,* he thought. He noticed several sets of brothers and sisters, all about the same age, all in the same class.

So far there had not been a hint of insurrection. Harry smiled at this. He knew they were feeling *him* out as well, and that eventually familiarity would breed insolence. By the second week his authority - his domination - would be challenged, and he would be ready. He slipped a finger into his vest pocket and stole a glance at his pocket watch. It corresponded precisely with the clock on the wall.

Three, he thought. *There are three possibilities in this room. Further investigation will allow me to determine which one would be best. Right now it's the Burns kid.* He looked down at his classroom roster. *Frank Burns.*

A week passed. Just as Harry expected, insubordination was beginning to crop up, as the students became familiar with Mr. Medwick. He remained deceptively lenient for now. The time to institute the new and improved *Medwick Theory* would come soon enough.

Casual conversation with Augie in the teachers lounge revealed to Harry that Frank Burns, undeniably the biggest kid in the class, was a farm boy. *Perfect,* he thought. *No influential father to worry about.*

Harry realized, however, as the days went by that there was a snag in his plan, at least insofar as it involved Frank Burns. While others in the class became bolder, challenging his authority, raising a ruckus when they could, Frank remained infuriatingly cooperative. He was courteous, attentive and quiet, and this irritated the hell out of Medwick. Things were not working according to his plan.

The beginning of the third week, Harry decided the Burns kid needed a little prodding. He started with subtle remarks, then as the week went on he graduated to good, outright insults. The whole class was aware of Mr. Medwick's behavior toward Frank. The boy seemed puzzled, but still showed no outright defiance. This made Medwick more determined to make his idea work. He concentrated all his efforts, all his concern, all his contempt, all his ridicule, on Frank Burns. Thus, the other kids in the class began to think they could do anything. Twice Medwick caught himself just before he exploded on someone else. No, it was Frank Burns now, all the way. The more of an angel Frank was, the more of a challenge he became in Harry's eyes. And Harry was nothing if not quick to rise to a challenge, particularly in light of his increased time at Ryman's Saloon. Now more than ever, he felt the need to prove himself, his theory.

The chance to lay some groundwork outside of picking on Frank came when he learned who Frank's parents were, and that Mrs. Burns attended all the church socials.

It was Augie Johnson who told him, during innocent conversation, and quickly regretted doing so. He had heard all too much about the *Medwick Theory,* and knew that Frank was easily the largest boy in the school, a prime target for Medwick's terrible ideas.

"Don't cause trouble," he told Harry sharply.

Harry shrugged. "Now why in hell would you think something like that?" he answered. He wasn't being coy. The question was intended to be serious.

Augie saw his indignation and said, "Harry, I just don't want there to be any *trouble."*

"Since when is going to a church social to meet the parents of some of my students considered trouble?" he said. "The only trouble there might be is if I die of *boredom* in front of everyone."

Augie frowned and walked away, muttering, "I just don't want there to be trouble."

Medwick attended the very next church social. He walked about, greeting the people he knew and making sure he was introduced to those he didn't know. Margie Johnson was there. She was tickled to see Medwick present and took to introducing him to everyone as if they were the best of friends, almost as if they were husband and wife. Augie stood by her side, frowning and bearing it.

All the while Medwick was waiting to be introduced to Mrs. Burns and it happened halfway through the evening. Margie grabbed his arm tightly and said, "Mr. Medwick, I would like you to meet Mrs. John Burns."

Harry turned and was instantly surprised by the almost glamorous attractiveness of the woman. He bowed his head slightly and took her slender hand.

"Mrs. Burns," he said in a low voice.

"Please, call me Agnes, Mr. Medwick," said the lady. "I understand you have my son in one of your classes."

He hesitated, scanning her eyes for any sign of reproach, but found none.

"Yes," he said, "as a matter of fact I do." He smiled at her and she smiled back. Her beautiful, youthful face (in stark contrast to the tired, dull faces of the other Fairchild wives) almost caused him to abandon his scheme right then and there. But he had carried it this far, he was determined to see it through.

"Perhaps at some opportune time," he said, "we could discuss Frank."

Agnes tilted her head slightly in concern. "Is something wrong?"

"Perhaps at some other time," he said, pretending to beg off. For the first time in Harold Medwick's adult life, he felt guilty.

"No," said Agnes, "if there is something I should know, please tell me."

He gave the appearance of being forced to divulge something he did not wish to. *That* was part of his plan. What was *not* part of has plan was the shame he was feeling on the inside.

He stifled the shame, took her arm, and led her to a more intimate corner of the church, where they could not be overheard.

"It's just that...well," he began, "Frank's not really a *bad* student."

She was quiet now, staring right at him, listening. And it tore Harry up inside. The arrogant disdain - which had always enabled him to pull off this type of scheme - was gone.

"But he tends to, oh, loaf, shall we say. He also, on occasion, disrupts the class." Agnes' eyes widened in disbelief. "Not that he isn't a good student," Harry continued, "it's just that he has showed - in the first few weeks of school here - a steadily increasing need for discipline."

Agnes was stunned that he could be talking about Frank. "I'm terribly sorry," she said, "we've *never* had a problem - any problem whatsoever - with Frank, at home or at school."

Harry Medwick believed that was true and that filled him with more shame.

"My husband isn't here tonight," said Agnes, "but he will be picking me up later and I will discuss it with him then."

Harry nodded and smiled politely.

"You can be sure," Agnes added, "that Frank will hear about this and be disciplined accordingly."

"No!" said Harry, stepping in quickly when he realized what she was saying. "Mrs. Burns, we teachers feel that home interference can be detrimental in some cases. We feel the discipline should be handled in the school, as it is a school problem, so the child can *recognize* it as such. As a school official I am obligated to discipline him, and if he were to be disciplined in school *and* then receive a similar or harsher treatment at home, we feel that can have a negative impact, cause the child to act up even more."

Harsher treatment, thought Agnes, as Harry spoke. *Negative impact? Act up? My word, what is happening!*

"I think my husband should know," said Agnes.

"Uh-huh, uh-huh," stammered Harry. "I can understand that. It's just imperative that neither of you mention the problem to Frank just yet. Allow me to try and deal with it effectively in the classroom first."

Agnes said nothing, unsure.

Harry added, "The teachers *also* feel - or should I say we are appreciative of the fact - that many of the families around here are struggling, and this is a way of correcting the problem without *adding* uneasiness or tension in the home."

"Well," said Agnes, "you don't have to tell *our* family about struggle."

"Well, that's what I'm referring to," said Harry. "It's best for everyone involved that a child's home life remain his home life and his school life remain his school life."

The notion - and the way Harry presented it - sounded silly to him. And Agnes was evidently *very* unsure about it herself, but finally she nodded her head and said, "I see what you mean, Mr. Medwick. I'll mention it to my husband, but neither of us will mention it to Frank. Hopefully the matter can be resolved at school, as you suggested."

"Oh it can, it can," said Harry. He took her hand again and said, "Now if you'll excuse me, there are some other parents I really should meet."

"Yes, of course," said Agnes.

Harry walked away, feeling satisfied, leaving Agnes numbed and silent.

Harry walked about the church social for another hour. As he talked his opinion of Fairchild dropped a few notches. He'd always heard (and felt) that small towns produced small people (and small minds), but Fairchild seemed to have its lion's share. Agnes Burns, with her lovely face and graceful demeanor, was but a shining star in an otherwise vast blackness of dull features and benign conversation.

He quickly grew weary of the talk and the people. He yawned a few times, spoke of an early rising, excused himself, and left.

As he walked along the streets of Fairchild that evening, a cold, autumn wind was blowing fallen leaves across the dusty street. Another wave of despair crashed over him. He headed for Ryman's Saloon again and attempted to forget where he was, and what he had just done to Agnes Burns.

Agnes moved through the rest of the evening like a woman in a strange dream, not knowing what action to take and wondering if it really *was* a dream. When she saw Augie Johnson enter the church to escort his wife home, she made a decision.

She approached the teacher and said, "Hello Mr. Johnson. May I speak to you alone?"

Somewhat surprised, Augie said, "Of course."

Agnes led him to the same secluded corner of the church. All of a sudden, like a flood, the words gushed from her. "I'm at a loss, Mr. Johnson," she said, "and I hope you can help shed some light on the situation. There's talk of my oldest son Frank having some behavioral problems in school, and I don't know what I should do!"

Augie looked bewildered. "I don't know what to tell you Mrs. Burns," he said. "Frank was never a problem when he was in my class, nor have I since heard of him being anything but a model student."

She held out her hands helplessly. "I just *can't* believe it!" Augie shrugged apologetically. "Mr. Medwick was so insistent. He seemed almost determined to discipline Frank."

Augie's eyes widened. "Oh, Mr. *Medwick!* Harry Medwick?"

"Yes," said Agnes.

"Then it makes sense," said the math teacher.

Agnes looked confused and said, "How so?"

Augie hesitated, tapping the tips of his fingers on his mouth in thought. Then he sighed deeply and said, "Mrs. Burns, it is seldom - if ever - that I interfere, or poke my nose into, another teacher's business. I believe the Fairchild school has some of the best teachers in the state, and I would never deem it necessary to criticize one of them. But this time, I feel I should. I must ask you *never* to repeat what I am about to tell you."

Agnes nodded her head in agreement, a look of terror sweeping over her face. Augie then quietly proceeded to tell her all he knew about Harry Medwick, including their first meeting and the dinner at Augie's house. He concluded with their last meeting at Ryman's Saloon, where Harry had explained *The Medwick Theory* in detail.

"The Medwick Theory," said Agnes distastefully. "It's absurd!"

"I don't know what you should do," said Augie. "Tell your husband, I guess. I've done all I can."

"Why does he hate Frank so?" Agnes asked in a shaky voice.

"He doesn't hate Frank," said Augie. "Ironically, he *respects* Frank. He considers Frank the biggest and the best and that's what Harry Medwick respects...a challenge. If he disciplines Frank - roughs him up a bit or otherwise picks on him - it follows that the *rest* of the class will fear Medwick and be meek as a lamb.

"Everybody likes Frank," said Agnes, "nobody is afraid of him. It doesn't make any sense."

"I don't think much in Medwick's mind makes sense," said Augie. "He gets an idea and he runs with it. He seems like that type."

Agnes thanked Augie for the information and left the church not knowing what she should do next. But knowing she should do something.

She watched the bobbing head of the mare, tinged with a silver lining of harvest moonlight. Her husband sat beside her, silent. John Burns had sensed something was wrong when he picked her up at the church. Now he waited for her to speak. He was a patient man, so he would wait as long as he had to, until his wife was ready to talk to him.

Finally she turned and placed her hand over his as he held the reins.

"John, I have something to tell you. Do not speak until I have finished."

She told him what had taken place that evening at the church; her encounter with Harry Medwick and what Augie Johnson had to say about Mr. Medwick afterwards. Throughout the telling she expected her husband's rage to explode. It did not. He remained strongly calm.

At the end she inquired, "Do we go to his superintendent?"

"No," said John, "let me handle it."

"How?" said Agnes nervously.

"I have an idea. Let me think about it for a while."

"John, I don't want you getting into trouble."

"I won't," he answered, as they pulled into the farmyard. *It's Mr. Medwick who's going to have trouble,* he thought.

Harry Medwick spent the next two days making life a living hell for Frank Burns. He picked at him incessantly; complaining about his work, ridiculing his clothing, harassing him with mocking remarks and then outright insults. Frank Burns could not make a move without Harry Medwick being right there with a contemptuous grin and remark. The shame he had felt at the church facing Mrs. Burns was forgotten. The old revolutionary anger and aggression came back to him. Twice he saw anger smolder in the eyes of the boy as well, but Frank fought for control.

Tomorrow he'll crack, Harry thought. *Tomorrow for sure. I know the whole class is watching and waiting to see what Frank does, and when he does it, I will demonstrate my dominance. All of these children who have been getting away with murder in the last month will learn a harsh lesson as soon as the Burns boy cracks. And he will! I'll make sure of that! I'll have the smoothest running, most disciplined class in the state!*

Harry was jovial as he cleared his desk and prepared to go home that night. He was looking forward to the following day with great anticipation.

Lightning flashed through the bedroom window in the pre-dawn hours. Rain had fallen most of the night. John Burns rose an hour earlier than usual, informing Agnes that he would be taking the children to school early as well. Already he was in the barn doing chores with the boys as she made the bed.

Two days had gone by and her husband had not so much as mentioned Frank's situation at school. Frank - for the first time in his life - was displaying irritability at home. It broke Agnes' heart to see the strain and frustration on her son's face and know why it was there.

She walked downstairs and into the kitchen, where the girls were starting breakfast. Moments later John and the boys came in the back door of the house. The boys washed up and sat down at the table. John walked right by and headed upstairs.

"Aren't you going to eat?" asked Agnes.

"Haven't got time," her husband answered.

Agnes knew something was astir, but she had to trust John. She busied herself by getting the children ready. All four children were out in the buggy when John finally came downstairs. In the front hall of the house Agnes met her husband to ask him once again not to overreact. But she was rendered speechless by what she saw.

"I'll be back," said John.

Outside, John Burns climbed into the buggy without a word. The children looked at him and then at each other in amazement. Frank looked at Whiley, and Whiley shrugged. Rachel started to giggle, but a sharp poke from Caroline's elbow sobered her. John Burns ignored the giggle and with a flip of the reins, they started into town.

Harry Medwick was also an early riser that morning. He was excited at the prospect of finding and flushing out Frank's boiling point. He spent the previous night shadowboxing and lifting weights, instead of heading to Ryman's Saloon. He shaved leisurely, examining his face in the mirror. He opened his mouth and checked his teeth. Looked good to him.

All in all, a fine specimen, he thought. *A symbol of power. A symbol my students will not likely forget.*

He looked in his closet, the sense of order back in his life. Four suits hung there, all cleaned and pressed. He chose the oldest, though it was not in excellent condition.

No point in getting a newer one torn if the boy puts up a struggle, he reasoned.

Then he thought about Agnes Burns and a slight twinge of regret sailed through him like a ghost. But like a ghost it vanished as quickly as it had appeared.

He dressed and examined himself in the dresser mirror. He had acquired a slight paunch since he'd come to Fairchild, and this dismayed him. He would have to do something about that. He picked up his gold timepiece and placed it in his vest pocket. Then he reconsidered and placed it back on the top of the dresser.

Just like the suit, he thought. *No sense risking it getting damaged if Frank puts up a fight.*

He left the room, locked his door and walked downstairs to enjoy breakfast with the rest of the boarders.

Everyone at the boarding house - and everyone on the street - noticed Harry Medwick's cheer. He whistled as he walked on the boardwalk down Main Street. Ahead lay the dirt street that led to school. He surveyed his course carefully and stepped off the boardwalk. Nimbly he made his way down the road, stepping only on the drier spots. Though the rain had fallen down in buckets all night, there always seemed to be drier spots to step to. By God, he was going to make it without even getting his shoes dirty. It was going to be a *good* day.

He was anticipating the coming attractions when a voice from behind startled him. "Mr. Medwick?"

"Yes?" he said, turning. The vision he saw before him made him step back involuntarily. He looked into the eyes of one of the biggest men he had ever seen. On his head he wore a black wool hat, pulled down below his ears. His ancient black coat was buttonless and open, revealing bib-overalls underneath. The man wore no shirt. The overalls were rolled halfway to his knees. An inch of mud clung completely around huge black boots. Harry looked at this apparition and almost laughed out loud. The man looked at Harry with a big, lopsided grin.

"Mista Medwick," the man said, "Ise John Burns. Ma boy Frank is a student iv yours."

Harry's mind flashed back to Agnes. Her petite, shapely body, gentle voice, and pure, raw beauty shone vividly. *Impossible,* he thought.

"You're Mr. Burns?" he said aloud, incredulously.

"Yup," confirmed the big man, grinning like a fool.

Harry cleared his throat and said, "Well, Mr. Burns, what can I do for you?"

The big man's face darkened and the grin disappeared.

"Weel, ya see," he said, "it's lak this. Ma missy says youse be havin' all dis' trabble with ma boy Frank." He frowned. "The boy shore needs a lesson if he been cawsin' you grievance. And Aggie, dat ma missy, she's got her son plumb-set on gadjiating..."

"Don't worry Mr. Burns, with a little discipline, I'm sure Frank will buckle down and do just fine." Harry Medwick had a frightening suspicion that his winning smile was not quite winning this dumb behemoth over.

"Weel now, dat kinda the poblem, Mista Meddick."

"How's that?" asked Harry.

"Well, ya see, my grandpappy, he always disapined my pappy, and my pappy always disipined me, and neithera dem *evah* needed no help. What would it lo' like, if I let someone else do what ma responbil'ty? Good God, what ma missy think? No sir! I not allow someone ess doin' what's ma doodie!"

Harry tried to think quickly. His plan was going down the drain. "I assure you, Mr. Burns," he stammered, "that many teachers take corrective action themselves in an effort to alleviate undue stress and worry at home."

"No sir, I tain't allow dat," said the big man, in a very serious tone.

Harry cursed to himself. He would not let this clown-like farmer interfere with what he had worked so hard at perfecting! Let him complain to the school. Nobody was bound to listen to him. He made the rest of the banal town's population look like renowned intellectuals. No, perhaps he would lay low for a week or two, but he would - he *would* - implement the *Medwick Theory* before the end of the semester.

For now, he said, "Well Mr. Burns, perhaps you're right. I'll let you handle the problem. For now."

The big grin returned to the farmer's face. He clapped his cantaloupe-sized hands together in glee, lifted his ponderous, mud-caked boots high and brought them down with terrific force into the mud-puddle between them. The water flew. Harry jumped back, but not quickly enough. Mud sprayed the front of his suit and ran down the front, covering his shoes.

Harry became inflamed. *You son of a bitch,* he thought. *You Goddamned son of a bitch!*

"Yays sir, ahse knew you undertand, Midder Meddick," said Burns, laying the ridiculous accent on even more thickly now. He extended his hand.

Harry looked at it. His initial thought was, *I would never grace this bastard by shaking his hand!* But then he caught himself, and took the man's hand anyway. There was an old trick he knew, a game of the mind, which he decided was worth a shot.

He could feel lumps of gruff, hard calluses on the farmer's hands. He grinned, and slowly he applied pressure, attempting to send just a shot of "unintentional" pain through the man's hand as they shook. No reaction. He squeezed harder. Nothing. Harry looked up at the farmer's gleeful face. He squeezed again and that was it. His hand was as constricted as it could get, the strain showing in his face, the cords in his own wrist bulging.

Christ, he thought. *This man's not human!*

Then he felt it. The farmer was tightening *his* hand, incrementally forcing Medwick to release his grip. It was barely noticeable at first, but it was growing. Then the first hint of pain came. Then - incrementally - more waves of pain. Soon a shot of unbearable electricity shot through Harry's arm, right up to his elbow. His face became contorted, first in discomfort then in pain. Desperately he tried to muster the strength to break free, but could not. He felt ensnared. Then his knuckles began to grind together. Harry panicked. *He's going to break my hand!* His eyes stung, a swallow was caught in his throat. Burns released his hand suddenly. He snatched it away and a wave of nausea passed over him.

"Weel, den," said Burns, "Ahse glad we come to dis here undertandin, and ahse must be goin' nah, so I'se see you...." Harry was looking at his mangled hand in painful horror. Gently John Burns grabbed his chin and lifted it so Harry was looking at him. "I sayed ahse *see* you awowned."

He let go of Harry's chin, turned, and walked away. Harry stared after him as he plowed through the mud, never thinking where he was going to step next.

When the feeling came back to his hand it brought a new wave of sharp pain. He could move his fingers...they weren't broken, but they were badly sprained. He grimaced. There would be no writing for a week or so.

That was the first time in Harry's life that anyone showed more physical prowess than he. It was also the first time in Harry's life that he was truly scared. It would be folly to provoke that animal further. Harry had not expected "Mr. Burns" to be like *that!*

And he doesn't even have the brains *to know that killing me would get him in trouble,* he thought distastefully. A block down Mr. Burns disappeared around a corner. *Hell with it!*

He would just have to teach the classes and get through the year. Next year, he imagined and hoped, another job would open up, somewhere, and he could get the hell out of that godforsaken town.

It was a full six weeks before Medwick had occasion to meet Burns again, at a school open house. Harry dutifully met all the parents who came, but when John Burns showed up as the quiet, well-groomed, conscientious and intelligent man he really was, he was informed by the superintendent, Mr. Holland, that Mr.

Medwick had suddenly taken ill and had gone home just minutes before.

Frank encountered no more problems with Harry Medwick, and would never realize fully the part that his father played in the brief episode.

Chapter Nineteen

The day was cloudless. The temperature was well above normal. The date was June 6th, 1915 - graduation day. Rows of chairs lined the grass in front of the hastily built platform that was to serve as the focal point for the ceremony. Before the pageantry began, John Burns stood talking with a small group of farmers. All showed concern on their faces as they discussed the weather. If ever it were going to rain, it would *surely* rain on graduation day. But the bright, blue sky proved them liars.

"Hell, if we don't get rain pretty soon, my fields are going to burn up!" said Chester White, knowing they all faced the same plight. And in some cases a *worse* plight. Chester's farmland was vast and he had money saved away. It was the smaller farms that were being hit hardest by the lack of rain - farms like that of John Burns.

Burns nodded gravely. Hooking his thumbs in his vest pocket, he looked over Roy's head. There was a stir of excitement as people began to mount the platform.

"Looks like things are going to get started," he commented. He hurried to a row of chairs right in front of the platform, where Agnes, Whiley and the girls had already seated themselves, and took his spot next to his wife.

The platform was a buzz of activity. School principal Harry Fisher talked excitedly to three of his teachers behind a highly policed podium. The graduating class sat to the left of the podium in alphabetical order. They sat in two rows, all twenty-two of them. To the right of the podium sat the teachers, and Horace T. Willoughby, owner of Willoughby's Feed and Hardware and the invisible mayor of Fairchild. Asked point blank, there were few people on the streets of Fairchild, Michigan who could name their mayor with any degree of certainty. Horace only showed *up* as mayor, only mentioned that he *was* the mayor, at graduations and other civic events, major crimes and minor disasters (and then it was Carmin and Charley whom people asked for information). The town pretty much ran itself.

The buzz of confusion silenced suddenly. There came the clearing of throats and the shushing of peers. Everyone made himself comfortable in his chair. Principal Fisher strode to the podium, beamed out at the audience (some 200 strong) and began, "Ladies and Gentlemen, distinguished guests (meaning Horace Willoughby, the mayor), we are gathered here today to honor the graduation class of 1915."

There was a smattering of what seemed to be half-hearted applause. Frank, seated in the front row, second chair, had to lower his head and suppress a grin. Lucy Carter, seated next to him, turned, looked at him intently, and batted her eyes. She had been doing this to Frank Burns since the sixth grade in an effort to get his attention. It had not worked yet, and she was not about to pass by what might be her *last* opportunity. Frank smiled at her and nodded politely (as *he* had been doing since the sixth grade) but felt uncomfortable. He turned and looked down at the faces of his family. His mother beamed proudly back at him. Even his father smiled broadly and waved slightly. He rose when his name was called, accepted his diploma, and walked down the steps of the platform into his mother's arms. On his shoulder he felt the heavy hand of his father and a slight, affectionate squeeze. That was it. Graduation was over. Around him, people milled. There was a lot of talking and laughter, but the affair was slightly subdued. Men came up to Frank, shook his hand and congratulated him, but Frank noticed their faces were solemn. He knew, like his father, they were worried about their fields.

Socializing continued for an hour or so after the ceremony. Doc Spencer walked around, speaking to different people, waiting patiently. He had offered the Burns family transportation on graduation day and they had accepted. Now he walked to his Ford, fidgeting. Relief showed on his face when he saw the family coming toward him. Soon they were off. A thick cloud of dust followed the Ford as they approached Hemlock's shack. The old bachelor stood by the side of the road and waved. Everyone in the car waved back. No one expected the old loner to come into town to attend the ceremony. They all knew this was his way of saying *Congratulations.*

At the farm, Doc was asked to stay for supper. He politely declined. When everyone else had started to the house, Doc called Frank back. Frank walked around the car and peered in Doc's window.

The old surgeon reached into his pocket, pulled out an envelope and handed it to Frank. "This is for you," he said.

"Thank you, sir," said Frank.

Doc watched him for a moment, then said, "Aw!" with a wave of his hand. The Ford lurched forward, swung around the yard and started down the road. Frank opened the envelope. Inside was a card of congratulations, and a five dollar bill. Frank looked up at the retreating cloud of dust and waved.

That night the supper table was filled with everything that Frank liked. The usual reserved discipline demanded by John at mealtime was flung to the wind. Everyone, *including* John, talked excitedly. When the meal was finished, John rose quickly and went to the cupboard. He returned with six glasses and a bottle of wine. Pouring a small amount into each glass, he passed them around. He stood straight and raised his glass in toast. Everyone did the same.

"To my son," said John. They all cheered and sipped their wine. He set his empty glass down and took a small, brightly wrapped package tied with a bow from a place behind the living room couch. "This is for you," he said, reaching across the table and handing it to Frank.

Everyone stared at this unexpected gift, including Agnes. Frank untied the bow carefully and tore away the paper to reveal a small, white box. He lifted the lid. Looking inside, his eyes widened in disbelief. He started to speak but his voice cracked. Tears stung his eyes. He set the box on the table for all to see and quickly dried the tears with his hands. Agnes' mouth literally dropped open when she saw the fabulous gold timepiece in the box. She looked at her husband. Their eyes met and hers quickly softened.

The box was passed from hand to hand for closer inspection by each person. Whiley looked at it and smiled proudly, without a hint of jealousy. Soon the initial shock lifted and the laughter and jubilation returned. John Burns even poured a second glass of wine for everyone. Frank, now composed, his belly warmed by the wine, decided this was the happiest day of his life.

That night Frank and Whiley lay in their beds, after having talked quietly for quite some time. The excitement of the day had tired them. Three times Whiley slipped from his bed and walked to the dresser to look at the gold watch, and each time he let out a new gasp of amazement.

Frank was nearly asleep when Whiley said, "You know, Frank, if ever there was anything in the world I'd want, it's a gold watch just like yours."

"Uh-huh," said Frank.

"That way we'd both have one," said Whiley.

"Mmm," said Frank, drifting off to sleep.

Chapter Twenty

Long thin strips of white clouds moved across the July sky, like bony fingers stretching to grasp eternity, but failing. The sun seemed to elude even these small filters and beat relentlessly upon the land. John Burns shaded his eyes as he looked helplessly at the woods along the edge of his pasture. The dark green needles of the small evergreens had turned a brackish brown. Even the leaves of the towering hardwoods seemed withered and dull, turning upward as if begging alms from the Gods of rain. Reports of some of the shallower wells running dry were becoming more frequent.

The drought of Summer 1915 was in its fifth week. On two occasions, large dark clouds amassed and rolled over the land threatening (or teasingly). There came the dark that always precedes a storm, a few claps of thunder, a droplet or two, and then the clouds would move on and the sun would come back, seemingly more merciless than before.

John Burns was thankful he had a good well, but now even he could be in trouble if the rains didn't come soon. And with each day that passed it would take more and *more* rain to repair the damage.

As it was now he and the boys were forced to fill large sprinkler cans to water the huge vegetable garden beside the house. The vegetables were to be canned and were a mainstay of the family diet in the winter. It was hard, tedious work carrying the heavy sprinklers to the garden, especially since it was not only dry, but hot as hell too. Everyone in the Burns family was expected to help, and the girls often staggered as they walked, both hands gripping the handle, causing blisters to form. But no one complained. John Burns knew when there was work to be done, the best thing to do was to do it right away, without thinking about it. And he had effectively taught his children this.

Then a new problem arose. The Wendell River ran through Cumberland County, and nearly parallel to the northwest end of John Burns' land. An offshoot of the river curved across a half-acre of the pasture, curved back, and rejoined the main river downstream some three hundred feet from the fence line. This produced a fine private brook, which John Burns took full advantage of and had come to depend on in large part. They called it the "cut", and it furnished water for his livestock. Never more than 12 to 14 inches deep (except during spring run-off or after an exceptionally heavy rainfall), it babbled on faithfully. Now it too was drying up, something that had *never* happened before.

John walked across the pasture, breathing heavily in the oppressive heat. When he reached the cut, he saw it was only a small trickle of water moving through. Here and there was left a deeper pocket, but it was apparent that the cut would be dry in a week or two, if rain did not come.

John could not understand it. Mother Nature seemed bent on destroying him. If he was forced to water his cattle completely from his own well, it might be more than the well could bear and he and his family could find themselves with no water at all.

He followed the cut to where it ran under the fence on its way back to the Wendell River. He climbed over the fence and continued following it. Fifteen minutes later he stood on the banks of the Wendell River. He picked a twig from a low-hanging branch and chewed it. What he saw amazed him. The river maintained an average width of about 40 feet. He judged the water to be down at least 2 feet from normal and he had never seen it move so lazily. He studied it, but could not comprehend the trouble. He knew the springs that marked its birthplace some twenty miles upstream produced a good natural flow even in times of drought. Certainly the river should not be down like this.

He took the twig from his mouth and threw it in the stream. It moved away slowly in the crystal clear water. As he stood there a gust of wind spread a thousand sunlight diamonds across the river. Birds rustled in the trees behind him, then one took flight. Then another, and another. He watched as the whole flock took wing. Then in unison they lighted in a tree fifty yards away. A thought occurred to him, and the more he considered it the more it made sense.

He watched the water plaintively. God, it had been so long since he'd actually *enjoyed* the Wendell River, which was so near and so convenient. Never any time to take the boys fishing or to camp out. Work, always work, *that's* what keeps a farm going.

And now it was too late. The boys were nearly grown up. Actually, Frank already *was.* And the girls, naturally, bonded with their mother. Had he been a good father to his family? He had *provided* for them, certainly. But, had he been a good father? Had he spent as much time having fun with them as he had teaching them? Was it love or respect they felt for him?

He walked upstream, moving as lazily as the river, to where the bank leveled off into a sandbar peninsula. He walked out on it. At water's edge, a log lay partly buried in the constantly shifting sand. He sat on it comfortably. He knew there was a lot of work waiting for him back at the farm, but he put it out of his mind. He unlaced his work boots, took them off, removed his socks and placed his bare feet in the cool, soothing water. It felt like heaven. He threw his head back and sighed.

After a while, melancholy overtook him, so that he almost wept. When this drought - when this *trouble* - was over, he and the boys would go fishing. Two, maybe three days they would fish and camp together. He'd get to know his boys again, really get to *know* them, not as his sons but as two boys quickly on their way to becoming men. As soon as all this trouble was over.

That night after supper was finished and the girls were heating water for the dishes, John Burns spoke to his sons at the table.

First he said, "Frank, you going over to Hemlock's place tonight?"

Frank nodded affirmatively. He had been visiting the old man two or three times a week. He enjoyed the old man's company and each visit reaffirmed his earlier suspicions that Hemlock had a lot to offer in the ways of knowledge and experience. More than most people in town knew.

"When you come home tonight," said John, "borrow the old man's gun and some shells."

Frank looked at him with surprise. His father continued. "I was down to the river today. It's two or three feet down, and the cut is almost completely dry. That's too much, even with the dry weather we've had. You *both* know the strain that would be put on our well if we had to water the cattle directly from it."

Both boys nodded solemnly. Whiley was proud to be included in this conversation.

"I figure," said their father, "we have some beavers working upstream. Day after tomorrow, I want you two boys to head upstream and see if I'm right. You might have to camp overnight."

Excitement showed in Whiley's eyes. Their father said, "I want you to find the dam that I think is there and take it out. We've *got* to have water back in the cut."

Chapter Twenty-One

The sun, like an orange ball, peaked over the tip of the horizon to the east, unfolding a curtain of light across the land.

Another hot, cloudless day, thought Agnes. She was in the kitchen stuffing two packsacks. Into them she put potatoes, bacon, salt, flour, bread, coffee and canned goods. She also supplied her boys with cooking utensils such as a skillet, two tin plates, an extra pan to boil coffee, cups, and soap. Her husband looked over her shoulder and remarked, "The boys are only going to be gone two days at the most."

"They have to eat," she replied, adding some raisins. John Burns smiled and shook his head.

He walked outside and met the boys, dressed, groomed and ready to go. Frank was explaining something to Whiley, pointing to the field and the unseen river beyond. Whiley was following Frank's finger and nodding. He was very excited. John Burns walked past them to the tool shed. When he returned, he was carrying two double-bit axes with rags tied around the business ends for protection.

"Be *careful,"* he said sternly, as he set them down. "They're sharp, and this is not a game." He handed Frank two small metal boxes. One contained stick matches, the other a coil of black fishing line and assorted hooks. "If you're resourceful," he said, "you just might catch yourself a nice supper." He grinned and the boys grinned back.

Then their father's face became sober again and he said, "Frank, the gun is to be used *only* in a case of absolute necessity. I only suggested it to make your mother feel better. She knows you know how to shoot. She's concerned about transients off the trains. If you run into someone in the woods move on. If they give you trouble, *real* trouble, the kind that could put you and Whiley in danger, raise the gun. If - and *only* if, do you understand me? - you have to fire it, fire it. But if you do, you better bring a dead transient out of the woods, or there'll be hell to pay. The gun has no other use than protection."

"Yes sir," said Frank seriously.

"What about the beaver?" asked Whiley.

"Leave them be," said John. "They will only rebuild the dam. By then, maybe it won't matter as much. It's *bound* to rain sometime. Besides, I'll get the word out about the beavers. When they come into prime, someone will take them out of there. Right now we just need the water to flow."

The discussion ended there. Agnes brought the packs out then and handed one to each boy. They lifted their packs, kissed their mother, hugged their father, and set off across the pasture to follow the cut to the river.

Agnes wiped a tear in her eye and said, "I feel like they're leaving home forever."

"They'll be all right," said John Burns. Together they headed inside for breakfast.

Chapter Twenty-two

The train yard at Timmins was busier than hell that morning. Three times, Rudy Carlson - the yard supervisor - had started to climb up and check the netting on the smoke stack of Engine No. 331, and three times he had been called away to lend a hand. Now the crews were arguing again. The last argument had come to blows. The heat and the heavy workload were getting to everyone.

Hell with it, he thought, moving toward the angry men to squelch the argument before it got ugly. *I'll check it next time. It's ALWAYS fine!*

The netting was, in fact, a wire screen that covered the stack to prevent burning clinkers from flying out. And it was not fine.

One hour later, No. 331 was chugging out. Her run that day was straight to Cedarsburg. A run that would take her through barren countryside, across the tip of Cumberland County.

Chapter Twenty-three

The day was hot and the boys were perspiring heavily by the time they stood on the banks of the Wendell.

Whiley was panting. "It's hotter today than it's *ever* been," he said.

"Nah," said Frank, panting himself, "it just feels that way because you've been walking so much."

Together they started upstream, passing the same sandbar where their father had sat two days before. Frank led the way and Whiley followed close behind. They both observed the quiet beauty of the land; silver streams ran into the river on both sides. Birds on the wing fluttered past the two interlopers. Squirrels paused in the trees to chatter indignantly. Crows cawed, first loudly then from a distance. On the wooded side of the river, small animals could be heard scurrying about over last year's dead leaves.

To Frank it was serious business as they picked their way through the sometimes heavy brush near the river. To Whiley, it was a holiday, a deliverance from childhood to adulthood. The land was fairly flat for the first mile, but then hillsides began to curl up around them and soon they were following the river through a deep ravine. Much of it was in shadow, where mosquitoes lay in wait. They paused to button their shirts to the top and pull up their collars, in spite of the heat. They were used to the heat, but the mosquitoes (and horseflies) in such black clouds were a new and miserable experience.

The river turned east abruptly, came out of the ravine and widened into a large open area, where they were once again bathed in sunshine. The mosquitoes disappeared. Frank decided this was as good a place as any to rest. They both sat down, unbuttoning their shirts in relative comfort. They had been walking for two and a half hours, during which neither had spoken more than a dozen words.

Now Whiley spilled out with conversation. "How much further, do you think?" he asked.

"Could be a mile, could be five," Frank answered.

"I think we'll spend the night out," said Whiley, nodding.

Frank shrugged. He knew Whiley was desperate to do just that, but he didn't care either way. "Let's move on," he said, standing up.

The river twisted and turned. One moment they were headed south, ten minutes later they were headed east. The breeze had picked up considerably, but it was a hot, blast-furnace breeze, that served only to remind them of how hot it was.

Frank called a halt. They had been on the river a total of six hours and they hadn't seen any sign of beaver or a dam. Frank was starting to think there might not be a dam. He mentioned it to Whiley, and Whiley rejected the idea. To agree meant that his father had erred and Whiley would not accept that. In addition, Whiley did not want to have to go back without spending at least one night camping.

"Well, let's rest again. Have something to eat." said Frank. They sat down and opened their packs. Frank sliced the homemade bread and cheese their mother had packed for them. Whiley took the tin cups and dipped some cool river water. They ate their sandwiches contentedly, self-assured that no matter what other men might be doing throughout the world at that very moment, there, wrapped in the solitude of the Wendell River, it could not affect them.

Chapter Twenty-four

Carl Echart snapped the lid on his pocket watch and steadied himself from the sway of the engine.

"Twelve o'clock!" he called to the fireman. No. 331 was running right on time, despite the five cars of heavy freight she was pulling. Ahead lay the Cumberland grade. After that it would be smooth running. The grade was the steepest on the run. It was a relatively gradual ascent, but very long - over two miles. The engine would be laboring by the time it hit the top.

"Give her hell, Oly!" he shouted at the fireman, who nodded silently and pacified his own thoughts by mouthing the words, *"piss on you"*, when Echart had turned away.

The small engine doggedly pulled forward up the grade. The engineer kept his eyes glued to the gauge. The engine strained and belched mighty chugs from the depths of her belly. Inside the firebox the coal dumped on the grates burst into hot flame. As it burned it split and fell apart. The forced draft caught the smaller pieces and shot them up through the flues into the stack. The unchecked netting failed to capture all of them and the escapees shot out into the air and landed unnoticed in the high, brown grass along the track as the train lumbered by. They turned a dusty gray - dying, but not dead. Moments later, a hot, sudden gust of wind breathed life back into them. Now a rosy glow, the same breeze that revived them also fed them, bending the grass to their fiery tongues. By the time the last car topped the grade and disappeared, the fire was feeding furiously on the plentiful brown brush of Cumberland County, acre by acre.

Far to the east, Frank and Whiley were just finishing their lunch on the bank of the Wendell. Revived by the food within them, they again struck out following the river, watching closely, keeping a keen eye for any sign of beaver. An hour later they still had found nothing. Outright skepticism had replaced suspicion in Frank's mind. Was their father wrong? It was possible, even likely. He was growing impatient.

He slowed and looked back at Whiley. His brother gave him a quick grin. No doubt showed on *his* face. Whiley was the eternal believer. He never questioned for a second that the dam was just ahead. Perhaps just around the next bend. If their father said it was there, it was *there.*

One thing that impressed Frank was that Whiley never once complained. They had endured discomfort, exhaustion, and bugs all day, yet Whiley - with the soft features of their mother - carried on as his father would have expected. Even Frank was beginning to get irritated, but Whiley showed no indication that he was anything other than willing and able to carry on.

It was Whiley who made the discovery. Frank had been watching the stream when Whiley saw the fallen trees a short distance from the bank, in the woods. There were several of them; muted stumps chewed to a peak. Scattered around were wooden chips. Nature's woodcutters had left their signatures as distinctly as any artist places his mark upon a work. A well-worn trail of grass showed where they entered and exited the stream. There was no sign of the beaver house or the dam. Once again Frank took the lead. Whiley, undaunted, followed closely behind. A sharp splash in the water ahead brought them to attention. They both stopped dead in their tracks.

"Beaver!" Frank said with excitement.. Together they moved in the direction they thought the splash had come from.

"Are you sure?" said Whiley.

"Yes! I heard the *splash!"* Frank insisted.

"So did I," said Whiley, squinting out over the water. "But I don't *see* anything!"

"He's swimming underwater," said Frank, "they can go long ways. You just watch the stream, he'll pop up soon enough."

"Where?"

"Oh, about there," Frank answered in a low whisper, as if they were waiting for something magical. And they were.

They waited. Nothing happened. They stood motionless. Minutes passed.

"Maybe he's drowned," Whiley whispered.

Frank looked at him and rolled his eyes. Suddenly, almost directly in front of them on the opposite side of the stream where it was deep and bushy, the water parted. He came straight into the air, the bright sunlight emphasizing his beautiful, iridescent color. The trout seemed to hang at the peak of its jump, then arched and fell back into the water with a loud splash.

"Wow!" said Whiley with a grin. "I never thought a beaver would look so much like fish!"

Frank reddened. "Let's go," he said, making a note of where they saw the trout jump.

Again they walked on. Five minutes later they found what they were looking for. The beaver dam stretched across the river like a bow, four feet above the water. It consisted of logs, alder brush, rocks, mud, leaves, and anything else its builders could find.

They stood silently, like archaeologists at a newly discovered site, something they had been searching for all their lives.

Frank looked at Whiley. "Well, we got a job to do," he said.

Above the dam lay a wetland. Water was backed up, creating a wide flood. Frank set the gun and the ax against a tree and took off his packsack. In the still water behind the dam, he counted three beaver lodges. He wondered how many beavers there actually were.

Now that they had found the dam, indecision set in. Whiley, though balking a little at the thought of destroying what the beavers had worked so hard at, wanted to start right away and get it over with. Frank had other thoughts.

"Why don't we catch some supper first?" he suggested. "I'd like to try my hand at fishing." Whiley consented, always agreeable.

Together they went into the woods, found a heavily shaded area, and began digging. The dry weather made worms scarce, but after much toil they managed to find a few. Armed with bait, they backtracked to the spot where they had seen the trout jump. Frank studied the fish's lair. It was on the opposite bank. Heavy with tag alder, it looked reasonably deep, perhaps four feet. Under normal water conditions it would have been much deeper.

Actually fishing it would be a challenge. Frank considered crossing the river and fishing from the bank above. But there were problems with that. First, he'd have cross through the water and crawl up on the bank, and the noise and motion would scare the fish. Second, he'd have to lean *over* the bank (which was steep) to get his line in, and with the sun behind him that would produce a shadow, which would also send the fish away.

No, he'd have to settle for fishing from the side they were on. But how? Fortunately, the river was extremely narrow where they stood, and the low water had narrowed it even more. *Probably not more than twenty feet,* Frank thought.

While Frank thought, Whiley waited patiently, confident that his older brother would know what to do.

Frank turned and went back into the thicket. In a minute or two he returned, holding a long, thick sapling with a crotch on the end of it. He opened the tin box and looked at the thick black line.

He frowned and muttered, "Damn!"

"What's wrong?" asked Whiley.

"It's the line," said Frank, looking at his brother, "he's gonna see it a mile away!"

"Who?"

"The fish!"

"Oh," said Whiley, embarrassed, "so what are we gonna do?"

"Go find a pole about so long," said Frank, indicating the length with his hands. "A *strong* one."

Whiley was gone in a flash. Frank took out the line, tied a hook, added sinkers and stretched it out. Whiley was back with a pole a few minutes later, holding it out for Frank's approval.

"That's fine," said Frank. "Now take off your shoes and roll up your pants."

Again Whiley obeyed without question. Frank did the same, removing his shoes and socks. When they were ready, Frank baited the hook.

Together they unraveled the line to the desired length - about 20 feet. Picking up the sapling, Frank lifted the line up in the crotch. When a length of four feet was hung over the end, he was ready.

He turned to Whiley. "You go up there," he said, indicating a spot upstream, above the hole. "Wade out as *quietly* as you can…quietly and *gently.* Put the pole in the water just as quietly. Stir the sandy bottom and keep stirring, gently."

Whiley was listening with such an intense look on his face, Frank felt like saying, *"Christ, not so serious, Whiley!"*

He settled for, "You understand?"

Whiley nodded.

"If you make too much noise, the fish'll be gone."

"Okay," said Whiley, in a whisper. He moved to the designated spot and gingerly waded in, like he was tiptoeing through a china shop. Frank watched. Armed with the sapling in one hand and the line in the other (running all the way down the sapling and extending over the crotch), Whiley crept into the water a few feet. He lowered the sapling into the bottom of the river, allowing the line to slip into the water. Slowly he began to work it through the water, bobbing it up and down slowly.

There was only a split second between the time Whiley lowered the sapling and when he felt a jerk at the line in his hand. He threw the sapling aside. Frank grabbed the line with both hands and pulled it back. Then all hell broke loose.

The fish naturally shot downstream. The line cut into Frank's hands, but he held on. His arms were jerking convulsively as the fish used its power to escape. Frank knew the line was strong and would not break, but he was worried that the hook might straighten. The fish shot out of the water, thrashing about, then turned and shot upstream. Frank pulled the line in as quickly as he could, hand over hand. For a moment he thought the fish was gone, but then he felt a new round of jerks that cut the line into his hands even more deeply. The fish turned again and headed for the brush on the other side. If he made it, they would never get him out of there. Frank held firmly, laying his trust in the hook. It was a standoff, neither side willing to give. Then in a frenzy, the fish came straight at him.

Frank turned and sprinted up onto the bank in a terrified, comical way, nearly knocking Whiley down. He kept running, pulling the fish through the shallow water, right up onto the sand. Whiley pounced on the fish. The battle now over, both boys started laughing. The fish was a four-pound rainbow trout. Supper had been secured and Frank, having mistaken the fish for a beaver earlier in the day, now had his pride restored. Almost.

Whiley couldn't breathe, he was laughing so hard.

"What's so funny?" said Frank, frowning.

At the end of his breath, Whiley gasped and said, "You looked like you were being chased by a bear!" Saying it spawned a new fit of laughter, forcing him to his knees.

"At least we have dinner," Frank said, turning red again. He knew Whiley meant no harm, and thinking back on his hysterical scramble up the bank, he started to giggle himself.

They went into the woods a short distance, cleared an area, gathered rocks in a ring, and built a fire. Potatoes were thrown right into the fire and the fish sizzled in the skillet. When they finished eating, they were so gorged it was a chore to take the utensils back down the river and wash them with sand in the clear water. They managed to do it, but working on the beaver dam was out of the question now. The wind died and nowhere could so much as a rustle be heard. They lay on the ground by their fire and watched it grow peacefully dark.

Stars were sprinkled across the sky like confectioner's sugar, starkly visible through the dry air. The night was warm and perfect. The two boys, living one of the most wonderful times of their lives, talked long into the night with that wonderful sense of freedom, of being (just for a moment or two) *nowhere in particular,* spilling from their souls. Finally Whiley nodded off, though he tried desperately to stay up. Frank leaned back and watched bursts of heat lightning until much later, when he too fell asleep, dreaming new dreams, the kind that come from new experiences.

Chapter Twenty-five

The morning sun burned through Frank's eyelids, and he stirred. The night had been warm and he'd thrown his blanket off in his sleep. He sat up and - instinctively - an uneasy feeling gripped him. He saw nothing amiss - in fact the beautiful night had unfolded into an equally beautiful morning - so he shrugged it off. The breeze was stirring again, from the west, and it seemed the day would shape up somewhat cooler than the previous. *Thank God,* he thought. They had a lot of work ahead of them that morning.

Whiley stirred. When he sat up Frank smiled at him and said, "You hungry?"

Whiley shook his head and rubbed his eyes.

"Good!" said Frank. "Let's get to work!"

They arrived at the dam and set to it promptly with axes, standing in the shallow water in front. They worked vigorously, but it was a slow process. At length, Frank pulled out a strong, sturdy pole. He began using it as a pry bar. Soon they managed to open a breach. To see the water begin to move more quickly invigorated them. They attacked the dam now, side by side. Together they worked like men possessed. Soon a steady flow of water was coming through. It remained hard work, but with the aid of the water, Frank found he could pry fairly large sections away at a time. Downstream, the water was littered with floating debris.

Frank refused to stop and rest even when Whiley did. He continued with a vengeance. They were both surprised by the fact that they had yet to see a beaver.

He finally rested when five deer came down to the bank, plunged in, crossed the stream, and disappeared into the woods. This sparked the uneasy feeling in Frank once again. He noticed that the birds were acting funny as well. Their normal conversation in the trees seemed to be elevated to an hysterical chatter and they were taking off and flying overhead in large flocks. The uneasy feeling grew stronger, but Frank still could not put his finger on it, so again he shrugged it off.

By noon the destruction of the dam was nearly complete. Frank wiped his brow, washed his hands in the water, blew a sigh of relief and said, "Let's eat." Whiley nodded gratefully. Frank could see that he was close to exhaustion, but still he had not complained.

On the bank Frank cut some bread and cheese. From the stream they dipped water into their tin cups and sat down, side by side, on the riverbank.

As they ate, Frank watched the unusual activity in the woods. At least he *thought* it was unusual. He hadn't spent a lot of time in the woods, and certainly wasn't experienced enough to know for sure, but there was an unusual excitement, like something was happening, or about to happen.

Then he caught it. It was faint at first. He almost thought he was imagining it, but a sharp a gust of wind brought it to his nose strongly. He stopped eating and summoned all his senses together. He breathed deeply - there was no doubt. He smelled smoke. Not domestic smoke, the kind coming from someone's house or yard, but wild smoke, with the taste of all things green.

He jammed the remainder of his sandwich into his mouth and washed it down with a gulp of water.

"Ready to head for home?" he asked, trying hard to hide the growing urgency (and fear) he felt. Whiley stopped chewing and looked puzzled. "The dam is pretty well destroyed," said Frank, "and I'd just as soon get going, we got a long hike ahead."

Whiley nodded in agreement. "Okay," he said.

Ten minutes later they were on their way, sticking close to the Wendell River. Frank set a pace that soon proved to be too much for the younger boy and he was forced to slow down. Forty minutes later, he unconsciously stepped up the pace again. The smell of smoke was strong and distinct now. Frank looked back at Whiley and saw perspiration running down his face. His younger brother was wiping his eyes and Frank knew that they were stinging. He groaned nervously, knowing Whiley would *have* to stop and rest eventually.

"Can you go another ten minutes?" Frank asked.

"Sure," said Whiley, grinning.

Ten minutes later they were in the ravine they'd traveled through the day before. They stopped. Whiley took his cup from his packsack and drank deeply from the river.

Frank watched him, his mind racing frantically. Where was the fire? In the ravine he couldn't even tell which way the wind was blowing. It seemed to be coming from *all* directions. He tried to figure out just exactly where they were - with regard to the fire - but he could only guess. He thought if they left the river and cut through the woods, they would hit a road. But he wasn't *positive.*

There's no room for error, he thought with a panic.

Whiley walked back to him when he was done drinking. "There's a fire burning somewhere," he said flatly.

"I wish to hell I knew where," said Frank.

"What are we going to do?"

Frank felt the sharpest indecision of his life. This was not a matter of left or right, but rather of life or death. Should they go west through the woods and try to find a road? He had heard stories about forest fires - how quickly they spread, how uncontrollable they could be. Heading west they could find themselves in front of a wall of flame.

It might be safer to stay by the river, he thought.

But there was an instinct in him, animalistic in nature. It was what all the other creatures in the forest were doing. *Run! Run! Run! Don't stay where your are! RUN!* It was panic setting in, and though he tried to suppress it, he couldn't.

Finally he decided to head west for the road, for *a* road. He didn't know which road it would be, or if it was even there. But the thought of staying put was maddening to Frank. They *couldn't* just sit and wait to be caught in the fire!

"Let's get out of this ravine and head west," he said to Whiley.

If Whiley doubted Frank's judgment at all, he did not show it. "Whatever you say, Frank."

Frank knew, with those words, that the heavy hand of absolute responsibility had landed on him. He knew it was not only important to get them out of the woods safely, but also to keep Whiley from panicking. Though it was hard to keep *himself* from panicking.

"We'll be home before dark," he said, in an assuring tone. Whiley grinned and nodded.

The side of the ravine was not as steep as it appeared from the bottom. It was an easy climb, but a long one. When they finally reached the top the wind was blowing directly in their faces, bringing the strong smell of burning timber with it. They halted. Frank looked around. Off to his left a short distance stood a small stand of pines.

"Come on," he said to Whiley. They headed for the tallest tree. Frank lay down his gun and ax and looked up to the top branches.

"You gonna climb it?" Whiley asked.

"Yup," Frank answered. He regarded the tree again, his eyes moving up the trunk steadily. *Lots of good, strong boughs,* he thought. Just as his eyes reached the top a long, thin cloud of smoke passed overhead.

At first he was forced to wrap his arms and legs around the trunk, slowly inching his way up. When he reached the first of the branches he moved quickly, with the dexterity of a trapeze artist. His hands began to sweat and once he nearly lost his grip. He did not look up or down, keeping his eyes firmly fixed on the branches and what he was doing.

When he was nearly to the top he stopped. He didn't trust the smaller branches to hold his weight. He had already taken some risks in that department.

Carefully, he positioned himself and looked to the west. What he saw hypnotized him; his eyes widening, his mouth going dry, the strength being sapped from his body. Before his eyes he saw a wall of fire...not just a fire, but a *wall,* stretching from the left side of the horizon to the right. How far away it was he could not tell. Two miles, maybe three. The only thing for certain was they were in grave trouble.

"My God!" he whispered to himself harshly. "We're trapped! There's nowhere to go!"

He looked down. Whiley was standing at the base of the tree, his arm around it, looking up at Frank with big, trusting eyes, hoping for some good news.

Chapter Twenty-six

Harry Medwick was in a good mood that morning. Three days ago he had decided to take a trip. *Detroit,* he thought. *That's where I'll go. A little theater, a little fine dining, some excitement. It's just what I need!*

Bored to tears in Fairchild over the last year, Harry had written a number of schools, applying for a post. But the only schools that showed him any interest were droll little towns dotted across the landscape. It was a frightening notion, but Harry knew it was true: There were towns out there that were duller, and more isolated than Fairchild.

A year had produced no decent prospects. Still, he held out hope. He planned to look around for a post in Detroit if he had time. Sometimes Harry Medwick was up, and sometimes he was down, but he always felt confident that someday, somehow, he would be transported from the deserted island he'd been marooned on for nearly a year.

He snapped the last suitcase shut. All packed, he did a quick mental checklist. *Landlord informed of his two weeks - check. Cash withdrawn from bank - check. Railroad timetable in pocket - check.*

That was just about it. It sure as hell didn't take much to just up and leave. That fact depressed him, a little. He didn't have any roots. He thought of the day he left college; confident, strong in body and mind, athletic hero, intellectual revolutionary. He was a young god set out to conquer (and change) the world. Now, five years later, the unthinkable had happened. Not only was he rotting into obscurity in this flea-bitten town (because the world never runs out of new revolutionaries), but he was starting to wish he had roots! *Roots!* The lull of the bourgeoisie!

No, no, he thought angrily. *To hell with those thoughts! This last year has been a mere respite, and an eye-opening one at that! I'll get out! I* will *get out!*

He checked his watch; three hours until train time. In anticipation he'd packed early. Now he had time to kill.

Ryman's Saloon, he thought automatically. Then he shook his head and said aloud, "No, no! Been spending *way* too much time in there as it is!"

He walked to the large bay window, which commanded an excellent view of the street. He was surprised to see an unusually large number of people below. They seemed excited.

Harry laughed out loud, as he surveyed the commotion. What the hell could cause so much excitement in Fairchild?

He let the curtain fall back. *Ah well, it's none of my concern. If I have to kill three hours I'd rather not do it cooped up in this dreadful apartment.*

He took one last look around. Then a pounding on his door startled him. He opened it to reveal a breathless Augie Johnson.

"Harry, we're meeting in the front of the town hall in an hour! Wear heavy wool clothes!"

"In this heat?" said Harry.

"If you haven't any, one of the merchants will fix you up with some!"

"What the hell are you talking about?" he asked Augie.

"The fire!"

"What fire?"

Augie struggled to catch his breath. "Harry," he said, "right now there are about two thousand acres of forest burning just to the west of here, and if the wind doesn't switch or we don't stop it, it's going to come *straight* through Fairchild."

Harry blinked. "How could this happen?"

Augie spread his hands helplessly. "We don't know yet! It's just a blessing that there's little population where it's burning now. See you at the town hall!" He turned and left as abruptly as he'd come.

"No, no, no," said Harry, his voice rising, "I'm going on a trip!"

Augie stopped and gave him a venomous look, which Harry would not have thought he was capable of.

Harry closed his apartment door and sank down to the floor. "My trip," he muttered, "my very own trip to Detroit!"

He slapped his face into his hands and wept pitiably as the excitement down on Main Street increased.

Chapter Twenty-seven

Carmin's office was a veritable circus. There were seven men crammed into the small cubicle, all talking excitedly. Carmin was on the phone, trying to hear above the din. He had the receiver pressed against one ear, and a finger in the other.

"Yes," he shouted into the mouthpiece protruding from the box fastened to the wall. "Yes, yes," he kept repeating. "Oh, that's wonderful. Thank you."

He hung up. The other men descended on him like jackals, looking for information.

"That was Mayor Paulson from Turnerville. He's got 200 men sitting on flat cars, waiting to come as soon as they get clearance from the railroad."

The men grunted approval and returned their attention to the map spread over Carmin's desk.

The police chief squeezed in among them and said, "Gentlemen, from the information we have right now, this is the situation. The fire is coming at us - straight at us - from the west." He used his fingers to point out the area on the map. "It looks like it's going to jump the county trunk and head for the Wendell River."

"Can we stop it from jumping the trunk?" asked George Ryman.

"No," said Carmin flatly. "You boys know the county trunk. It's narrow and there's a canopy of foliage overhanging it. We'd never get all of it cleared out in time."

"So what the hell are we going to do?" asked Moses Clark.

"Nothing! We're doomed!" said another town merchant.

"I say we all get the hell *out!"* another chimed in hysterically.

"If you'll all please settle down and not turn this into a panic situation," said Carmin, "I'll show you what we're going to do."

He placed his finger at a particular spot on the map. A line had been added in red pencil. It was east of the county road where the fire was expected to cross.

"This is the logging road that leads into the old Gunderson camp," said Carmin. "And it's where we're going to fight it."

There was a titter of disbelief and skepticism among the men.

"That's damn close to town," said Horace Willoughby, the mayor.

"I know," said Carmin, "but it's the best place. The logging road is much wider than the county trunk, and we'll have a little more time to clear it out. We should have close to 500 men on that logging road by the time the fire gets there, if the boys ride in from Turnerville."

"They better ride in," said the mayor. "The only thing between that road and the town is the Bedlow swamps, dry as a bone this summer. If it gets past them and through Fairchild, God help us all!"

A wave of silence fell over the room, each man considering the potential for loss, not only on a personal level, but for the town as a whole.

Then the door to the office jerked open. It was Charley Lambert.

"Can I speak to you for a moment?" he said, addressing Carmin.

"Of course," said Carmin. The two men left the office. A few minutes later Carmin returned, looked at the men and said,

"The two Burns boys are out there, in the woods. Somewhere on the Wendell."

"Jesus," said George Ryman.

"They went out yesterday to investigate a beaver dam upstream and have not returned."

Mayor Willoughby cleared his throat. "Surely they must know there's a fire."

Carmin let out a sigh. "Perhaps, but *knowing* about it isn't going to help them."

"Anybody search for them?" asked George.

"John Burns searched all morning. Couldn't find them. They must be far up the river."

"Is he still searching?"

Carmin shook his head. "I don't know. Probably not. He has to think about the rest of the family."

George looked down at the map and said, "If they're *that* far up the river, they must be..." He looked up and his voice trailed off.

"That's right," said Carmin. "In the center of it all."

Chapter Twenty-eight

Harry Medwick shouldered his way through the crowd in front of the city hall. Around him, men were being loaded onto every kind of transportation that could be mustered up: automobiles, wagons, buggies, and hayracks - anything that could carry men and equipment. He was surprised to see over a dozen automobiles, and wondered where they had come from. *Only Doc Spencer and the postman have automobiles,* he thought. I *don't even have an automobile yet, surely no one else in this town has one!*

He spotted Augie Johnson and worked his way over to him.

"I see you made it," said Augie indignantly. (And making no effort to hide it.)

Harry did not reply. Together they stood, waiting to be loaded up and shipped out to the Gunderson logging trail with the other men.

A train whistle blew and Harry looked longingly in the direction of the train depot, thinking of his foiled vacation plans.

They don't have *to be foiled,* he'd thought earlier. *You can leave. There just might not be anything left to come back to.*

That last thought is what prompted him to stay. It wasn't so much a desire to join the team of gallant firefighters and save the town, as it was the unsettling idea of traveling to Detroit and having his two weeks ruined with thoughts of what was going on back home. The idea of *not* knowing for all that time and then returning to find a black, charred pile of ruin where once there stood his town (his *home,* however displeased he was with it), disturbed him. No, if Fairchild burned to the ground then he would carry on, perhaps move on...but he wanted to know about it.

And hell, he thought wryly, *I guess my ultimate wish will be fulfilled. I'll get to watch the town burn.*

That was mostly a joke. He just didn't know how *much* of a joke it was.

"That must be another load of men coming in," said Augie of the train whistle, which sounded for a second time. "Probably lumberjacks from the camp at Pleacher's Lake."

The two teachers were loaded on the back of a Model T truck with others, mostly strangers. Augie was filled with brave determination. Harry shoved his hands in his pockets and wondered what the hell he was doing there.

The ride out proved to change Harry's attitude, however. There was no talk among the individuals on the back of that truck (Harry didn't recognize anyone other than Augie), no idle chatter. They all looked and acted as serious and determined as Augie. It was then Harry Medwick began to realize the seriousness of the situation. Excitement started to grow in him, slowly.

The truck turned onto the Gunderson trail.

Holy Christ, Harry thought. The trail seemed hardly wide enough to accommodate the truck. This was their line of defense? *This* was the road that everyone was talking about? The one that was supposed to be so much wider and a safer bet than the county trunk?

The truck stopped abruptly and the men began to jump off the back.

"What's going on?" asked Harry.

"We walk from here," said Augie. "The truck has to go back and pick up more."

They jumped off together and began walking down the trail, which was marked with deep wagon ruts. The grooves in the middle were trampled down by the scores and scores of men who had come before them that afternoon and were already further down the trail at their designated spots.

After about five minutes of walking, men appeared, then more men, then over a hundred seemed to be everywhere. Like ants, they swarmed the woods on the west side of the road with saw and ax. Trees were falling everywhere. The woods were in a constant motion; downward. More and more sunlight was allowed to spill directly on the road as each tree fell. It was all completely disorganized.

"Christ," said Harry, "someone's going to get killed...not by the fire, but by falling trees!"

Augie did not answer.

Harry asked, "Is this where they expect the fire to come through?"

Augie shook his head. "Not really, Harry. They're just not taking any chances. They figure the fire will break through about half-way down the road."

"How far does the road go?"

"About twelve miles," said Augie. "The old logging camp is at the very end of it. That area's pretty well cut out already."

The first twinge of worry flamed inside Harry Medwick. "How big *is* the fire?" he asked.

"Right now, about four miles wide, from what I've heard. And she's burning straight as an arrow because of the wind. That's actually a good thing, because it's not getting any wider.

Both men quickened their step. Eventually they reached the area where the lines of men ended. A hand signal from a man in front of them indicated this was where they would start. Harry and Augie took their positions along the trail with the other men. Soon new men appeared, passed Harry and Augie, and took *their* positions further down...and so it went, on and on.

An army is being amassed, Harry thought. His worry turned into nervousness.

Then a wagon appeared, pulled by mules, bouncing over the ruts in the road. From it two men handed out saws and axes to anyone who had come unequipped. Harry and Augie each took and ax.

The work began. Harry and Augie were set to cut brush. Only the experienced woodsmen worked on timber. Soon axes were ringing all around them.

What had seemed so disorganized to Harry before did have a pattern to it after all. It was like a ballet; all the men, cutters and brushers, moving in time with the falling trees. When they were down, men working teams of horses swept in from the road and pulled the timber out. Harry found himself part of an organized, almost rhythmical dance.

It was also a strenuous dance. Harry huffed and puffed, finding himself having difficulty keeping up with Augie.

Then the men caught the first faint odor of smoke in the wind. The axes fell silent for a moment, as each man raised his head in unison, like a herd of startled deer. They stood still for a moment, listening, watching, and sniffing the air. Then the axes fell to chopping once again.

At an even quicker pace.

Chapter Twenty-nine

In Fairchild, Carmin and Charley supervised the movement of all the men. In kitchens all over town, food was being prepared and boxed. Blankets were being gathered from everyone. Doc Spencer rushed about, setting up first-aid stations and seeing that they were properly staffed with people who knew what they were doing. There would be a lot of men unaccustomed to strenuous labor swinging axes in the woods that day. Doc knew that could (and probably would) cause injuries. There could also be burn victims, fatigue, dehydration...the list could be extensive, and he wanted to be prepared.

Too old for this, he thought. *Where in hell are the young men of medicine, the young doctors?*

Indeed, the call for additional medical help had been sent out at the same time as the call for firefighters. There were several women in Fairchild who knew some basic emergency procedures, and they were staffing the first-aid stations. But if more trained professionals did not arrive, Doc feared he might be overrun, and that thought sent a chill down his spine.

God in heaven, give me the strength to stand up to the task before me.

Everyone in Fairchild would be tested before this ordeal passed. Even if they managed to stop the fire and save the town, it would be a hard winter ahead. Larders were being stripped to feed the influx of men and the drought had already cut sharply into the upcoming harvest. If they could stop the fire with no loss of *human* life, they could still expect loss of stock and equipment on a grand scale.

And there was the matter of Frank and Whiley Burns. Doc thought about the two boys - *especially* Frank - and his shoulders sagged visibly.

Chapter Thirty

"What do you see?"

The question brought Frank out of his hypnosis. What Frank Burns saw from the top of that pine tree had numbed him speechless. He looked down at his younger brother.

"Frank," said Whiley again, "what do you see?"

Quickly Frank backed down the tree, jumping the last eight feet to the ground. He scrambled to his feet and said, "Leave everything but your bedroll."

Whiley stripped off his packsack. His face was ashen, fear building up in his eyes. He said, "How bad is it?"

"Bad," said Frank. "Let's go."

"Where?"

"Back to the river."

Together they ran back down the ravine, where they found the smoke to be thick. The ravine was trapping it.

"Okay," said Frank, "let's stop running and catch our breath." Running only made them breathe heavily. Whiley began coughing, panic written on his face.

Frank grasped his shoulder. "Walk," he said emphatically. "Walk."

They followed the river out of the ravine. Above them smoke billowed thickly. The sky was noticeably darkened. Frank could taste ash in his mouth.

After a few minutes of slow, frantic walking, Frank found what he was looking for; a break in the woods, a small meadow. The large timber stood well back from the river and the bank was low and sandy, sparse of grass. Without the danger of burning trees falling down on them, perhaps they *would* survive.

Frank stopped, but Whiley kept walking ahead blindly. He ran to the boy and tackled him as gently as he could, just to get him to stop.

His face close to Whiley's, he spoke in a low voice. "We *have* to stay here, Whiley. We can't outrun the fire. It's too big and it's moving too fast." Whiley didn't seem to understand. Frank shook the boy angrily. "Listen to me!" he screamed. Tears started to run down Whiley's face, and Frank regretted his harshness.

He began again, in a softer, more reassuring voice. "We can make it, Whiley! We are not going to die! But you have to do everything I tell you, do you understand that?"

Slowly, Whiley nodded his head.

"We are going to stay right here. When the fire comes, we'll wade out into the deepest part of the river, wet our blankets down, and cover ourselves. We'll keep only our heads above water. See the trees?" Frank pointed. Whiley turned his head and looked. "They are far enough back so that they will not fall on us." Whiley nodded again, this time more comprehensively. Then he grinned. Frank grinned back and said, "We'll make it." He patted his brother's shoulder.

His outward calm and enthusiasm belied his inner feelings. Frank Burns was scared to death. The midday sun had turned to dusk. Bits of gray ash now fell all around them like snow.

Then they heard it.

It sounded like a steady, fierce wind, broken only by what seemed to be small explosions. Frank dipped his handkerchief in the stream and covered his nose and mouth. His throat was already starting to ache. Whiley did everything Frank did.

Suddenly, behind and *above* the tree line, they saw fingers of flame shooting into the sky. Their throats and eyes were burning as they waded into the river. Soaking their blankets, they draped them over their heads and shoulders. They moved toward the deep part of the stream, but had to retreat to shallower water because the current was too strong in the deeper water and they could not maintain their balance. Huddling in the river, submerged up to their chins, the boys waited and watched.

Between the thinning trees at the edge of the forest the wall of fire unfolded into view, in ever-inflating contortions. It was such a strong fire it seemed to be rippling like lava. The small explosions of super-heated timber were numerous and loud now, so loud both boys felt the desire to plug their ears, but both were too terrified to move.

Choking, they covered their mouths with their handkerchiefs. The heat seared their faces. Nether spoke. Occasionally Frank would duck his head under for quick relief and Whiley took the cue to do the same.

Frank knew that in order to survive they would have to protect their lungs. Breathing in the heat and ash would be as fatal as being caught in the inferno. He motioned to Whiley and they both turned their backs to the fire, drenching themselves continuously.

Then Frank noticed something, and it spawned a new wave of terror. The cold water in the river was not so cold anymore. It was warming. Was it *possible* that the fire could actually heat the stream? Was the only refuge they had to save them from the fire going to turn around and do them in?

No point in thinking about that, Frank thought, shutting his eyes with a shudder. *If it happens it happens. And if it does, there's nothing we can do.*

Behind them they heard terrible explosions rise above the already deafening roar. They watched as showers of sparks and glowing ash drifted over their heads. Now was the critical time. The next five minutes would tell them if they were to survive or perish. Frank drew his body inward and shut his eyes tightly. Clutching the blanket around him, he could feel his temples pounding. One word was pounding just as hard in his head: Survive. Survive. *Survive.*

Sparks, ash and debris formed into a whirling dervish around their heads. Soon the woods on the opposite side of the river - the side they were facing - caught fire, submitting itself to the fire's furious wrath.

After twenty minutes, Frank dared open his eyes. He peeked out from beneath the blanket. The water was filled with half-burned debris and covered with a thick, gray-colored paste, all of it floating downstream at a very quick pace. He looked over at Whiley, and could see his eyes blinking inside the wet shroud covering his head. They had done it. They had survived. The heat was still intense, but had diminished a bit. The worst was over for *them,* but Frank was worried about his family and the people of Fairchild. He could not imagine any power of man being able to stop the fire.

He started to speak, but it was impossible. His voice was hoarse, his throat charred to the core. His lips were full, thick and stiff. He pulled the blanket off his head and did the same with Whiley's. He looked at his brother with horror. His face was flushed, and long strips of white skin were beginning to raise and flake on his cheeks and forehead. There were also blisters about his mouth and lips. Frank knew he did not look any better.

But they were alive. *Goddamn, they were ALIVE!*

Frank wondered how long they would have to stay in the river before it would be safe to leave. They certainly could not risk it before tomorrow morning. It was still hot, and small, smoldering fires still burned all around. Frequently they heard the violent explosion of super-heated timber. In addition, the smoke was lingering in thick clouds. Together they huddled in the water, dipping their handkerchiefs and trying to preserve themselves as best they could.

After a couple of hours Frank's legs began to cramp. He wanted desperately to move, but it was still too hot. Then he noticed something strange: Smoke coming up from the ground. *My God, is the Earth itself on fire?* He watched in amazement for a minute, then it came to him. What he was seeing were peat bogs. There were peat bogs burning in the ground. In a sense, the Earth itself really *was* on fire! Occasionally, a burning tree would fall to the ground amid a shower of sparks. By morning, what had once been a rich, lush (if dry) forest would be a complete wasteland.

Then, out of nowhere, something struck Frank hard, knocking him forward in the water. He regained his balance and saw an enormous log slide past him. The log was driven by a strong current, and it had shoved him aside like a small child. Whiley let out a barely audible shriek and moved toward the opposite bank to escape. As soon as he tread into deep water the current caught him and he was pushed downstream. Splashing and kicking frantically, he managed to gain purchase on the opposite side of the river, clinging desperately to the ash-covered embankment. A second log appeared, this one more than ten feet long and very thick. It seemed to be gouging into the sandy bottom of the river. It got held up for a moment, but the current and its tremendous weight soon broke it free and it gained speed, heading straight for Whiley. Frank bounded awkwardly across the river and grabbed at it, but it only pulled him along.

"Climb the bank!" Frank screamed, his throat being ripped into painful shards. Whiley tried, but the bank was steep. He grasped at some charred brush growing out of it, and managed only to uproot it. He could not find a place to pull himself out of the water.

Frank wrapped his arms completely around the log and dug his heels into the loose bottom of the river, but to no avail. He lost his grip on it and watched helplessly as it moved toward the bank in a spinning motion toward Whiley. One end of the log struck the bank just upstream from the boy and held fast. The current swung the other end around. Whiley was caught in-between it and the bank, as if trapped in the pincers of a giant crab. In the last seconds, Whiley looked back and flung himself at the log in a desperate attempt to climb over it, but he wasn't strong enough and managed only to get his shoulders over before it pinned him to the bank with a forceful crunch. Whiley only grunted softly. He was caught fast.

Frank rushed to the point where the log had originally caught the bank. Some tangled brush was keeping it there. He ripped all of it out and pushed the log as hard as he could away from the bank to the middle of the river. He watched it float downstream benignly.

Frank returned to Whiley and held him in his arms. "Oh Christ Whiley," he croaked. He remembered the power with which the first log had knocked *him* aside. Whiley was much smaller than Frank, and the log that had pinned him was bigger than the first one. The boy was unconscious, his breathing rattled. Frank knew he needed help desperately, but he did not dare leave the river. The ground was still scorched and inflamed, and all around trees were still falling or exploding. When night fell, Frank's suspicions about leaving the river were reaffirmed: All around the dead forest glowed brightly. The river water began to fall back to its normal cool temperature, and the resulting steam brought a chill. Soon Frank's teeth were chattering. All night long he huddled in the Wendell River, holding his unconscious brother.

Chapter Thirty-one

Harry Medwick worked harder that afternoon than he had in his entire life. No amount of exercise, mentally as a student or physically as a boxer, could have prepared him for this. He marveled at how well Augie was holding up. He knew the little mathematics teacher was tired, and yet he was working as hard and with as much determination now as he had when they'd started five hours earlier.

Much had been accomplished in those five hours. With the help of ax, saw and horse the men had produced a no-man's land as far as the eye could see up and down the logging road. Stripped down and cut up, most of the foliage had been hauled several miles away. It was hard for Harry to believe that when they'd arrived they faced a lush thicket. For close to fifty yards off the road the land was bare, as if the fire had already come through. At least five hundred men (and probably close to a thousand - Harry couldn't be sure), many who didn't live in Fairchild and were in no danger from the fire, had given it their all. They had stopped only for two minute drinks of water, the water being hauled to them in large milk cans brought by local boys.

The first water break was a religious experience for Harry. Everyone drank from the same dipper. *Not very sanitary,* he thought at first.

But it did not stop him from drinking, and drinking heartily.

A whistle blew and everyone turned to face the road.

"Come on boys!" called Bill Sorensen, an experienced jack who was managing the crew. "We break for a little lunch! I think we got it pretty well cleared!"

A wagon came down the road, stopped, and the driver rang a small school bell. The men all headed for the chow wagon. One by one sandwiches were doled out to the men.

While Harry ate his sandwich, he learned from other men that the whole road had been effectively cleared.

When dinner was finished they all returned to work.

"It isn't over yet Harry," said Augie, finishing his sandwich.

"More clearing?" Harry asked.

Augie nodded. "Uh-huh. We're going to be clearing out the brush and pushing the foliage back as far as we can, until we can't anymore."

"When will that be?"

"When the fire gets here," said Augie.

Two hours later, the smell of smoke was strong in the air. Harry took in a deep breath of air and dropped an armload of brush at the designated pick-up spot. The whistle blew once more and again the men turned and faced the road, waiting for instructions. Some sat down and rested, including Augie and Harry.

"Are we done?" Harry asked. He didn't want to sound impatient. This was like any other challenge to Harry - in fact, the greatest of his life - and he wasn't about to quit. He just was hoping the fire would come soon so he could see if all of this was going to work.

"Not quite," said Augie.

"You certainly know what's going on," said Harry, "have you done this before?"

Augie nodded. "Once, up in Honey Bush County, where I got my first teaching job."

More horses were being led down the road. Harry noticed that plows had been situated every fifty feet or so and the horses were being hitched to them. In the distance he saw a familiar figure approaching. He squinted his eyes and looked harder.

Then his eyes widened. It was John Burns approaching. His stomach sank a little, but he maintained his composure. He watched John take a position behind one of the plows. He set the horse out, plowing the remaining foliage across the road to the opposite side. Harry *still* did not know that he had no reason to fear John Burns, and he was thankful John was not placed beside them to work. In that year of school he had managed to avoid the big crazy farmer successfully, in spite of the fact that he seemed to turn up everywhere.

It was the job of John Burns and the other farmers to plow the remaining foliage and cut a trench along the west side of the road. It seemed to take a long time. Augie, Harry and the other men who had worked so hard on clearing the area, were allowed an extended time for rest, and for waiting.

Just before dark, yet another wagon came through. A bale of gunny sacks was thrown off and one was given to each man. Harry eyed his, puzzled.

"Soak it in the water barrel," explained Augie. "The ground is dry as hell. If any small fires pop up before the backfire, we'll stamp them out with the burlap."

Darkness unfolded. The smoke became thicker, causing the moon to rise blood red in the east. Harry's throat began to ache. Then they saw a glow in the distance. It grew brighter. The men watched and began to stir nervously. Sacks were soaked in water over and over in preparation. It grew warmer and brighter. On signal, torches were lit and the piles of brush - which Burns and the other farmers had plowed into the trenches - were lighted. They burned slowly and produced a lot of extra smoke. Everyone was forced back.

The roar could be heard, like something swooping down on them. Flames leaped high into the night sky, some thirty feet above the tree line. This was no longer the glowing infant that had jumped the Wendell River eight hours before. This was an alert monster, in full maturity. Like cannons going off, the pine trees exploded, sending fiery arrows in all directions. The intense heat burned the oxygen from the air, seeming to rob the men of their very breath. Hot ash fell.

The men retreated in as orderly a fashion as possible. Tiny fires did indeed pop up from the burning debris, but were quickly snuffed out with the wet burlap sacks. The advancing wall finally reached the backfire. The meeting flames danced around each other in a sharp-tongued embrace, swinging back and forth hypnotically. Then the flames became one, grew smaller, and began to burn out. Everyone knew the fire would take days to subside entirely, but the men started to rejoice. It had been stopped, bringing an end to the danger to Fairchild, Cumberland County, and the next county after that.

The work didn't stop however. All night long, right to the very break of sunlight, Harry, Augie and the rest of the men battled small fires that popped up. This went on all the way up and down the road.

In the thick, gray light of early morning, Harry was exhausted. He was also a changed man. He realized that it was he who had a lot to learn about the world, the world beyond the university walls he was accustomed to. These men (all the citizens of Cumberland County really, but particularly those along Gunderson Road) had fought a revolution all their own, against insurmountable odds.

Bill Sorenson blew his whistle and said, "We got her boys! There's replacements arriving now. They can fight whatever pops up. Go home."

The thought of a hot bath and food cheered Harry Medwick. He hoped he could catch a ride into Fairchild - he was too damn tired to walk. Sometime during the night he had lost track of Augie. They had been working side by side in the darkness, and then he was gone, just like that. The sense of loss he felt shocked him. *Damn, if I don't miss the guy!*

He wanted to find Augie. Harry Medwick would have given *anything* to find Augie then. He wanted to apologize to him for a year's worth of bad behavior. He scanned the crowd of dead-on-their-feet men. Apologizing was something Harry was not accustomed to doing, nor was he good at, and he knew if he didn't do it then he might never. But the brave, strong little math teacher (whom Harry had come to admire) was nowhere to be found in the chalky morning air.

Chapter Thirty-two

Slowly the night drained away, but it was a silent dawn. No birds, no small animals scurrying about, even the river was quiet. The strong current that had helped cause so much harm the day before was gone. It moved slowly now, as if tired and wounded.

Frank walked to shore with Whiley cradled in his arms. They had spent the night in the river. He laid him down gently on the sand and examined him anxiously. Whiley moaned, seeming to fight for consciousness. Frank winced when he saw the amount of blood dried and caked around his younger brother's mouth. He stripped off his belt and lashed Whiley's wrists together. Pushing his hands and head through Whiley's arms, he rose slowly. Reaching back he caught the boy's legs in each arm and hoisted him up. He would have to carry Whiley all the way home piggyback, not knowing if *he* even had the strength to make it. His legs were cramped and swollen from spending the night underwater.

His first instinct was to move as fast as he could, but he quelled the desire. He had to move at a moderate, steady pace to conserve his energy. If his calculations were correct - that is, if he had any sense of anything - the road leading to home was about six miles west.

He started out. He had taken about ten steps when Whiley suddenly thrashed to the side. The buckle of the belt fastening Whiley's arms dug into Frank's neck. He fell to his knees, stifling a scream. The belt buckle had not only choked him, but cut *into* his neck. He felt like vomiting, and did not stand up until the urge passed. He withdrew his head from the belt and set Whiley down.

Jesus, he looks awful, he thought. In addition to the blood around his mouth, the boy's skin was ghost white and his breathing was shallow. Despair swarmed in on Frank. Tears filled his eyes. He felt something running down his neck. He rubbed it, thinking it was water or perspiration, but when he took his fingers away and examined them, he saw that it was blood, his own blood.

He looked up at the clear blue sky. In between sobs he shook his fists and said, "Damn it, why don't you *help me!"*

After a while of helpless indecision, he was able to compose himself enough to get Whiley hoisted up on his back again, this time with the belt (and buckle) situated in a different way. He started out again, with absolutely nothing in the world to encourage him.

The going was easy in the cool morning, as he plodded through the charred, barren wasteland. But soon the sun was high in the sky and the temperatures soared as they had been doing all summer. Sweat poured down Frank's face in wide streams until his hair, face and shirt were soaked. His legs - particularly his calves - screamed in painful protest. In front of him for as far as he could see the ground was covered with gray ash. The only landscape was the skeletons of trees, standing mute, like black, unmarked tombstones. His body called out for rest, as he plowed through the ash. It was like lumbering through deep snow. He knew that if he rested he might not get up again. He tried leaning against a charred tree and was shocked when it broke in half in a cloud of black powder. The barren landscape stretching to the horizon kept reminding him that there was no help forthcoming. This demoralized him even further so he walked with his head down, eyes on his feet.

Then a grisly thought struck him and he stopped cold in his tracks. Was Whiley still alive? He hated thinking it, allowing such a thought to make an appearance in his mind, but it was possible, terribly possible. Frank could remember watching in horror as the log swung around, pushed by the strong current, and crashed into Whiley. There had been no movement, and no sound, from the boy since they left river.

No, no, he thought, tears welling up again. *Stop it right now. Stop, stop, stop!*

A sharp gust of wind kicked up at that moment, bringing with it a storm of ash. It whipped around him in tornado-like eddies, flying into his eyes, blinding him. He could taste the bitter powder as it turned to paste in his mouth. Within seconds he was covered in it, from head to toe, choking and coughing, tucking his head into his shoulder for protection as he walked.

It was over in a few minutes, but it didn't matter then. Tears made dark lines down his ash-covered face. He was finished. He was not going to make it. Neither of them were going to make it.

He thought of the deer that he and Whiley had hunted in early November of last year, how it had run in a vain attempt to escape its fate. That's what he was doing. He, like the deer, now ran on instinct alone.

When the wind died down he brought his face away from his shoulder and opened his eyes. Through blurred vision, he thought he saw something. He blinked his eyes, trying to tear the ash out of them. Yes, there was something. Dark images. He squinted. My God, they were moving!

He quickened his pace, frantic that they would not see him and disappear as quickly as they'd appeared. He tried to scream but his voice was simply not there. He moved faster, staggering under Whiley's weight. *Not much time, not much time,* he thought. *God Whiley, stay alive, stay alive, stay alive!*

The figures he saw became larger and more definable. Soon it looked like they were approaching *him.* Soon Frank realized they were. Soon it sounded like they were shouting to him. Soon Frank realized they were.

He broke out into a full-tilt run, which lasted about four steps, before he fell face first into the ash and could not see, hear or taste anything.

Chapter Thirty-three

The kerosene lamp burned slowly. The soft light illuminated only the immediate area around the bed. Doc stood back, in the shadows. He watched the bed, and the disconsolate family gathered around it. Caroline and Rachel Burns sat and cried without hiding it. Agnes sat and stared blankly at the boy lying in the bed. John stood behind her, his big hands resting softly on her dainty shoulders.

How small he looks lying there, thought Doc. He turned to the window and looked out at the night. His eyes caught his Ford down in the yard and memories of Frank cleaning it on Saturdays came back vividly. Those memories seemed years ago now. He blinked his eyes in an effort to wake himself up. He hadn't slept in forty hours, and was near collapse. He had no idea how many people he had treated in that time. Way too many for a man *half* his age. No medical help had arrived, and the burden had fallen on him entirely. When he got some sleep he would raise hell about that, but now he was just too tired.

He made his way to the bed. He reached under the covers, exposing the boy's arm. He pressed his thumb on the boy's wrist. He tucked the arm back under the covers and straightened. His eyes locked on John Burns for a moment. Then he walked to the dresser, picked up his bag and left the room.

Down the hall he opened another bedroom door. Peeking in he saw another lamp glowing softly. He tip-toed in. Frank's face looked pale. Ointment glistened on his torn, blistered lips. He stirred, but did not awaken.

Doc left the room and continued down the hall. At the stairs he had to grasp the railing tightly to steady himself. In the parlor, the smell of coffee greeted him. Half a dozen neighbors, including Chester White and his wife, sat quietly, sharing the midnight vigil. Their eyes followed him as he passed through on his way to the door.

"Doc?" said Chester.

Doc Spencer paused at the door, his hand on the knob. Without looking at them he said, "Whiley Burns is dead." Then he walked out, closing the door behind him.

Chapter Thirty-four

The news of Whiley's death spread like a virus through the town. It seemed to touch everyone, blotting out their own problems - at least momentarily.

Frank awoke the next morning. When he was finally cognizant enough to where his inquiries about Whiley could no longer be evaded, he was told of his brother's death by his father. The news seemed to confuse him. He rose from his bed and began pacing. Several times he tried to speak, but no words would come. His behavior became erratic.

"He might be delirious," said John to Agnes. Agnes was in no better shape. She sat with her hand in John's, staring.

Doc returned at mid-morning, examined Frank again and immediately returned him to bed.

"He seems agitated," said John, when Doc came down the stairs to the parlor. "Is he all right?"

"He's fine," said Doc. "But he may be affected by this more than we realize. He's very restless. I'd keep a close watch on him."

That day passed slowly. Several times John Burns entered the room to find Frank pacing back in forth in front of Whiley's bed, tears streaking his face. He put him to bed, only to find him doing the same thing in an hour.

Late in the afternoon, Frank finally fell asleep, and John sat beside his bed all night, watching him toss and turn, calming him when he cried out. John prayed for strength. Tomorrow morning he would bury his youngest son in the ground, and he was nearly at the limit of his endurance as it was.

The church was packed, more than it had ever been on Sunday. Outside, latecomers - unable to enter - talked in hushed voices. Inside, the Burns family sat together silently and solemnly.

John cast a glance at his oldest son, sitting beside him. Frank had aged in the last two days, there was no doubt about that. His eyes were sunken, his face seeming to wrinkle before his father's very eyes. Everything had changed and the future was as uncertain as it had ever been. The pain and anger over what happened had subsided, and been replaced by a sort of nether world; a stretch of time that was both real and a dream. It felt, at least to John, that time wasn't moving in a straight line anymore, but bending and contorting violently, taking the long way to get around each and every painful moment.

There was a titter of commotion in the back of the church. John turned around and his eyes widened. Coming down the center aisle was a little man dressed in a neat, brown suit. His white beard was carefully combed. Hard scrubbing had transformed his ruddy face to a glowing pink and his bald head fairly shined. New shoes squeaked, as he seemed to tiptoe down the aisle. He stopped in front of the coffin. Everyone in the church whispered to himself in amazement as Hemlock looked down on Whiley and paid his last respects. When he was through, he turned and left the church. Another murmur went through the congregation.

Frank rose suddenly and walked to the coffin for a second time. Looking down at his brother, in perfect, peaceful repose, he reached into his pocket and pulled out his gold timepiece. He could remember Whiley's words on the day of graduation: *"You know, Frank, if ever there was anything in the world I'd want, it's a gold watch just like yours."* Frank had been nearly asleep and had barely heard his younger brother, but now he could remember the words vividly.

In a moment of grieving pageantry, he had decided to bury Whiley with the pocket watch, which his brother had admired so greatly. But now, at the right moment, his resolve began to crumble. It was his most prized possession. He wanted to keep it. What good would it do to bury it with Whiley? He looked at the watch and bit his lower lips anxiously.

He couldn't do it. Not that. He returned the watch to his own pocket and returned to his seat. He lowered his head, a profound sense of guilt weighing down on him. Then the minister appeared and the service began.

Chapter Thirty-five

Three days after Whiley's funeral, rain swept over Cumberland County in broad, wind-driven sheets. But it was too little and too late. The farmers had watched their gardens and fields shrivel and die for most of the summer. This spelled disaster for those who counted on the fall canning. Local cupboards, usually filled to the brim with canned fruits and vegetables by the time the first snowflakes fell each year, would be bare. Without these, a long, hard winter lay ahead. In a domino effect, the merchants in town were also going to be hard-pressed. Furnishing credit to the farmers would be out of the question. September saw many farmers selling cattle for whatever they could get, not only because they needed money, but because the parched fields simply would not be able to sustain a large herd, and the animals would be more trouble than they were worth.

And so it was - autumn descended on Fairchild, Michigan. The mood of the people, usually jubilant at this time of year, was subdued. Charley Cullen, local farmer, said it best: "This winter is gonna be a real pisser!"

Frank had always loved the golden days of autumn, loved to revel in nature's painted landscape. For Frank, autumn was a time of rebirth - or a *sense* of rebirth - rather than a time of decline.

But not this year.

Trout splashed, fighting their way upstream. Deer were appearing in the open fields more frequently, in large numbers, and with less trepidation. The majestic bucks came right up to the gravel roads. Pawing the dirt, they proclaimed their masculinity. Brandishing their new racks, they warned, "Beware! This is *my* time!" Soon the calm, sunny skies echoed with the sound of geese, heading south in long, earnest formation. To watch the geese migrate is a sight to hold any man in a profound moment of reflection. These were the days Frank loved.

But not this year.

The deep, stabbing pain over Whiley's death had slowly turned into an all-encompassing grief. In some ways, the grief was *worse* than anger and pain. He could not escape his brother's memory. At night he had terrible dreams. During the day he helped his father with chores and that was maddening. It was his and *Whiley's* job to do chores in the barn, and now he and his father were doing them. Frank would break down often in the middle of work and would have to sit down. His father had not yet showed any outward emotion, any apparent signs of grief. This surprised Frank, and angered him a little.

In October Frank Burns made a decision. In fact, it really *wasn't* a decision. There was no choice involved. He *had* to leave.

Once he resolved to go through with it, he began thinking up reasons to leave - reasons he could give to his parents, for they would surely object. The strongest argument he could think of was the drought of that summer. John Burns, like every other farmer, had been hit badly. The family faced a long, hard winter. One less mouth to feed would stretch their already meager food supply. He could also send them money when he found work. He *would* send them money.

Armed with this argument, he confronted his father one evening after dinner. John Burns said nothing for a long while, staring intently at his son.

After what seemed to Frank to be an eternity, the man spoke.

"All the reasons you give me for leaving are valid," he said, "but are they the *real* reasons you want to leave, Frank?"

Frank shifted uncomfortably. His father had looked right into him, right through him. He could not admit the real reason, not even to himself: He was running away. Running away from a terrible thing, but nevertheless running away.

"Are they the real reasons?" his father asked again.

"No," said Frank, with a frustrated sigh. There was no lying to his father. He never had, and things were bad enough already. He knew lying (about this or anything) now would just make things worse.

His father nodded. "Where do you want to go?"

"Blackwing."

"Blackwing?"

"Yes sir," said Frank. "I want to go work in the camps."

A look of displeasure unfolded across John's face. Blackwing was a notorious lumberjack town, forty miles to the north, filled with saloons, gambling and whores. It was a very rough scene, but it was also the hiring point for the many lumber camps that surrounded it.

"Why Blackwing?" said John, his face flushing red.

"Because it's close and I know I can find work there."

"It's a hell hole," said John angrily.

"It's work!" said Frank, with the most defiance he had ever showed his father.

The defiance, and the look in Frank's eyes, stopped the big farmer. *He's going,* he thought. *No matter what I say, he's going. If I argue or try to force him to stay, I'll lose him...I'll lose another son.*

"All right," he said, "I'll speak to your mother."

"Explain to her that I *must* go."

The big man nodded resignedly. "It's not going to be easy for her, especially now."

"I know," said Frank.

The next morning Frank looked into his mother's face. She averted his eyes. Her face was drawn and she looked tired and old. Frank knew she had been told. The breakfast passed in silence, with Frank unable to find anything to say to his mother. Later, in the barn, he told his father he would leave town at the end of the week. Burns nodded silently and kept busy.

Chapter Thirty-six

In his office, Carmin Jones sat at his desk, toying with a pencil. This became tiresome after a moment so he threw it on the desk and frowned with irritation.

He was seriously contemplating a trip. *Dozens* of times he had thought of going to Birchwood to investigate Millard Hoffman's family ties, but with so much else having gone on that summer in and about Fairchild, it had been an easy idea to shrug off. Yet, something inside would not let him forget it completely. He had no delusions of finding out what *happened* to Millard. That secret had died with Millard, and the perpetrator was long, long gone. It was the nagging feeling that someone ought to *at least* inform his family. That is, if there even was a family, and if they even lived in Birchwood. He had gotten no help from the boys in Lansing, just an absurd letter suggesting that *he* journey down and look through the records himself. Lansing was too far to travel. Birchwood was not.

A day going, he thought, *a day around the town asking questions, and a day back. Three days total. Not* too *bad. Fairchild can spare me for a little while. Charley knows how to take care of things.*

There was another reason for going, hiding back in the far reaches of his mind. The *urge* was once again creeping up on him. It had been nearly three years since it last seized him. He reckoned it was the goings-on of that summer, the misfortune fallen on Fairchild, that brought it on. Long ago he had learned to curb it, but he knew he could never conquer it. Never had he yielded to it in Fairchild. But whatever the reason, it was coming up strong, and going to Birchwood would provide the perfect opportunity (and the proper discretion) to satisfy it.

He made the decision, and resolved to stick to it. Carmin Jones was going to Birchwood to find out what he could about Millard Hoffman. Then he would go on one hell of a rip-roaring drunk.

With the weight of that decision lifted off his shoulders, he sat back and smiled. Tomorrow he would tell Charley he'd be running the show for a few days.

Chapter Thirty-seven

Frank was being torn up inside. For two days his mother barely spoke to him, and when she did she said as little as possible. His *father* seemed to understand, and appeared to have accepted it. In fact, in those two days they had grown closer than ever before. Now, as they worked side by side in the barn on a beautiful morning in late October, Frank brought up the subject of his mother.

"You have to understand," said John, "she's terribly disappointed and frightened, especially after...." He stopped, unable to speak of Whiley's death.

"I know Pa," said Frank, "but I *must* make her understand. I can't leave her like this."

"I know."

"But I *will,*" he added, "if I'm forced to."

John paused. "I know. Try after supper tonight. But remember, her silence is only her way of fighting this. With it, she is trying to get you to change your mind. It's the only way she can think of. She doesn't want to lose another son."

Frank nodded silently.

"And neither do I," said John. Frank stopped his work and looked at his father for a moment. Then they continued in silence.

That night after supper, Frank went to see his mother. She was alone in the kitchen, washing dishes.

"Where are the girls?" he asked. It was their job, usually, to do the dishes. Caroline, like their father, showed no outward grief over Whiley's death. Rachel had drawn into herself completely. She rarely spoke now, and the rest of the family was worried about her.

"Mom?" Frank said again, softly. "Where are the girls?"

"Visiting friends," said Agnes, without taking her eyes away from the dishes.

Frank took her by both wet hands and led her to the kitchen table. When they were both seated he began to explain. He repeated all the reasons he had given his father, emphasizing the importance of the money he would be sending home, and the fact that he would only be forty miles up the road. When he finished, he looked at her expectantly. She rose without a word and returned to washing the dishes. Frank went to bed feeling worse than ever.

Friday night of that week, Frank stuffed a few remaining articles of clothing into a canvas bag. His packing was complete. He reviewed his travel plans. He had thought about taking the train to Blackwing, the road and tracks ran parallel to each other nearly half the way, but he decided against it. The road was a fairly busy one and he was confident he could find a ride. Besides, train tickets cost money and Frank had thirteen dollars to live on until he found work.

He looked around the room that had once been his and Whiley's. He shuddered, relieved that soon he would be away from it. Had he forgotten anything? He had seen Doc and told him of his plans. Doc's parting words rang in his head: "Don't let anybody get the best of ya, or make a dern fool out of ya!" He had traveled across the field and through the pine forest to Hemlock's shack and paid a painful, emotional farewell visit to the old man.

That was it. He was set. Tomorrow he would leave. Only one thing dimmed the excitement mounting inside him: His mother's feelings remained unchanged.

Saturday was one of those mornings that only come in October; when it's comfortably warm and refreshingly cool at the same time. The sun rose and set the changing leaves on fire.

John Burns picked at his breakfast with little interest. He had been up since before dawn doing chores with Frank. By now his appetite was usually ravenous, but he was not hungry today. He too had noticed the strengthening bond that had cropped up in the last couple of days between Frank and himself, and that made Frank's leaving all the more bitter to swallow.

The girls ate nervously. All week long they had sensed the tension in the house. Agnes stood next to the sink, packing a lunch, her back to the rest of the family. John occasionally glanced at her, his heart breaking. He knew she felt betrayed. Not only by Frank for leaving, but by her husband for not stopping him.

He rose from the table and said, "I'll get the buggy ready."

No one answered as he left the house.

Frank looked at the girls with a false smile on his face. "I'll get my things," he said. Again, no answer.

When he returned with his duffelbag, the kitchen was empty. Everyone was outside in the yard. Frank walked out and joined them.

Taking Rachel's face in both hands, Frank leaned down and kissed her forehead. Her lips quivered and she hugged him tightly for a long time.

Looking into Caroline's face, Frank saw her eyes beginning to water. They had a look that cried, *"I wish I could go with you! I'd give* anything *to go with you!"* This broke Frank's heart. He knew how trapped Caroline must have felt. The farm was his parents' life. They would go on. They had no desire to leave. And Rachel was still too young. But Caroline, sweet Caroline...Frank knew she was getting restless.

"Don't worry," Frank said, kissing her cheek.

"I know," said Caroline.

His mother's eyes were cold and vacant. He kissed her without response. She stood frozen in his hug. Frank waited to see if her response would change, but it did not.

"I love you mother," said Frank.

No response.

Dejected and crushed, he turned and walked to the buggy. All his life he had only known love, kindness and tenderness from his mother, and now when he needed it the most she was oblivious to him. He had never felt more lonely in his life.

John Burns waited patiently in the buggy. As if to question her behavior one more time, Frank turned and stared intently at his mother. This time their eyes locked and she flew at him. Her arms went around his neck with incredible strength. Relief and gratitude flooded Frank's soul. Tears welled up in his eyes.

"Be careful," Agnes whispered in his ear in a sobbing voice.

"I will," said Frank.

He climbed aboard, beside his father. John looked down at his family and said, "I'll be back."

He snapped the reins and they were off. Agnes, Caroline and Rachel stood by the road and watched, waving, until the buggy was completely out of sight.

Chapter Thirty-eight

Carmin Jones stood on the platform of the depot, suitcase in hand. He watched as the buggy crossed the tracks, stopping at the road that ran parallel. Moving ahead of the chugging engine for a better view, Carmin watched with interest when it stopped. A large bag was taken from the buggy. He watched as the two talked for a time, then shook hands. Abruptly John Burns started back across the tracks in the buggy. Frank hefted the duffelbag and started down the road on foot. It didn't take a genius to figure it out. Frank Burns was headed for Blackwing. When boys left Fairchild to become men, they either headed south to Detroit or north to Blackwing.

Striking out on his own, Carmin thought. *Gonna go work in the camps.*

Down the platform came the cry, "All aboard!" Moving quickly, Carmin boarded the train and sat down in a window seat. Looking out he could still see Frank Burns walking down the road. He continued watching until the sudden lurch of the train set him back in his seat.

They were two men on a journey, both headed in a different direction, on a different road, neither knowing where it would lead.

Carmin leaned back in his seat. Slowly he became accustomed to the rocking motion of the coach. Beneath his feet he could hear the *clickety-clack* of each new length of rail.

Deliberately, he had chosen the third and last coach. Already he could smell the faint odor of smoke from the engine. He hoped it would not get any worse. And he liked the privacy as well. There were only two other travelers in the coach with him, and they were seated up in front. Carmin could only see the backs of their heads, but their thick, cotton shirts with collars faded from sweat told him they were lumberjacks. *Probably coming from Blackwing,* he thought, *bound for God knows where.*

He thought about his own destination, Birchwood, lying on the shores of Lake Superior. Carmin had always liked the town, liked how possessed it seemed by the great lake. It had been over twelve years since his last visit. He imagined its population must be eleven or twelve thousand by now. *That* was a town going places, not like Fairchild. But like Charley Lambert, that suited Carmin just fine. More people meant more problems. Increased commerce meant increased crime. And if Fairchild *were* to suddenly boom, Carmin and Charley would be the *last* to be compensated for their extended responsibilities, in the way of pay raises or being able to take on extra help.

He looked out the window. The land that sailed by him was bright with fall color. Carmin could almost smell the leaves. It was a smell that was at once sweet and acrid. When the train reached Lake Superior he marveled at its vastness. *It's like viewing the ocean,* he thought, wanderlust gripping his soul. *It stretches on forever!*

He was glad to be on this trip. Now that he was growing older it seemed his list of priorities was ever changing. He wondered how many more times after this he would be able to marvel at Lake Superior. How many more fall seasons would be his to enjoy with late night walks in the cool breeze? How *much* more color would he see?

Carmin Jones had never married, something that he occasionally regretted, especially during moments of reflection such as this. He was generally a solitary man, like Hemlock. But *unlike* Hemlock, Carmin was not averse to human contact all together. Carmin simply enjoyed his solitude, preferred the company of no one. As an officer of law enforcement, even in a small town like Fairchild (or perhaps *especially* in a small town like Fairchild) Carmin felt it was appropriate to stay somewhat aloof anyway. Carmin was friendly and kind to the people of Fairchild, but he always kept enough distance so that when a dispute arose (usually over something mundane) he could not be accused of playing favorites. Carmin was liked by all, but if someone needed a night in jail, Carmin gave it to them, whether it was the likes of Millard Hoffman or some influential businessman. He maintained this policy of aloofness (and, he thought, fairness) in every aspect of his life.

But now it was getting near the end of the trail. As far as work was concerned, Carmin was nearing sixty and they (the government of Cumberland County and even the people of Fairchild) would want a younger man eventually. Carmin didn't know what he would do then. He had some money. Not a lot, but enough.

Maybe that's why I'm making this trip. If I *were to pass on, I would want* my *kin to know!*

"What kin?" he said out loud, chuckling. This prompted one of the lumberjacks to turn and look at him. Carmin grinned and waved, knowing the chances of him finding out anything about Millard Hoffman were slim at best. But if there *were* someone out there, some distant relative who had once known and liked Millard and who now sat and wondered what ever happened to him, Carmin felt that person had the right to know.

And the urge to drink was stronger in Carmin than ever.

The train turned away from the lake and traveled due east for three hours, then pulled into Dexter. Carmin spent a half-hour layover at the tiny lunch counter at the station. He ate a dry beef sandwich and a piece of cherry pie, washing it down with two huge mugs of steaming coffee. He bought an apple to eat on the train, just in case, and boarded the northbound for Birchwood. This time, much to his dismay, the coach was almost full. He found a seat in the back and sat down. He placed his transfer in the breast pocket of his suit, three-quarters of it sticking out, and closed his eyes. When he awoke, his transfer was gone and they were pulling into Birchwood.

Chapter Thirty-nine

An hour after leaving the train, Carmin stood at the entrance of the Hotel Wellington. The Wellington was, by far, the most impressive building in Birchwood. It was an enormous sandstone structure that covered almost an entire block. Ornately detailed, it was an architectural masterpiece. It rose five stories into the sky, twice the height of any building in the town (or the region) at the time. Inside the Wellington the weary traveler could indulge in a variety of amenities, including a hair cut, shave, shoes shined, hat blocked, and clothing cleaned and pressed. There was also a billiard room, barroom, ballroom and dining room, all extravagant, both in how they were decorated and operated.

Carmin entered the lobby. He had stayed at the Wellington years ago, but now he gazed around the lobby (with its vast ceilings) in awe, as if it were his first time. He had spent too much time in Fairchild. He was not used to this. Clustered about the marble floor were large, leather easy chairs, the kind ideal for smoking and reading in pure comfort. The smell of cigar smoke hung in the air.

Carmin walked to the desk. A neat, impeccably dressed desk clerk gave him an appraising glance. "May I help you sir?"

"Yes, I would like a room please," said Carmin.

"Very good sir," said the clerk, pushing the register in front of him. "How long will you be with us sir?"

"I'll be checking out Tuesday morning," Carmin replied, wishing he had the money, the time and the wherewithal to say, *"Two weeks, my good man!"*

"Very good," said the clerk. He turned and scanned a large board lined with room keys, hanging on the opposite wall.

"Something I can see the lake from," Carmin added.

"Yes sir," said the clerk, smiling. The clerk gave him his key with a sharp flick of his wrist and rang the desk bell. An anxious bellboy appeared. He too was dressed impeccably in red uniform. He picked up Carmin's suitcase and together they headed for the elevator.

Carmin was well satisfied (to say the least) with his room. The bed was soft and spacious. The furnishing was elegant. He took off his coat and hurried to use the convenience. When he returned, he took the chair from the room's writing desk and set it in front of the window. From the fourth floor of the Hotel Wellington he looked over the rooftops into the cool blue waters of Lake Superior in the distance. It was a hazy day and Carmin had trouble telling where the lake and the sky met. He sat in the chair and stared for a long time. Water had an almost hypnotic effect on Carmin. When he was young, he had considered going to sea, but...well, that was a long time ago.

He changed his thoughts to Millard Hoffman, which is really what had brought him to Birchwood. On Monday, he would learn what he could. Until then, there was the *urge* to contend with.

"Or submit to," he said out loud. He shook his head. *Later. Later. Not now, not when it's still daylight.*

His eyes returned to the water.

It was nearly dark when he walked through the lobby and into the dining room of the Wellington. Most of the tables were filled with people already in the process of dining. About half an hour later he was enjoying the finest lake trout he had ever eaten, the specialty of the house. He luxuriated with every bite, eating very slowly. The dining room was empty when he finally finished.

Returning to the lobby, he bought a paper and, from the glass counter, an expensive cigar. Occasionally, the otherwise reserved Carmin Jones enjoyed a good cigar. Armed with his paper and his cheroot, he found an easy chair with decent lighting. Sinking back into it, he lit his cigar and opened the paper.

He scanned through the paper, but couldn't seem to focus on anything now except the urge. He readjusted himself in the chair and fought to find something in the paper, something of interest to take his mind off drinking. He wasn't really *resisting* the urge, just waiting, waiting like a child waits to open the biggest Christmas present last. It would be sweeter if he waited. He forced himself to stay in the chair for an hour. Then, when the anticipation and the raw urge were at their peak, he rose.

Leaving the lobby through a large archway, he turned to the right and moved down the corridor to the barroom. The bar was long (longer than even Ryman's Saloon) and it was busy. The man behind the bar was young and once again dressed immaculately. Carmin walked up and ordered a bottle of expensive whiskey. He paid the barman and was off.

In his room, he returned to the chair in front of his window. It was stuffy in his room, so he opened the window. A cool lake breeze swathed his face. He breathed in deeply, opened the bottle and brought it to his lips. The liquor was smooth. *Good whiskey,* he thought. *Very good.* He remembered the old adage: There is no such thing as bad whiskey - some are just better than others. He brought the bottle up to his mouth and took another drink.

Three hours later he lay on his bed, fully clothed. Only his tie had been stripped. It lay on the floor by the window. Next to the tie lay the empty bottle. Carmin snored loudly and erratically, the sound broken only by an occasional moan. The smell of whiskey hung heavily in the room. The curtains billowed in circular contortions in the lake breeze. Carmin snored on, his drugged mind unable to catch a dream.

The morning sun touched his face and he stirred. He was incredibly sick and he ran for the convenience. When he finally returned to the room, he plucked himself despondently into the chair by the window. There were always these feelings of depression and regret afterwards. Carmin hated himself for it, but he'd learned long ago that although he could control the urge, he could never defeat it. No one in Fairchild knew of this vice. He had been very careful about that.

He cleaned up, put on new clothing and went for breakfast. In the dining room he toyed with his bacon, eggs and cakes, but eventually left them virtually untouched. He returned to his room, sent out his suit to be cleaned and left the hotel.

For that entire Sunday he walked about town, trying to put his thoughts together. He felt much better when he returned to the hotel around sundown. He went back to the dining room and enjoyed a meal equally as fine as the one the night before. When that was over he returned to the barroom, ordered another bottle of whiskey and brought it up to his room, where he took the same position in the chair by the window and eagerly raised the bottle to his lips.

It was nearly ten o'clock the next morning when Carmin finally came to. He was sick again, this time *deathly* sick. He forced himself up and spent the next half-hour on his hands and knees in the convenience. Then he stood before the mirror, examining the image that stared back at him. His skin was a grayish pallor, his eyes dull and glossy. The skin around his eyes was taut and puffy-looking. As he touched the puffiness around his eyes his fingers trembled uncontrollably.

"Well, that's it," he said. "The urge has been satisfied. No more for me."

And he knew he was speaking the truth. He would drink no more, at least not until the urge overtook him again. And that would probably not be for years. Feeling and looking like death warmed over helped his resolve.

He cleaned up and went down to the dining room. Once again he toyed with his breakfast and left it.

On the street he walked with shaky legs, but was determined to do what he set out to do. The six blocks to the courthouse were almost unbearable. And his head, Christ! It felt like an overripe tomato...a *painful* tomato.

The courthouse was a large gray stone building with a huge front lawn. It, like the Wellington, took up all of the block, and from both corners, sidewalks ran over the grass diagonally, coming together in front of the door.

Carmin entered the building. The wide corridor was lined with offices on each side. Straight ahead a stairway as wide as the corridor itself led to the second floor. Carmin scanned the frosted glass windows of each office door. The title and function of each office was stenciled in gold and black lettering on the windows. The third door on the right happened to be what Carmin was looking for. *Public Record.* Carmin walked inside.

No one was at the greeting counter. Carmin looked at his watch. It was 12:15. *Lunch hour,* he thought. *I suppose it's no surprise. I guess I'll have to wait.*

Then he heard a noise. It came from an open door on the far side of the office. Leaning far over the greeting counter, Carmin was able to peer into the room. Behind a desk sat a large, balding man eating a sandwich intently.

"Hello?" said Carmin.

The man looked up from his lunch with surprise.

"I'll come back," said Carmin.

Unable to speak with his mouth full he waved Carmin into his office. The man washed down his food with a long drink of milk from a mason jar. From his lap he snatched a white linen cloth and wiped his mouth quickly. He stood up and extended his hand. Carmin took it and they shook.

"Cecil Whitt," said the man, "what can I do for you?"

"Carmin Jones. I'm a peace officer from Fairchild. I'm hoping your records can help me."

"Well," said Cecil, who seemed jolly, "we got 'em! What do you want to know?"

Carmin sighed and said, "Well, we had a man die in Fairchild late last year, and he may have lived here in Birchwood at one time. Might even have some relatives. I'd like to get in touch with them."

The clerk nodded. He grabbed a pencil and poised his hand, ready to write. "What's the family name?"

"Hoffman."

"Hoffman?"

"Yes," said Carmin. "The deceased man's named was Millard Hoffman."

Cecil put down his pencil. "I'm sorry to hear that," he said, a genuine look of regret on his face.

"You knew him?" said Carmin.

"Oh yes," said Cecil. "Millard was a fine man!"

Carmin thought about Millard; the drunk, the vagrant, the derelict who had been lying dead in the snow. He wondered if he and Cecil were talking about the same person.

"How did he die?" Cecil asked. "Heart?"

"Something like that," said Carmin. He'd decided not to go into the details of Millard's death, just to keep it simple.

"Yes, yes," said Cecil, "I knew Millard. A good man, and a *hell* of a Mason. Knew the whole family!"

"Good," said Carmin, "maybe you can help me then."

Cecil shrugged and shook his head. "I don't know how! They're all gone! All except Tom, of course. He's the eldest brother. He's in a boarding house outside of town. Senile, you know."

So that's it, thought Carmin with frustration. *The end of the line.* Then a thought struck him. "When we went through Millard's things, we found some letters from a woman named Matilda."

A pained look came across Cecil's face. "Matilda?" he said. "Now *there's* a saint, a beautiful girl if ever there was one!" Carmin nodded and waited. "She was Millard's sister. The youngest of the Hoffman kids," Cecil went on. "Must be dead, now, about sixteen or seventeen years. That *bastard* killed her!"

"Who?" asked Carmin with a newfound interest.

"I can tell you about it," Cecil offered. "You got a few minutes?"

"Sure," said Carmin, taking a seat in front of the desk, "go ahead."

"Well, like I said, it was a long time back. In those days, *most* of the young men had a fancy for Matilda." Carmin watched as the man paused and thought back, almost like *he* once had a fancy for Matilda. Then he snapped out of it and continued. "Anyway, about this time this fella blew into town and got himself a job at the sawmill. Big and burly bastard, he was. A real hell raiser. First thing you know, he's got his eye on Matilda." He sneered and shook his head slowly. "That was the sorriest day of *her* life. At first he treated her nice as pie, and she fell for it. One thing led to another and they got married.

"Things were goin' just fine until she became pregnant. Then things got bad. He didn't care about her once she was with child. He left her alone for days at a time when he was drinking. Wouldn't even have had food on the table if it hadn't been for Millard. They were real close, her and Millard. Old Millie worshipped his sister...woulda done anything for her. He tried many times to convince Matilda to leave this guy, but she wouldn't. Millard hated him like poison. Then one night it all came to a head when Millard found him in a saloon, drunk as usual. Called him every name in the book. Never heard nobody cuss like that! Of course, the two men went crazy, but this man was big and ended up beating Millard to within an inch of his life. Old Millard didn't have a chance, but he fought his heart out, I'll give him that."

"What happened after that," said Carmin.

Cecil shrugged. "Millard just up and left town a few days after that. When he could walk straight again, that is." He laughed weakly at this and drank some more of his milk. "Guess he couldn't stand to see what was happening to his sister. He left her quite a bit of money when he skipped town, and told her that he didn't want her to spend the money unless it was to get as far away from this guy as possible."

"But she never did," said Carmin.

"Nope, never got a chance to. She just kept going down, the situation between her and her husband draining her of all strength. Then the day for the baby to be born came. The baby was just fine but Matilda was not. She didn't make it. Just too weak, because of that bastard."

Cecil looked sad now as he reflected. "Millard came back for the funeral, and that was the last we ever saw of him around here. Now you tell me that *he's* dead too."

Cecil Whitt seemed exhausted from telling the story, and at the same time unburdened, as if it were a story he had to tell. That was all fine, but it did not help Carmin any.

"Well," he said, rising, "thank you very much for your time and information." Cecil nodded. "Matilda's husband, is he still around?"

"Naw," the clerk answered, "he left right after Matilda died. He wasn't too much liked around these parts. He came back a year or so ago and collected the boy. The boy was raised by a farm family just outside of town, and he just shows up after nearly twenty years of being away. That rose one *hell* of a stink, but what could they do? He was the boy's father, and the boy *wanted* to go with him!"

Carmin thanked him again and they shook hands. Halfway to the door of the office Carmin turned and asked, "I don't suppose anybody knows or cares where to find the boy and his father."

"No, I doubt it," said Cecil.

"You remember the man's name?"

"Yeah, Dumont," the clerk answered.

Carmin froze. His stomach dropped out. He could not *believe* what he had just heard.

"Dumont? Are you sure?"

"Yeah," said Cecil, looking puzzled. "Matilda's husband."

"Not *Alex* Dumont!"

Carmin walked back to Cecil's desk, sat down, took a deep breath, and said, "Tell me more. Tell me all you can!"

Cecil, very surprised, did as instructed. By the end, the case of Milllard Hoffman's death was as new and fresh as the morning he'd been found dead in a snowbank.

Chapter Forty

Charley stood beside the desk, staring at Carmin in amazement. His mind was struggling to process everything his boss had just told him.

"You mean to tell me," he said, "that Frenchy and Millard were brothers-in-law?"

Carmin nodded. "Yeah, it looks that way."

"But they *hated* each other!" Charley cried. "Damn, you just never know what the hell is going on, even in a small town! Just think what they must have thought when they happened together on the street. And long as I've been around I don't remember *anything* actually happening between them. I knew - everyone knew - that Millard didn't like Frenchy, but *no one* likes Frenchy!"

Carmin shrugged silently.

"How come Millard never had anything to do with Dumont's kid out at the White farm, if he cared so much about his sister and the child?"

"I don't know," said Carmin, shrugging again, "maybe he didn't like the boy either. From what I've heard he's just as mean as his father. Maybe Millard didn't even know he was here. Frenchy only brought him down from Birchwood a year ago. Who knows, Charley, who knows?"

"And why," Charley continued, "did Frenchy take him off the farm in Birchwood, bring him down here, and put him on *another* farm? That doesn't make any sense!"

Carmin shrugged silently and elaborately. "Frenchy's crazy!" he said. "Probably took the kid from the family in Birchwood just because he could."

"You think Frenchy did Millard in?" Charley asked.

Carmin considered the question and said, "Yes, I do, Charley. But we could never prove it, not now. We can't even prove that Millard's death was anything other than an accident. *Way* too much time has gone by."

Carmin was more upset by the thought of Frenchy Dumont getting away with murder than he let on. But there really was nothing he could do. If Frenchy ever came back to Fairchild, Carmin would see to it that he was sent packing by the next day, but other than that it was too late.

He leaned back and sighed loudly. He had followed a small thread to Birchwood and a web had been exposed. The question now was where was the spider?

Chapter Forty-one

The road was hard clay and uncomfortable to walk on. *Must be a real dandy,* thought Frank, *after a hard rain.* He could visualize the mud.

The sun was directly overhead now and he chewed his lunch while sitting on his canvas bag. Three vehicles and about a hundred buggies had passed him that morning and none had slowed down. Frank was beginning to think he might be spending the night beneath the stars. Just as he was considering this, he heard the *putt-putt* of another vehicle. He stood up and watched as the black Ford approached, making no indication that he needed a ride. The Ford blew by him, but then braked suddenly, coming to a stop in a cloud of dust. Frank grabbed his bag excitedly and ran.

"Hi Bucko! Need a lift?"

"You bet," Frank answered. He lifted his bag into the backseat, next to three very expensive leather suitcases and a cased rifle.

Slamming the door he looked at his newfound benefactor. Behind the wheel was a young man - about twenty-four, Frank judged. He was dressed in a neat black suit. Laid back on his head was a black derby, and beneath it, tight curly black hair. He was handsome and had jolly, dancing eyes. Clenched between two rows of perfectly white teeth was a cigar.

"Hi Bucko," he grinned. "I'm Chris Huntington." He shot out his hand. Frank took it. The grip was firm and surprisingly strong.

"Hi," said Frank, "I'm Frank Burns."

"Where ya headed Bucko?" Chris asked in a perpetually cheerful tone of voice, which would take Frank some getting used to.

"Blackwing?"

"Well! You're in luck! That's where I'm headed!"

"Salesman?" Frank asked, taking a shot in the dark.

"Hell no! I'm going to work for a lumber company."

"You're going to work in a labor camp?"

"No, no," said Chris, watching the road as he talked, "I'm going to work in the office in Blackwing."

"Oh," said Frank.

"Banishment!" said Chris, with a sudden grin.

"How's that?" asked Frank.

"That's right," said the man in the black derby with a laugh, "I've been out east in school, *couple* of schools as a matter of fact. Too much of a monkey brain to stay in either one of them. You know, the old *heave-ho!* Father says I'm immature and lack substance. Maybe he's right. I sure do have a way of getting into trouble." He flashed another quick grin. "Anyway, here I am, on my own, about to go to work for the Calvin Lumber Company, presumably to get some substance."

Frank had never met anyone like Chris. Nobody in Fairchild talked of such negative things with such enthusiasm. But he liked him. "How did you get the job?" he asked.

Chris looked at him with surprise. "Why, through my father, of course."

"Oh," said Frank, still not understanding.

"My father," Chris announced, "is a broker. He owns shares in a lot of companies. The Calvin Lumber Company is one of them. So it was *arranged,* my banishment. Say, Bucko, you want to drive?"

"Naw," said Frank, too embarrassed to tell him he didn't know how.

"Okay then," said Chris, dismissing the question with a wave of his cigar.

The Ford bounced and lurched its way down the road, leaving a long-hanging cloud of dust behind it. Not once did Chris ask Frank about his family or where he was from. He seemed perfectly happy talking about himself. But he seemed sincere, and this comforted Frank. There was only one thing he did not like about his new companion, and that was his constant reference to Frank as *Bucko.* Frank didn't know what *Bucko* meant...nobody had ever called him anything but Frank. He let it pass, however. Chris' easy-going demeanor and cheerfulness assured him that it was not meant as an insult.

Eventually the conversation died. Chris took to driving and chewing his cigar. Frank looked out the window and studied the land. Both sides of the road were lined with thick, heavy timber now. Big stuff. The kind that would bring money to the lumber barons, and the brokers who invested their money in it. Frank thought about this and looked over at Chris. Chris noticed he was being watched. He glanced back at Frank and a grin exploded on his face like a firecracker.

Frank thought about the first people that had owned this land. He thought of the Indians who had hunted and fished it. Then came the trappers, working their trap lines for fur. Now the timber was coming down. People were already burrowing into the ground for minerals. When the timber was gone, mining would be the rule for as long as the land could give it. Then perhaps all this land would be cleared and farmed, like it was down by Fairchild.

Frank thought (though he would never have been able to articulate it in conversation), that there was something unnatural and wasteful about Man's use of the land.

It was sunset when the Ford chugged into Blackwing. Chris smiled at Frank. "Goddamn, Bucko, we found it!"

What they had found, Frank noticed, was a town that had only one road running straight through it, and that one road was lined with saloons. Closer inspection revealed a few houses scattered helter-skelter, off the main road a bit. There was also a blacksmith, hardware store, clothing store, and a café; all sandwiched in-between saloons. Frank had never seen so many saloons in one place in his life. Chris stopped the Ford and the two got out to look around. Chris whistled. "She ain't much, is she?"

Frank didn't answer. He was busy staring in amazement at the gaudy buildings, that somehow lacked permanence. *That* was what struck Frank as odd: Blackwing seemed to be just a camp itself, rather than an established town. As if it were ready to pack up and disappear at any time.

Chris walked up on the sidewalk and headed for the nearest saloon. Frank hesitated. "Well," said Chris, "let's have a look!" Together they entered.

The barroom was full from wall to wall. Big men pushed and shoved up and down the bar, laughing, cursing and singing. These were hard men, smelling of the woods. Few of these men would bother to step aside for another. And yet, as tough as they acted, there seemed to be a comradeship between them.

Standing at a small open area at the bar, Frank and Chris surveyed the patrons. More than a few eyes were lifted at the two strangers, particularly at Chris with his black suit and derby. This unnerved Frank a little, but Chris simply smiled as he stood there, like he was having a dandy time. The bartender appeared and looked questioningly at the two.

"Beer," said Chris. He looked at Frank. "You, Bucko?"

Frank nodded. To Frank this world was surreal. Here he was, standing in a saloon for the first time in his life, about to drink his first beer. He thought of his parents and how vehemently they would have disapproved.

Chris paid for the drinks, grabbed his schooner and turned his back on the bar. His eyes were scanning the room intently. Pushing his derby back on his head with his thumb, he took a sip. He spotted six men at a round table, throwing money in the middle. His eyes lit up.

"This may not be so bad," said Chris. "You play poker, Bucko?"

"No, we never played cards…" Frank's voice trailed off.

Frank had to admire Chris. *He's got guts,* he thought. *Already acts like he owns the place.* He lifted the schooner to his lips and took a drink slowly.

Surprisingly, the taste was pleasant. He took another sip, smacked his lips and smiled. *Not the poison Father always said it was,* he thought.

"Come on, Bucko, one more!" said Chris when they had finished their beers. "Then we'd better find a place to sleep." Frank nodded approvingly.

Leaving the Ford in front Chris pounded on the door. The small sign nailed to a pillar of the porch said, **ROOMS**. A large, burly man about fifty opened the door slowly and peeked out.

Chris smiled brightly. "Got a room for a couple of weary travelers?" he said. The man looked them both over, nodded silently and stepped back, opening the door the rest of the way.

They followed him down a short, dimly lit hallway to a large roll-top desk. Behind it, a stairway led to the second floor. Frank could hear laughter coming from somewhere. Turning around to investigate he looked through an archway into a bright parlor. Seated on the couch were two girls. They were absorbed in talking about something that was apparently funny to both of them. Frank couldn't make out what they were saying, but one was strikingly attractive, with black hair. She stopped talking when she noticed Frank watching her. The other girl, with blonde hair, stopped talking and looked at him with bright, blue eyes. She smiled. She was prettier, in Frank's opinion, than the other, and he felt a nervous twinge he had never felt before. He stared at her intently.

Chris' voice shook him from that moment. He turned to Chris quickly. In his hand his companion held a skeleton key.

"You fellas need anything besides the room?" the burly man asked.

Chris and Frank looked at each other. "No," said Chris. The man shrugged and walked away.

The upstairs was one long hallway, with doors on both sides. "We're room number three," remarked Chris. "Here it is."

He flitted the key. "I'll bet every room here has a skeleton key just like this one," he laughed.

The room was nearly bare except for two small beds. But it was clean.

Frank took a red handkerchief out of his satchel. Tied inside was all the money he had. After much insistence, he paid a reluctant Chris for his half of the room.

All through the night, the sounds of doors opening and closing and people running up and down the halls disturbed his sleep, as he dreamed of laughing girls.

Chapter Forty-two

The following morning, as they sat eating breakfast in a small restaurant, Chris asked, "Did you get any sleep last night?"

"Well, yes," said Frank, "I always sleep well." He could not remember if the opening and closing doors and the people in the hallways were real, or just part of his dreams, so he didn't mention it.

"I didn't sleep well at all," said Chris. "Too much damn noise. I'm a light sleeper." His voice seemed pained, as though he were admitting to an imperfection.

After breakfast, Chris decided to look for the office of the Calvin Lumber Company. Being Sunday, he really didn't expect to find anyone there, but he wanted to see where he would be working anyway.

Together he and Frank found the right building, wedged thinly between a tobacco store and a vacant building. If the Calvin Lumber Company was a prosperous, growing concern, its Blackwing office did not indicate it. The single-story building appeared to be standing at a slant (like the buildings on each size were holding it up), and was badly in need of paint. The best looking part of the whole structure was the sign, and that was removable. The two men peered in the window.

Noting the look of disappointment on Chris' face, Frank could not help saying with a grin, "Just how much influence did your father have to exercise to get you *this* job?"

"Very funny, Bucko," said Chris. They noticed movement inside, and Chris' face brightened. "Hey! Somebody's in there! I may just as well go in and introduce myself."

Frank bid him enter with a sweep of his arm. "I'll wait here."

Chris went in. The whole building was one large, long office. Three desks occupied the room. Two were vacant. Seated at the third was a square-shouldered man around fifty. He wore no coat and his shirtsleeves were rolled up to his elbows. His face, like his body, was square and clean-shaven. A thick batch of white hair crowned his head. The fact that he combed it with his fingers rather than with a comb was obvious. Below a curling wave of hair on his forehead, were two deep blue eyes. Advancing on him, Chris said, "Hello, I'm Chris Huntington."

The man rose and shook Chris' hand. "We've been expecting you. I'm Vincent St. Claire. I run this little office."

Chris took out the letter his father had given him and handed it to St. Claire. "Have a seat, Mr. Huntington," St. Claire said, opening the envelope. From it he produced a large sheet of paper and unfolded it. Both sides were completely written in.

Good God, St. Claire thought. *Is this a letter of introduction or a treatise?*

He put on a pair of reading glass, sat down, and began reading. By the time he had finished reading the first side, a smile was tugging at the corners of his mouth. The more he read the more his eyes twitched with humor. He flipped over and continued reading the other side.

When he finished, he folded the letter and put it in a drawer of his desk. He made no comment on it and his face gave no clue as to what the contents were.

"Tell me Chris, what do you know about lumber?"

Chris looked at the man. On his trip to Blackwing, he had come to a decision: No matter what frivolous or outlandish escapades might ensue in Blackwing, there was *one* thing of which he was determined - he would be successful at this job. To be successful, he knew he had to be honest with everyone, including himself. He had learned *that* from his father anyway.

"Nothing," he said.

St. Claire nodded and smiled amicably. "Well, that's about what I knew when I started in this racket. It says in the letter that you spent some time in the halls of higher learning, so the office work should not present any real problems to you, correct?"

Chris nodded.

"However, there are some basic things about work in this field that you should know. I think a couple of tours through the camps should give you a general idea how we operate, but that will come later. For now, we'll just keep you around the office. That will be your desk." He pointed to one of the vacant desks. "Mr. Kennedy, who previously occupied it, has been transferred back to civilization with your coming. You made him a happy man!" Vincent St. Claire smiled and Chris did too.

"Where are you staying?" St. Claire asked.

Chris explained the noisy antics of the night before and then said he was open to suggestions.

"Mrs. Wallace's," said St. Claire. "She runs a nice, clean place. She serves a morning and evening meal, and it's quiet. You tell her I sent you." He gave directions to Mrs. Wallace's, and then said, "Seven o'clock tomorrow morning," in a dismissive tone of voice.

Chris thanked him, rose and turned to leave. At the door he stopped and said, "Oh, by the way, on my way up here I chummed with a young fellow and he's looking for work in a camp."

"Bring him in with you tomorrow," said St. Claire. "Jack Kelly, our man-catcher, is coming in. If he looks good to Jack, he's got a job." Chris nodded and left.

Out on the sidewalk, Chris told Frank about the possibility of a job and Frank thanked him enthusiastically. He had been worrying about finding work since leaving Fairchild. In the short time the two men had known each other, a strong bond had grown between them.

Chapter Forty-three

The following morning Frank sat in the corner of the office, his gear at his feet. As he waited, he watched St. Claire familiarizing Chris with the office and his new job. The fourth man in the office was seated at his desk working quietly. His name was Tom Reynolds. A tall, sandy-haired man about 30, Tom sat hunched in his chair, his head forward, rubbing his hands in the oddest way. Frank couldn't figure it out. It was like he was doing it without *realizing* he was doing it.

The door opened and a small runt of a man came in. Frank blinked. The man was no more than 5-foot-2, and could not have weighed more than 120 pounds soaking wet.

St. Claire saw him come in and moved to greet him. "Hello Jack!" he said. The little man acknowledged him with a silent nod of his head. The two men talked quietly by the front door and then moved toward Frank. Frank rose, and towered nearly two feet over the man who would decide if he had a job or not. For the first time in his life, Frank felt awkward about his height and size.

"Jack," said St. Claire, "this is Frank Burns."

The little man did not offer his hand, but scrutinized Frank from head to toe. Finally he said, "So you're looking for work then, eh?"

"Yes sir," said Frank.

"Ever work in a camp before?"

"No sir," said Frank. "But I've worked on a farm all my..."

"Okay, we'll give it a try," said Jack, cutting him off.

Frank relaxed, feeling fortunate to be accepted. The little man turned to St. Claire and said, "I'm going over to Elmer's. Got a line on a couple of *experienced* men."

Or maybe he didn't stress the word "experienced", Frank wasn't sure. In any case the little man, quick as a cat, scooped up Frank's duffel bag and threw it into his arms.

The quick motion surprised Frank and he just barely caught his bag. "Let's go," said Jack, leading the way out.

Chris and St. Claire moved to the window and watched Frank and Jack move away down the street.

"I'm glad Frank looked all right to Jack," said Chris. "He was really counting on that job."

St. Claire smiled broadly. "He would have *`looked all right'* if he was a one-armed dwarf. We're damn short in the camp. Jack just likes to make a big production out of things."

St. Claire spent the rest of the morning explaining to Chris exactly what his duties were. "Limited for now," he said, "but after a while you'll know this office inside and out. I won't even have to *come* into work!"

At noon Chris and the Tom Reynolds went to lunch at a café down the main street. Chris had noticed - like Frank - Tom's strange habit of continuously rubbing his hands together.

"What's with the hands?" he asked flatly.

Tom looked up from his desk and said, "Aren't *you* cold?"

Chris shrugged. "No, not really."

"I am," said Tom. And that was the end of it. Other than the hand rubbing, Chris didn't see anything peculiar or unpleasant about Tom. In fact, he was lively conversation, which is one of the things Chris delighted in.

Over lunch Chris learned from Tom that an office in town, away from the camp, was quite unusual.

"Most companies run their office right at the campsite," Tom said. Chris thanked his lucky stars for that, at least. Being stuck out at camp would have been more than he could have handled. He wondered if, perhaps, his father had known that when he sent him to Blackwing.

"How come the office *is* in town?" Chris asked.

"St. Claire," said Tom, rubbing his hands. "Somehow he talked the company big boys into renting space in town. I would bet St. Claire has a lot of pull in the company, probably more than he lets on."

"You get along with St. Claire?" Chris asked.

"Yeah," said Tom, "he's a decent fella."

The rest of the day went smoothly. Chris caught on very quickly to his new duties. By the end of the day, his inherited intelligence was evident to St. Claire, and he told Chris this. Chris left work that night feeling good.

Frank followed Jack to a saloon called Elmer's. There, two other men were hired. They merely nodded when introduced to Frank. They were hard-looking men and apparently had been buddies for quite some time. Frank felt like an outsider around them, but resolved not to let it bother him. By late afternoon they arrived at camp number twelve. It consisted mainly of log and shanty-type buildings, situated on either side of railroad tracks.

Jack assigned Frank his bunkhouse and Frank was glad that the other two men were given another.

"Tomorrow you start on as a road monkey. Your job will be to keep the logging roads in repair," Jack said.

And so Frank Burns had his first job.

Tiers of blankets lined both sides of the bunkhouse. At the far end stood a wood stove. It was going to be meager living. Frank felt his first wave of homesickness.

That night, summoned by a loud horn, he ate his first meal at the cook's shack. This brought on more homesickness. He missed his mother's succulent, well-prepared and well-presented dinners. Following the lead of the other men, Frank gulped down his meal hastily and left.

Later in the bunkhouse, after dark, only two men took any interest in him; Curly Bill, a bald, stocky man about fifty, and another man whom everyone referred to as Pumphandle, due to his nervous habit of bobbing his head up and down when he spoke to you. It wasn't until he actually lay down that Frank realized his mattress was made out of straw. This prompted yet another wave of homesickness.

Weeks passed and slowly Frank became accustomed to camp life. The work was hard, but he had grown up on a farm and was used to that. His *specific* job came very easy to him. At night he was part of the group with Curly Bill and Pumphandle. When he received letters from home, the memory of Whiley would slip back to haunt him. Then he turned melancholy, afraid of the future. He tried to fight it. *I* have *to fight it,* he thought. *The memories of my brother will be with me for the rest of my life. If I can't learn to accept that, all is lost.*

It was during one of these blue moods that Curly Bill announced he was going into Blackwing. "It's Saturday night, by Christ! I'm *not* going to sit around here! You want to come with me?"

The question was directed at Frank, and it made Frank realize that he had been in camp seven weeks. He hadn't left once. At that moment, a night in town was just what he needed.

The thought of going into town made him think of his appearance. A look into Pumphandle's hand mirror actually shocked him. He was staring into the eyes of a stranger. His thick black hair, always cut and groomed, was long and shaggy now, hanging over his forehead into his eyes. Two months of beard had grown on his face, robbing him of his youthful look. He was stunned. Damn, it was *definitely* time to go into town.

Blackwing, Michigan was America's mini melting pot. Gathered there were men of every nationality in the world, hundreds of different cultures, languages, and skin colors. The only thing they had in common was the ability to cut and move timber. After leaving Curly Bill at a saloon, Frank found a barber shop open. Thank the Lord, a haircut and a shave! Afterwards he headed for the bathhouse. An hour and a half after *that,* smelling like a French whore, he walked into Elmer's saloon. A quick inspection told him that Chris was not there. He moved on.

Four taverns later, at one called the Silver Dollar, he spotted his friend at a table playing poker. His hat was cocked back on his head and he was hunched back in his chair, peering at the cards in his hand. On his face was the look of a fox eyeing up fine, big hens.

"Straight," said Chris, laying down his cards after the last caller. He flashed a smile that was at once triumphant, sympathetic and disingenuous.

"Flush," said a big man sitting across from him, laying down his cards and sweeping the pot. The smile drained from Chris' face. "Son of a bitch," he muttered.

Frank walked up to the table. "Hi, Chris!"

The young gambler turned his head and looked up. A *genuine* smile appeared.

"Bucko, how are you!" he asked. He jumped up and they shook hands.

"Pretty good," Frank grinned.

Chris turned and scooped up his money. "That's all for me. You boys are just too damn lucky tonight."

The two men pushed their way up to the bar, ordered beers and talked. Frank told him about life in camp. Chris mentioned that he had been out there with St. Claire a time or two, had met some people, but had not seen Frank.

As they talked, Chris studied his friend. He seemed to have changed in his two months in camp. Frank Burns seemed more confident, more adult-like. He had even changed physically. His face was thinner, his whole body leaner. The cords in his forearms bulged and yes, by God, he even seemed taller to Chris, and that would have seemed impossible before.

Good Christ, he's still growing, Chris thought, marveling at what two months of working sun-up to sun-down can do for a person.

"Say, Bucko!" he said. "This calls for a celebration!" He ordered two shots of whiskey. He slid Frank's over to him and said, "You ever drink it before?"

"Nope," said Frank.

"A toast, then," said Chris, raising his shot glass, "to us! May we both be in heaven an hour before the devil knows we're dead!"

Together they downed their shots. The liquid burned all the way down Frank's throat, like nothing he had ever experienced before. He gulped for air and his eyes watered.

Chris grinned and said, "How do you like it?"

"Good," Frank croaked.

"The next one won't be quite as bad," Chris assured him.

And he was right.

It was the cold that first stirred Frank. He was uncomfortable as hell. His entire body cramped up stiffly, he lifted his head and looked around. Light was sneaking in through the heavily-frosted car windows.

He felt terrible. The heavy scent of the hair oil from the barber shop nauseated him. He was in the back seat of a car, he could tell that much. But whose car? Chris' car? Most likely.

Loud snoring echoed from the front seat. He leaned forward and peered over. Indeed, Chris lay across the seat sideways, his head against the door, his feet propped up against the opposite window edge. On his right shoe, his hat hung precariously.

Despite the cold, Frank felt a sudden sweeping urge for more air. He opened the door and stuck his head out. It was crisp, clear, cold air. All was very still. Across the street, the door to the Silver Dollar opened and the swamper threw a large bucket of dirty water into the street. Steam rose off it slowly, but steadily. In a few seconds Frank caught the smell of mop water and pulled his head back in.

A half-hour later, they were bumping their way to camp, Frank's stomach tumbling unpleasantly (to say the least) all the way. Chris was rambling on about how much money he had won playing poker, since arriving in Blackwing.

"You ought to learn the game," he said, puffing on his cigar. "I could teach you!"

"No thanks," said Frank, waving away the smoke that was beginning to get to him.

Chris dropped Frank off at camp and called out to him as he was turning the Ford around. "Next time you get into town, we'll have to do it again!" he yelled out the window, his voice obtrusive in the cold, early morning air. Frank thought he might wake up the whole camp.

He nodded dryly and waved goodbye. Then he walked to the edge of the woods, in a dark, secluded spot, and forced himself to throw up for several minutes.

Two nights later the first snow flakes fell. It was a late snow, and it had a sobering effect on the crew. In the bunkhouse men began to check their winter gear in anticipation for the very rough months ahead. Neglected clothes were mended and torn gloves and mittens were stitched carefully. Any man caught unawares or unprepared would regret it.

Frank knew that he had to prepare as well. With the help of Curly Bill, he made a list of clothing he would need to combat the winter. This would necessitate going back into Blackwing, and soon.

He finished the list and sat down to write a letter home. It was only the third one he had written since he'd left. He felt a twinge of guilt. One previous letter had contained money. In this current letter, he explained that the clothing he had to buy would be cutting into the amount of money he could send home next.

Frank wondered if the money he sent was even being used. He knew his father's pride.

He said hello to his mother and the girls, tried to explain what new things were going on (although that was difficult, because day-to-day, very little ever changed in camp), and that was that. He re-read the letter and sealed it.

It was late when at last he turned in, the December wind beating hard against the side of the bunkhouse, interrupted only by the low rhythm of snoring men.

Chapter Forty-four

The old man stood looking out the window at the low, gray sky. He remained motionless. Small white flakes fell, one at a time. Two days earlier snow had come to Cumberland County from the north. All of it melted upon hitting the ground. But eventually, sometime very soon, it would not melt and would begin to pile up, plunging the Upper Peninsula of Michigan into the winter of 1916.

The old man's eyes were sad. *How many winters have I endured,* he thought. *Can't remember. But what does it matter, anyway? My whole damn* life *has been one continuous winter, and there's nothing I can do about that anymore. It's too late. It's too late.*

Frank Burns was gone now. There would be no more visits from the boy to ease the loneliness. Whiley was gone, too. For good. Any hopes that he might take his older brother's place in keeping the old man company died along with him. John Burns stopped by occasionally to check on him, appearing out of the darkness like an apparition. That was the best he could hope for: John (meaning well, of course) tapping on his door. He would answer it, and the conversation was always the same.

"Hello Hemlock."

"Hello John."

"Everything all right?"

"Yup."

"Need anything?"

"Nope."

"Okay, then," John always said. "I just thought I'd make sure. Good day."

The old man appreciated John's concern, but his visits didn't make him feel any less lonely. In fact, they made him feel *more* lonely.

And there was the pain...every winter the pain. And it got worse each year. He could already feel it growing in his fingers. By January it would be spreading like a racehorse through his shoulders, arms, and down toward his legs. The copper band around his wrist could no longer ward off the rheumatism and arthritis in his old bones. It was as if his body were *telling* him (screaming for him to listen!) that he had lived out his magic.

There was also the dream, recurring and hideous. For three weeks straight it had invaded his sleep every night. Thinking about it in the waking hours made him question his own sanity. It always started the same. He was standing on a hill beside a charred, shattered tree. Dawn was forcing a gray light through a thick, sullen fog. He was alone. Below him, at the foot of the hill, ran a muddy, wagon-rutted road. Then he saw them, coming out of the mist along the road. Their heads were bowed, their shoulders sagged. They moved before him, an endless line of men in blue uniform. In the dream, they were young men (the dead of war), his former comrades, looking as they had during the war, like young men. Yet *he* was old. *He* was the pitiful old hermit he'd become in the next century. As they marched they did not turn. They did not seem to notice he was there, on top of that hill.

Then he saw Cody's face, one in a long line of thousands stretching all the way down the road to the left, and all the way down the road to the right.

"Cody!" Cody!" he would cry from atop the hill, waving. "It's me! Peter! It's Peter!"

This young soldier turned and stared up at Hemlock with no expression. And he kept marching. And he disappeared into the long line.

That he should dream of Cody, and dead Union soldiers, was not *that* surprising to Hemlock. What was disturbing about this dream, in addition to its recurring nature, was that in the dream he was *aware* that what he was watching was a death march. Worse yet, he felt an urge to join it.

And in very recent days, as the winter sky mounted for its assault, that urge to join the death march had crept from his dream into the waking hours.

The winter sky hung low in color gradients ranging from blue in the east to gray in the west. Hemlock turned from the window, where he'd spent the day (like every day in the last month), looking out at the field in front of his shack. It was the same view he'd watched for nearly seventy years.

I can't live with that anymore, he thought. *I've spent the last seventy years in this very shack, staring out at that very field. And I can't accept it anymore.*

A brown suit lay neatly on his bed. On top of that a white envelope. He felt the fabric of the suit between his fingers one more time. He looked at the lamp. No need to light it *tonight,* in a sorrowful attempt to avoid the darkness.

Tonight, he thought, smiling nervously, *I'm going to let the darkness catch me.*

Walking to the chair in the middle of the floor, he stepped up on it. The noose was tied securely to the rafters of the shack. He placed it round his neck tightly and stepped off the chair with a gasping sob, into the darkness that is stronger than all mortal light.

The following day, John Burns came by to check on the old man and found him. Looking in through the open door he merely stepped back and closed it. When he returned to the shack, he was accompanied by Carmin, Charley and Moses Clark. They did not talk much. Together, they took the old man down.

Before leaving, Moses took the suit from the bed and handed the envelope to Carmin. Carmin looked at both sides of the envelope. Seeing that it was blank, he slipped it into his jacket pocket.

John Burns took a long, sweeping look about the cabin and started for the door. Carmin followed him. Then Moses. Then Charley, who did not look well at all.

In his office, Carmin sat behind the desk and took out the envelope. He had deliberately waited until Charley left to view it. It would have been nothing to let old Charley see the contents, but Carmin was in a foul mood, and did not want to endure Charley's sincere but dullard-like questions: *"You think this letter means something, Chief?"* or *"What are you gonna do about it now, Chief?"*

It was actually Doc Spencer, not Charley, who had put Carmin in such a huff. When he'd gotten in touch with Doc about Hemlock's death, the damn old quack said, "Is he dead?"

"Certainly," said Carmin.

"You sure?" Doc said.

"Uh-huh," said Carmin.

"Well, what the hell do you want me for? I'm here to treat the *living!* Get the undertaker! I'll look at him when Moses gets him down to his place!"

Carmin argued, but Doc would not budge. He had never been so angry with Doc Spencer as he was then.

For now, he tried to sweep the anger from his head by examining the envelope. There was no name on it. Carmin decided this gave him reason to - as a peace officer - examine the contents, since no instructions were left as to whom the letter was for. He opened it, confident in his rationale. His eyes widened.

There wasn't a letter, but three documents. The first document was the deed to the forty acres of land on which the shack stood on. The second was the Last Will and Testament of Peter Christian. It had been drawn up by a lawyer over in Benson. All duly witnessed and notarized. The will had been written two years before. The completeness and legality of it all didn't seem like Hemlock, but there it was in black and white. The fact that Hemlock had traveled all the way to Benson, that he *owned* the land on which the shack stood, and that his name was Peter

Christian, was surprising as well, at least to Carmin. What was *not* surprising was the name of the sole beneficiary in the will.

Carmin had to read the third document twice. The information it contained was *totally* new to him (to the point of being downright unbelievable), and he doubted anyone else in Fairchild knew it. While he considered it very strange, he didn't - at the time - think it was all that important. Only a small handful of men knew the enormity of it, and they were definitely *not* in Fairchild.

Chapter Forty-five

The camp swelled to twice the size it was when Frank first arrived. The winter's work was in earnest now. The daylight grew shorter, and everyone felt urgency to accomplish as much as possible. At night, Frank listened with interest to the stories the men told. He learned how logs were floated down the rivers in spring's high water to Lake Superior. There they were formed into rafts; rafts held together by booms. Booms were logs chained together end to end, forming a large corral. Inside the floating corral, thousands of logs were encircled. A tug would pull the raft across Lake Superior to a port with a pulp hoist. There they would be loaded onto the pulp trains and transported to the paper mills of the north.

Frank heard stories of logjams in the rivers; *millions* caught in low water, tangled and not moving an inch. Men risked their lives, and sometimes lost their lives, trying to pull the logs free.

"Driving the river must be exciting," said Frank to Curly Bill.

Curly Bill gave him a sober look and said, "Stay in the woods boy, you'll live longer."

In truth, Frank had no intention of becoming a permanent woodsman of *any* kind. He had become accustomed to his job and life in the camp, which - especially now with so many men and so much going on - had become enjoyable, but he planned to remain in camp only as long as absolutely necessary. When he felt his family had recovered sufficiently from the losses incurred during the drought, he would be off to the city, where he felt his real future lay.

Still, looking at these simple men telling stories, smoking cigars, and continuously mending their clothes, Frank felt a deep respect for them. Courage did not belong only to men storming up a hill in battle, or men trapped at sea with a gale bearing down. No sir, these men faced equally dangerous and frequent trials furnishing the timber needed to build a nation, and were not given nearly as much - if any - credit.

Two weeks before Christmas time, the letter came from home announcing the death of Hemlock. Frank had been leaning against the wall by his bed reading his mother's words, and suddenly felt weak at the knees. Reflections of the old man's constantly jolly face and the knowledge he had given to Frank, came back vividly. The news weighed down even more heavily on him because he had never written to Hemlock since leaving.

Two days later twelve inches of snow fell. It seemed to enhance Blackwing, bringing a false sense of purity to the town. Hidden beneath the as yet clean white sheath, the clapboard buildings looked almost quaint. Only when one got close enough to hear the rinky-tink piano and the inebriated laughter echoing up and down the main street, did the illusion dissolve. Frank peered in the window of the Silver Dollar. He had come into Blackwing after the storm to find Chris. Chris was there, seated at a table playing cards. A light snow was still falling peacefully.

Frank turned to walk inside and stepped directly into their path. The black-haired girl managed to side-step him but the blonde girl walked into him. Frank caught the startled girl before she fell.

"Oh! I'm sorry!" said Frank. He steadied her on the snow and ice, and released her. When the surprise left her, she smiled. He recognized her right away. She was the girl he had seen at the boarding house his first night in Blackwing.

"I'm sorry, ma'am," he stammered, blushing.

The girl smiled flirtatiously. "That's quite all right, accidents will happen."

"Yes, they will," said Frank, frantically at a loss for words. "I'm Frank Burns." He extended his hand like he was meeting a business client.

She blinked a moment, took his hand, shook it, and said, "I'm Angela Stevens. This is my friend Mary-Ann."

Frank nodded to the dark-haired girl, who looked extremely bored and impatient to leave.

"You live at the boarding house," said Frank, "I remember you. I remember both of you."

"Yes," replied Angela, "I remember you too. We live with our uncle."

"Oh," said Frank.

"Well, it's been nice meeting you," said Angela sweetly. "Perhaps we'll meet again sometime."

"Yes ma'am," said Frank. He watched the two girls continue down the street. Mary-Ann said something to Angela sharply, then glanced back quickly to see if Frank was watching. They disappeared into the flickering snowfall, and Frank again felt that mysterious, uneasy feeling in his stomach.

He walked into the Silver Dollar. "Hey Bucko!" said Chris. He quit the card game and joined Frank at a separate table.

As always, they talked of trivial things, but Frank could not concentrate on the conversation. Thoughts of Angela kept coming back to him, *especially* now that he knew her name and had spoken to her. Chris noticed too, that something was distracting his young friend, but he said nothing. They talked for an hour. Frank suggested he should be getting back to camp. They talked for a few more minutes, and then Frank left.

Chris watched from his chair as Frank began picking his way through the room to leave. But his eyes were not the only eyes following Frank Burns across the room of the crowded bar. A large lumberjack watched as well. Recognition crept into his wide eyes, and look of rage swept over his face. He turned back to the bar and seized the glass of whiskey, downing it in one gulp. Slamming the glass down hard on the bar he croaked for another in his unnatural voice. He turned again to stare at the now vacant door, with tiny beads of whiskey glistening in his black beard.

Chapter Forty-six

Life in camp had become routine to Frank. He never thought he would at first, but eventually he grew accustomed to the ever-present smell of wet clothing and sweat, not to mention the continuous swearing, smoking, spitting and scratching that went on around him. He was even able to listen to the outlandish tales that men told about drinking and women, and still keep a believable look of interest on his face.

But there was one thing that he could not accept, one thing that disgusted him now just as much as it had his first week: lice. It was everywhere, on all the jacks, and little or nothing was done about it.

"It's in *every* camp," said Curly Bill, who didn't have to worry about lice on his head, being bald. "Hell yes, just as sure as the sun rises every day, you're gonna be a boarding house for bugs!"

Frank used every method he was told about (fact or fiction, he didn't care) to stay free of the insidious insects. He was successful to a certain degree, but not entirely. One time he scratched his head without thinking about it and produced a tiny lice crushed beneath his fingernail.

"Damn," he said, nervously. He spent the next six hours with lard from the kitchen smeared in his hair (advice courtesy of the worry-free Curly Bill). Sitting up straight and uncomfortably on his mattress he thought longingly of his clean, decent bed at home, and his clean, decent family. But with these thoughts came the memory of Whiley, so he shut them out.

Later that night he had one hell of a time getting the lard out of his hair.

Chapter Forty-seven

When the meal was finished and the waiter had cleared the dishes, two of the three well-dressed men lit expensive cigars. They were sitting beside each other. The third man sat across from them, alone, and simply sipped his coffee, his thin, shaven face lost in thought.

Finally he spoke, and his voice was troubled. "You *sure* he's dead?" he asked.

Nods to the affirmative.

"Jesus Christ," he moaned, "we have to be very careful or this could cost us a great deal of money."

Again, the silent nods enshrouded in smoke.

"You say we have people checking to find out who owns it now?" he asked, lowering his voice and looking around the expensive restaurant.

The man across from him on the right puffed and said, "The best. We're moving as fast as we can, Paul."

"Good. When you know anything, notify me immediately." He cast a stern glance at the two men. *"Don't* do a thing. Just notify me. This has to be done correctly or not at all!"

The other man spoke. "We should know everything in a few days, Paul. Relax."

"I'll relax when the plan is executed effectively."

For the next hour the three men talked quietly, their conversation guarded. When the two cigar-smokers left, Paul sat and thought some more. Paul Kristov Calender did his best thinking, his best planning, alone.

It'll work, he thought. *It* has *to work.* Then he smirked to himself and smiled broadly.

Either way, I guess, we're going to make a lot of money - a fortune. Several fortunes, in fact! And if we're clever enough to pull this off just right, more money than we could spend in a lifetime!

It took three days to get the information he sought. Paul sat behind the desk in his office and read the report carefully. It was complete and very professional. It *did* lack one important fact - the most important - but Paul knew how to get that. He took a business letterhead from his desk drawer and examined it. Then his careful, cunning mind told him no, this wouldn't do. He called in his secretary, explained to her what he wanted, and dispatched her on a specific errand. While he waited, he composed the letter in his head with carefully chosen words.

Michael Tyler stood at the window of *his* office. He looked out at the snow-covered streets of Benson, Michigan. Down on the sidewalk, men labored with shovels to clear paths to their shop doors. Fourteen inches of snow had blown off the lake and fallen overnight. For Benson, that was not a lot, but the wind had a cute way of blowing the snow into formidable banks.

Michael Tyler was a tall, thin man. His face was white, almost anemic-looking, serving only to emphasize his bright orange hair, heavy with oil and combed neatly. On his desk, yesterday's mail sat unopened. He sighed, sat down, and began the chore of going through it. With each passing year his mail became less and less interesting. Or maybe he became less and less interested in it.

When he came to an envelope from the office of P.K. Calender, he became interested, because he had never heard of the man. He opened it and read it through. He was about to put it back in the envelope, but stopped and re-read the letter. It was written on cheap, blank stationary. He picked out key sentences.

"It is my information, you will be handling the will," it read, *"would appreciate the address of heirs, if any. Will offer reasonable price for section 14, Alamde County on timber speculation."*

Tyler sat back. He could vaguely recall the grisly little man seated across from him two years before. He could remember part of what the man had told him:

"I know it ain't much," he'd said of the land he planned to bequeath, "but it's all I got. Had it for a long time, it might be worth something."

They had made out the will together, and Tyler never saw the man again. Only recently had the news come that he was dead.

What the hell have I got to lose, he thought, reviewing the letter from Calender. *It's only a telephone call.*

He dug out an address book and thumbed through it. Tom Whitney, City of Lanchester, Alamde County. Tom Whitney was him roommate in law school. They had kept in touch for a few years after graduation, but time and distance had diminished their relationship to only an occasional hello, and then only when their practices crossed paths. Still, he knew that if Tom could help, he would. After a long delay, the call was put through. He was lucky to get through at all, with the storm having incapacitated much of the Upper Peninsula.

Tom's familiar voice came over the line. They caught up in a perfunctory way for five minutes, then Tyler asked straight out, "Tom, how familiar are you with the area north of Lanchester?"

"Not too familiar," Tom replied, "what area are you talking about?"

"Section 14 in Alamde County."

"Let me check my plat book," Tom said. Tyler waited. There was a shuffling sound on the other end, then Tom came back and said, "Okay, I've got the books in front of me. Hell, that's pretty desolate area up there. I can't really help you, I don't know it. Why do you ask?"

Tyler explained the letter he had received and the unusual request. "I'm just wondering what a fair price for timberland up there would be."

"I didn't even know they were logging up there," said Tom.

"Okay," said Tyler, "I was just hoping to get some information on it. Thanks anyway."

"Well now," said Tom, "wait a minute. Maybe I *can* help. Old Sam Coffey has trapped most of the county at one time or another. He should be able to tell you something about the land up there. I'll talk to him the next time I see him and get back to you. Might be a while, though...Sam has a way of disappearing for days at a time."

"That would be fine, Tom," Tyler said. "Get back to me when you can."

It was two weeks later when Tom Whitney called back. He went straight to the point.

"I got in touch with Sam Coffey. Like I said, he knows the county top to bottom and left to right. Sam said there's no logging going on up there because there are no concentrated stands of timber and your section - section 14 - is the worst."

"Hmm," said Tyler. "Interesting."

"But he also said that he was up there in October and ran into a crew of men. Sam asked them what they were doing and they gave him the run around. Kind of secretive, he said."

"What was his impression?"

"Well, they had surveying equipment."

"Surveyors, eh?"

"And it's my understanding that a lot of land up there has been bought up.

Tyler scratched his head. "Something is funny," he said.

"I agree," said Tom, "but that's all I could find out. Help you any?"

"I don't know, but thanks. I owe you one."

They said goodbye and hung up. Tyler sat rubbing his head, slicking the oiled hair as far back on his head as it could go.

He could not understand it. Right out of the blue, he gets an offer for land where there is no timber, from a man he's never heard of. Land in the area *is* changing hands, surveyors are sneaking around…

He wanted to know what the hell was going on.

Then it hit him, and he actually jumped up. He grabbed the telephone and made another call. In a few minutes he was talking to his brother Kenneth.

"Listen Ken," he said, "you still dabble in mining stocks?"

"Sure," Ken said.

"You ever hear of a P.K. Calender?"

"Oh, you must mean Paul Calender."

"Okay, who is he?"

"The president and major stockholder of Consolidated Mining."

"Big outfit?"

"Big enough, and getting bigger."

"What do you mean?"

"I mean he mines mostly copper."

"Pretty shrewd fellow then, eh?" Tyler asked.

"One of the shrewdest."

"Not above taking advantage of another's ignorance?"

"Do you know somebody who is?"

"No," said Tyler, "no Ken, I don't." He chuckled as he hung up. He retrieved Peter Christian's folder from his records, and from it produced a copy of the deed to section 14.

"I know it ain't much," rang the old man's words again, *"but it's all I got. Had it for a long time, it might be worth something."*

Tyler shook his head sadly. "If you only knew, old man," he said aloud. "If you only knew."

He took the old man's will from the folder and examined it.

We'll just sit on this for a while, he thought with a smile. *At least until I get a chance to bone up on mining laws and contracts in the State of Michigan.*

The new heir to section 14 was about to become his most important client. His heart raced just thinking of the fees. The country was about to go to war, he was sure of that. Then the sky would be the limit for copper prices.

He read the Last Will and Testament of Peter Christian thoroughly that afternoon, three times over.

At the end he laid it on his desk, leaned back, and thought, *You're going to come into a lot of money, whether you know it or not, Mr. Frank Burns. Whoever you are.*

Chapter Forty-eight

The wind streaked down the main street of Blackwing, locking its inhabitants in the firm, icy grip of winter. It was not just impossible to go outside, it was also inadvisable. The temperature this mid-January day was 26 degrees below zero at dawn, and in spite of bright sunshine, the mercury did not rise above ten below.

Inside the office of Calvin Lumber, the stovepipe glowed a bright red. There was no comfortable medium in the building. If you fired the stove excessively it got burning hot. If you didn't keep up with it, it became downright cold. And there was always a draft as the brutal wind blew outside.

St. Claire sat behind his desk. His mind was not on business this morning. He looked over at Chris Huntington (sitting at *his* desk, absorbed in his work) and wondered what he could do about the young man.

Since coming to the office, Chris had done everything expected of him, at least in a business sense. St. Claire recalled the letter Chris' father had sent along with him. "*Teach him responsibility,*" Mr. Huntington (who was an old friend of St. Claire's) had written. "*Teach him respect. Christopher is a good boy, he just needs to grow up. He's intelligent and perfectly capable of carrying on after me. I've just been too lenient with him and now he's lost respect for me. Help him to understand what I want for him. He's all I have. Do it, Vincent, and I won't forget it.*"

The old banker had been desperate in that letter. He had expected many things of Chris and when it came to work he had gotten them. Chris *was* intelligent, and certainly - in St. Claire's opinion - did not belong working in a run-down office in the middle of nowhere.

But Chris' father had expected - and wanted - something else: a son. And he had failed at that. Subsequent letters St. Claire had received from Mr. Huntington revealed that Chris had not written him or attempted to call, not even at Christmas time, and it was obvious the banker was agonizing over it. Now he was entreating St. Claire, in no uncertain terms, to do something about it.

Vincent St. Claire was no good at such dealings. But he was a very direct and honest man, so, knowing he had to do *something,* he decided he would do it his way.

That evening, as Chris and Tom were preparing to leave, St. Claire approached Chris and said, "Chris, you wanna stay behind for a moment?"

"Sure," said Chris. He turned to Tom and said, "Guess I'll talk to you later."

Tom nodded. His eyes moved to St. Claire, then back to Chris. Then he left.

When they were alone St. Claire went directly to the heart of the problem. He told Chris of his father's feelings.

"Your father expects you to take the reins of the family business once he is gone." Chris opened his mouth to speak and St. Claire raised his finger. "He *also* wants his son back. I don't know what things have been like in the past, but I know how your father feels now, and it's tearing him up inside."

"Where was he when I needed him?" Chris blurted out suddenly. The bitterness in Chris' voice surprised St. Claire.

"What do you mean?"

"I mean where the hell was he when I was growing up? He never had time for his family, for *me!"*

Taken aback by this, St. Claire could not think of anything to say.

"Hell with it," Chris added.

"Someday," St. Claire said finally, "you'll realize what your father *has* done for you, and will stop dwelling on what he hasn't done. He doesn't want a partner half as much as he wants a son. I just hope you get your head straight before it's too late."

Chris looked at him. "Before what's too late?"

"Your father is not a young man," St. Claire said pointedly. Chris looked as though he hadn't thought of that before, and St. Claire felt they had made some headway.

The winter of 1916 was rough; lots of snow and long stretches of cold. In the camp, the men simply added extra layers of clothing and worked their way through it stoically. The harsh weather and the confinement to camp (due to the snow) frayed nerves, but generally tempers were kept in check. The letters from home that Frank received from his mother spoke only of generalities, but the separate letter he received from his father as January slipped into February were the words of a troubled man. The letter spoke of young stock he was forced to sell in a depressed market because he simply could not feed them. Fields lost to drought and fire were just *now* - nine months later - taking their toll. Farmers who normally sold oats and hay through the winter had barely enough for themselves.

Frank shared the helpless feelings of his father. He too was living on bare minimum, sending every penny he could spare home. And still it was not enough. Another even marginally poor summer could mean the farm, and both men knew it.

Chapter Forty-nine

Paul Calender was burning mad. The ability to keep his cool in all situations, especially business situations, had enabled him to become successful.

But now he was furious. Three letters of inquiry had produced no reply with regard to Section 14, wherein lay the very *heart* of the copper deposits. If he didn't get Section 14, there would be no point in continuing with any of it. And Paul Calender had not become successful by walking away with his tail between his legs. He was a man used to getting what he wanted.

But he was smart, as well as aggressive. A casual approach had produced nothing. An aggressive approach might arouse suspicions as to the true value of the land. He shuddered at the thought of *that* happening. He would, of course, cut any deal within reason, to option the land, but only as a last resort. In his career Paul Calender had had to go to his last resort very few times.

"Goddamn it," he muttered sharply, alone in his office, staring straight ahead. "Time for a war council."

He picked up the phone and rang.

The two men called to Calender's office were the same men who had been in the restaurant with him, his junior partners. Outside the office they were independent and ruthless men, but here under Calender's gaze of anger and frustration, they were reduced to the mere underlings they were. Like everyone else they collapsed under the sheer dynamic force of the man. Besides the vulgar verbal abuse Calender could dish out (making some men cry), he was also not above a physical attack if angered enough.

"This goddamn thing is going *sour!"* he screamed, kicking the wall behind his desk. "I wanna know why the *hell* we don't know more now than we did the last time we met!! Anyone want to explain it to me?!"

Neither man spoke. This was not the time to speak, even if Calender was asking a question.

"All right, all right," Calender said. "Let's go over what we *do* know. We know an old man owned the land, and he's dead. We know a lawyer in Benson represented him in other minor legal matters with the state. So chances are, if there's a will, he's got it. But the *bastard* won't answer my letters or return my calls. Son of a bitch!"

"Sir," said one of the men.

"What!"

"May I suggest we meet with the man face to face?"

"What, travel all the way up to Benson and speak with him in person?"

The man nodded.

A smile unfolded over Calender's face. "All right then, let's do it. I *knew* you were good for something Bernard!"

"Thank you sir," Bernard answered.

Calender's smile broadened. "Yeah! *Yeah!"* he said excitedly. "I like that! I didn't want to have to take the trouble of a trip, but hell, I think that's the way to go!" He smiled broadly. "Boys, the land is as good as ours, I can feel it!"

Tyler closed the book on his desk. He looked around his office and rubbed his eyes. Outside the street was deserted and quiet. Gray light was beginning to come through his office window. He had burned a lot of midnight oil, and he was exhausted, but it would be worth it. He was ready for P.K. Calender.

A thought struck him. *What if this is all for naught? What if I've read something in this report that isn't accurate?* He shuddered. *No, it* has *to be true. This is my ticket OUT of Benson!*

His fee for negotiating a deal such as this would buy his way into a good, established firm. Ideally a firm in a warmer climate. In recent years, his health had been declining steadily, and his doctor had warned him of the toll the winters of Benson, Michigan (wet, cold and endless) were taking on him. He had always been frail, a sickly child. His whole future was on the line with this. One way or the other, he would *have* to find a warmer place to live. And if this deal could make that happen *and* make him a lot of money to boot, he was prepared to make sure everything went just right. This truly was the chance of a lifetime for Michael Tyler.

The three letters he'd received from P.K. Calender (which he had purposely ignored until he could study up on everything there was to know about Section 14 in Alamde County), each one more urgent, filled him with confidence. Mr. Calender seemed desperate.

Four days later, on a gloomy, cold Tuesday morning, a man walked right past his secretary and into Tyler's office. Tyler stood slowly and said, "Hello?"

The secretary appeared at the door with a helpless look on her face.

"It's okay, Phyllis." The secretary nodded apologetically and closed the door as she left.

"Mr. Tyler?"

"Yes."

"I'm P.K. Calender."

"Yes," said Tyler, his heart in his throat.

"Mr. Tyler, I have written to you three times regarding property owned by Peter Christian, now deceased. Mr. Christian was your client, correct?"

"Yes," said Tyler, "he was."

"I realize you lawyers are busy and I apologize for the unannounced visit, but I'm the type of man who goes right to the heart of the matter. I figured I would save you the trouble of calling or writing back."

Tyler swallowed. "Yes," he said, his voice croaking, much to his dismay. "I understand you're interested in purchasing some land from the heir."

"That's correct," said Calender. "If the price is reasonable, of course. I'm only speculating."

Tyler mustered up some confidence and said, "Oh I don't think you're speculating, Mr. Calender. I think you know damn well how much copper is in the ground up there."

Calender hesitated, and Tyler was triumphant.

"All right then," said Calender after a moment, "here's what we'll do. We will schedule a meeting a week from today, in Lansing."

"Lansing?"

"I took the trouble to meet you here," said Calender, "I'm sure you can find it in your heart to respond in kind."

"Fine," said Tyler. "Of course, I'll want to see all your geological survey charts, everything pertaining to your study."

Calender sighed. "Of course, of course. Will the owner of the property be present?"

"Probably not," said Tyler, "but rest assured I have his every confidence."

Calender suggested a good hotel in Lansing and parted with, "See you in seven days, my friend."

Odd, thought Calender, as he walked out of the office and down the hall. *The person with the most to gain from this will not be there? Hmm...would he trust his lawyer that much? Would* anyone *trust his lawyer that much? Not likely.*

When P.K. Calender was gone, Tyler dropped down into his chair, feeling like he had just given birth.

When he had gotten hold of himself, he reached into his desk drawer and pulled out the will. He thought back to the day, two years before, when the old man had been in his office. It was a rather routine matter to Tyler, thus he had not paid too much attention. What had the old man said? *"No kids of my own..."* *"A neighbor..."*

Yeah, that was it. Frank Burns was his *neighbor!*

"He should be easy to find," he said aloud to himself.

But not yet. Not until *he* met with Calender himself and could see what the shark was willing to lay on the table.

Chapter Fifty

Tyler sat at the table in Calender's hotel room, with no expression. He was greatly impressed with the spacious, luxurious hotel (Calender had footed the bill), but he was trying desperately not to show it.

The table was littered with surveys and legal documents. Seven men were seated around it. Two had been introduced as lawyers, three as junior partners, Calender and himself.

The heavy artillery, Tyler thought. Calender sat directly across from him. During the introductions Tyler had said as little as possible, trying to appear confident. Inside, his stomach was hollow. Calender had not taken his eyes off him for even a second. Now he was sitting silently, watching, letting his lawyers and junior partners speak for him. Tyler wished *he* had someone to speak for him, but he was in this alone.

They discussed the anticipated amount of copper that could be extracted from the section in question, Calender's men taking great care to emphasize the risk Mr. Calender would be taking. Tyler brushed this aside, pointing to the geological survey that indicated perfect conditions for a large, large deposit. His late night studies had paid off. *They would have walked all over me,* he thought, *if I hadn't done the research on my own.*

Nevertheless, the two lawyers took exception to Tyler's contention that the mining endeavor was a sure thing.

"Nothing is guaranteed," one of them said. "Until Mr. Calender spends the money to start digging into the ground, we will not know what's down there. There's no way to know what's down there! Speculation: it's just *that!*"

He had a hoarse voice and a mocking tone. He kept looking at Tyler and rolling his eyes, as if Tyler were being outrageous in his statements.

"I don't appreciate your tone," Tyler said.

"Well I don't *care* very much," the lawyer shot back, "if I must take issue with what you say, I damn well will!"

"Gentlemen, gentlemen," Calender chimed in, "this bickering is not going to get us anywhere. This is simply a preliminary meeting. Mr. Tyler, is your client interested in selling the land outright or could a leasing agreement be worked out? With royalties, of course."

"I shall go over both proposals with my client," Tyler said. "A decision will be reached. Future negotiations will then be geared in that direction."

Calender nodded and studied Tyler. He was getting tired of the man's posturing. He stood up abruptly, stretching to his full height, and leaned over the table. "We have to have an answer in a week."

Tyler said nothing.

"Certainly, you should be able to consult with your client and reach some sort of decision in a week's time."

"I'm not sure," Tyler stammered, "there are options to discuss, there are..."

"I'm sure you've discussed the options with your client. He must have *some* idea of what he wants."

"Yes, certainly," said Tyler, "I just think we'll need more time."

Calender sat down and stared at Tyler. No one in the room said a word. Then Calender spoke. "Gentlemen, will you allow us a moment alone?"

The other men looked at each other, rose, and left the hotel room.

Alone, Calender said, "You want to know what I *really* think, Tyler? I think that you are *not* representing the owner of the land. I think he doesn't even know about any of this. I would dare say you have not even gotten in *touch* with him yet."

Tyler was frozen.

"I think your client is probably some backwoods yokel. I think you're here cutting a deal on your own. A deal that you're going to take back to him and - in his ignorant surprise and gratitude - he's going to pay you a big fat fee. Maybe even hire you permanently to look after his concern. Am I right, Mr. Tyler?"

Tyler was shaken, and could not say anything.

"Well that's fine," said Calender after a moment. "I don't mind that. I admire an enterprising young man like yourself. In fact, I *hire* them whenever I find one."

"You're mistaken!" Tyler blurted out.

Calender smiled. "Just in case I'm not," he said, "hear me out, please. Now, let's say - *hypothetically* - you have no agreement with the new owner, as I suspect. Written or verbal, your *only* agreement was with Mr. Christian, the deceased. Once the will is processed and the land is turned over to the heir, your responsibility in the affair is finished."

Tyler kept his head down, looking at his feet.

"Yes sir," Calender continued, "I need more men like you. How in *hell* did you find out about the copper? What put you on to it?"

Tyler said nothing.

"Hmm? I didn't hear you."

Tyler kept looking at his feet.

"Does the heir know anything about the copper?"

"No," said Tyler, weakly.

"And why's that?" Calender asked, cupping his ear to hear the answer.

"Because," said Tyler, swallowing hard. "I haven't talked to him yet.

"Okay, that's fine. I'll tell you what, Mr. Tyler, suppose that you do what you were hired to do. Simply execute the terms of the will, hand over the land to the heir, and walk away with no mention whatsoever of the copper that may - or may *not* - be in the ground up in Section 14."

Tyler looked up and was about to object.

Calender raised his hand. "Hear me out, my friend," he said. "If you do this, I will give you an iron clad contract to serve as one of my legal advisors for a period of five years."

Tyler pursed his lips tightly, not wanting to submit.

"Incidentally, I pay my inner circle of employees well," said Calender. Tiny beads of perspiration began to form on Tyler's forehead. "And to sweeten the bargain, I'll give you a ten thousand dollar *cash* bonus for signing the contract."

Tyler was shocked. He could not believe what he had just heard.

"Is this contract iron-clad even if you don't get the land?" he asked.

Calender shrugged. "Is there any reason I *shouldn't* get it...cheap?"

"No," said Tyler, "none that I can think of."

"Don't miss this opportunity," said Calender. "This is a sure thing for you. If you go with the new owner, you're gambling that he will retain you in the future. He may, he may not. You may tell him everything and he may leave you in the cold. Then *I'll* find him."

"When do you want my decision?"

"I *told* you when I want your decision," said Calender. "One week!"

"It's too soon!" Tyler said, trying to regain some bit of his former confidence. "Way too soon to work everything out, now that you know I have not spoken to the heir yet."

Calender knew that more time would probably benefit his own interest, by allowing this weak man's greed to get the best of him.

"Very well," he said, nodding, "I'll need your decision by May 1st. No later."

Tyler rose. He couldn't wait to get out of the room.

"I'll be in touch," he said.

"Fine," said Calender. He stood and they shook hands. Calender's grip was swift and strong. "We want you with us. You're a damn good man!"

Calender watched Tyler leave, called the others in, and told them what had just transpired.

"Do you think he'll take it?" asked Bernard.

"Take it?" said Calender, grinning maniacally, "that *mouse?* He'll *grab* it!" He burst into excited laughter, making the others a little nervous. Calender was unpredictable when he was angry, and he was unpredictable when he was jubilant.

Then an angry look swept over Calender's face. "Goddamn it!" he screamed ferociously, kicking the table, nearly knocking it over. "I SHOULD HAVE OFFERED HIM FIVE THOUSAND, INSTEAD OF TEN THOUSAND TO SIGN ON! WHOSE IDEA WAS THAT?!!"

He looked at each of the men severely. They all laughed nervously and looked around, shrugging. Then Calender let out another burst of laughter, heaving and hoarse. The others laughed along with him, in great relief.

Inside his hotel room, Tyler closed the door with his back and leaned against it heavily. His face stung with shame. He whispered, "Oh God, oh God." He wished to the very depths of his soul that he had not come. Calender had chewed him up and spit out the pieces. It was like the whole thing was a terrible dream, and he wished it were. Trying to bluff his way through a dealing with P.K. Calender had been insanity on his part.

He's out of my league, he thought sadly. *I'm just a hick lawyer, in a hick town, that's all I'll ever be! And his offer...it isn't a contract, it's a* bribe! *Here's thirty pieces of silver to stand by and let one man steal a fortune from another!*

Tyler knew the Calenders of the world. He had just never been involved with any of them, until now. They were the men who twisted and corrupted everything they touched. Calender was probably up every night praying for war; war that would enhance his fortune by sending the price of copper into the heavens. The worst thing was that Tyler had gone to Lansing attempting to *act* like Calender. For a while, he too had been dreaming of war and copper prices. And this made him feel ashamed.

And if he took Calender's offer? He didn't want to *think* about the abuse and contempt Calender would heap on him during those five years of employment.

"But what can I do?" he said, sliding down until he was sitting on the floor. "I can't afford to stay here anymore! The winters are going to kill me! I need to be able to afford to leave! I *have* to think about myself!" His voice echoed unnaturally in the quiet hotel room. Tears welled up in his eyes and burned as they streaked down his face.

If I stay in Benson, they're gonna bury me in Benson.

He sobbed violently. "I'm sorry," he said to the heir of Section 14, whom he had never even met. "I'm sorry I can't help you!"

Chapter Fifty-one

The weather broke at the tail end of February, turning unseasonably warm. The great drifts of snow began to settle noticeably around the camp. *"Early spring!"* the old-timers predicted.

That meant the camp would break early and Frank would be out of work. That worried him. Recent letters from his father told him that the situation at home was getting worse. The letters never mentioned the money Frank sent home, but Frank knew it was both appreciated and badly needed. He could not imagine the impact losing the farm would have on his family, especially his father.

Huge piles of logs dotted and dashed the riverbanks now. The winter's cutting was situated and ready, awaiting only the ice break-up and the high waters of spring. Down the tributaries they would go, emptying into the Great Bear River. There they would join thousands of other logs on their way to Lake Superior, and to the mills. For the white water men, this was an exciting and dangerous time. But Frank was not one of them. For him, and others like him, employment was winding down for another year. Now he brooded as each passing day brought him closer to the end. It was getting steadily warmer. New snow was failing to stick. The ground began to thaw. The river opened up and at last - in mid-March - standing shin-deep in mud, Frank Burns was paid off.

Frank, Curly Bill, and the rest of the crew rode into Blackwing on one of the flatcars the camp used to transport the men out.

Blackwing was a sight to behold. The streets were packed with jostling men. The railroad normally ran only a freight from Blackwing, but now they were running a temporary passenger train also. Sixteen hundred men would eventually leave the camps and swarm into Blackwing, almost all at once, all of them needing (sooner of later) transportation out of the northwoods.

Not, however, before the saloons and other establishments took in a great deal of the money the men were carrying. If it weren't for the mass influx of men every spring, Blackwing would be little more than a boarding house or two. It was springtime that allowed the businesses to carry on for the rest of the year. It was a safe bet that every saloon's whiskey stock was at an all-time high. And the ladies! Oh, the ladies! Every saloon imported two or three extra to meet the heavy demand. Back rooms were transformed into mini-brothels for the ladies to ply their trade. None of them were blushing beauties, but to a man seven months in the bush, they were angels, each and every one of them. For the next week at least, Blackwing would become Boomtown. After that, things would slow down to a mere riot.

Frank jumped from the flat car, grabbed his duffel and followed Curly Bill and Pumphandle. Groups of men sat waiting outside the already packed barbershops. The same situation existed in front of the bath houses. It was not a great devotion to cleanliness that led the men there, but rather the knowledge that cleaning up somewhat was a requisite for visiting the ladies.

"Oh boy, oh boy!" Curly Bill cried, with a glint in his eye that bordered somewhere between lust and pure insanity. Eyeing the lines and calculating the wait, he said, "Let's get us a drink or two before we line up, eh?"

Pumphandle nodded enthusiastically. Frank shrugged and said, "Sure."

He followed the two into the nearest saloon. The place was packed, of course. Chunks of dried mud on the floor were being ground into a fine dust, but no one seemed to notice. In the corner to the right of the door, luggage of every description was piled haphazardly. Curly and Pumphandle threw their bags into it without thinking. Frank debated throwing his into such a hodgepodge, but decided it was safe. Anyone in that saloon thinking he would take something that didn't belong to him would probably be murdered on the spot.

After much jostling at the bar, the three stood with schooners of beer in their hands. It truly was standing room only. There was no room at the bar, no tables that weren't completely encircled, and barely any room to walk. Two waiters worked their way through the crowd, filling schooners of beer as quickly as they were being emptied. Frank studied the faces of the men. In them, he saw little more future than the next drink.

A sharp elbow in the ribs brought his attention back to Curly Bill. His eyes were fixed at the other end of the bar. Frank turned and looked. Approaching the bar from the back was a woman. Frank judged her to be somewhere around fifty. Heavy make-up had been applied to conceal her age. Her hair was a dim blonde color and faded. Her eyes were hard. When she smiled, enormous teeth seemed to jump out at you. The swearing at the bar decreased noticeably. These were men who would walk on your face with caulked boots, but they would not swear in front of a whore.

Frank watched as she bargained and then left. A big lumberjack followed her, looking somewhat silly.

"Now there's a *woman,*" Curly Bill sighed wistfully. Pumphandle's head bobbed up and down in agreement. Frank bought another drink.

As he drank his beer, Frank's attention was drawn to a table where two men were seated. The men were complete opposites. One was a six-footer, at least 300 pounds. He was around thirty, and his bright blonde hair was cut close; a Swede if Frank ever saw one. He wore a checkered wool shirt and heavy dark pants, held up by bright red suspenders. Across from him sat a thin, swarthy little man, twice his age but about a third his size. The only similarity was the way they were dressed. Each man's coat hung on the back of his chair.

Camp buddies, thought Frank.

The big man was getting louder and the little man seemed to be getting nervous. After downing each beer, the big Swede would slam the schooner down and roar with laughter, then reach across the table and give his little buddy a sharp knock on the arm. Then, to boot, he'd hook a big finger in the little man's suspenders and give them a good snap, following it up with more heaving laughter.

"Drink up Toivo!" he hollered. To the Swede it was all good-natured fun, but to Toivo it was getting painful. Several times the little man tried to leave, only to be pushed back into his chair by a big hand on his shoulders.

Frank turned away, not wishing to get involved. He felt sorry for the little man.

Three ladies returned to the bar, over and over. Each time a new customer would follow each one back, only to return a short time later looking rather sheepish, but happy. Frank periodically checked his watch. He wanted to catch Chris at the office just before closing time. He still had a bit of a wait.

"You goin' back?" Curly Bill asked him, nodding pointedly to the back of the bar where the whores were located.

Frank shrugged. "No," he said.

"Aw!" Curly Bill cried, "me and Pumphandle are! Ain't that right Pumphandle?"

Pumphandle bobbed up and down and grinned broadly.

Frank shook his head.

Curly Bill gave him a silent wave of his hand, then he and Pumphandle walked toward the back of the room, being led by two whores. That made Frank sad. Since coming to Blackwing, he had indulged in some things which his parents would have staunchly disapproved of, but he drew the line at prostitutes and gambling. Not for fear of his parents, but because he simply was not interested. Especially in the whores. They were vulgar, hard women, and though he would *never* discuss it with anyone, he could not understand the need for intercourse consuming a man *so* much that he would do it without love, without verbal or eye contact, without a connection made. A connection like his father and his mother had.

A while later the big Swede was slouched down in his chair, his head tilted back, his mouth open, snoring loudly. Toivo recognized his chance. He reached across the table and with a bony finger, dabbed the Swede's nose a couple of times. The sleeping giant did not react. Lightly he tapped on his arm. No response. Satisfied that his companion was indeed passed out (rather than *almost* passed out), Toivo jumped to his feet and looked around the room with a toothless grin. He spit on his hands, rubbed them together, then reaching over the table he seized the Swede's suspenders, one in each hand, and began drawing them back, actually walking backwards until the suspenders were stretched as far as they would go. The whole bar had quieted, watching. With a flourish Toivo let go of the suspenders. They flew toward the Swede and snapped loudly against his chest. The Swede flinched violently from pain and surprise and fell backwards on his chair, onto the floor. Mumbled swearing could be heard from beneath the table, then the top of the Swede's head appeared, followed by two groggy and angry eyes searching. Alas, the little man had grabbed his suitcase and blown out the door and down the street like the wind. He was out of sight before the Swede even got to his feet. Nearby men who had witnessed the Swede's behavior earlier started cheering. This prompted the rest of the bar to join in, though not knowing exactly why. The big man clamored to his feet in a rage, but, clearly outnumbered, he found his own luggage and left.

Frank was waiting outside the office of Calvin Lumber Company when Chris came out. The two men shook hands and walked down the street, deep in conversation, each bringing the other up to date on the latest happenings in their lives.

Chris asked, "Where are you staying?"

It was a question Frank had been wondering about himself. "I don't know," he said, "looks to me like the town is all full up."

"Don't worry Bucko," said Chris, "you can stay with me! I've got plenty of room. That is, if you don't mind sharing a bed."

Frank expressed his appreciation and added, "I'd better get cleaned up then."

"You can do that at my place," said Chris. "I have a bathroom with a big tub."

Frank looked at him skeptically. He was not any more optimistic when Chris introduced him to Mrs. Wallace at the rooming house. She looked at Frank with obvious distaste. Chris was quick to explain that Frank was a good friend with nowhere to stay.

Mrs. Wallace nodded with a frown "Just in from the camps, are you?"

"Yes, ma'am," said Frank, twisting his fingers nervously. He was painfully aware of his ragged clothing, muddy boots and overall unclean appearance. She looked at him closely, and despite his appearance decided she liked this big, good-looking young man. She noticed his nervousness and had come to realize over the years that this was a good sign. A person who was nervous was respectful. Under the weight of her maternal instinct, she caved in.

"Well, I suppose it would be all right for a couple of days," she said. "As long as you're a good friend of Mr. Huntington's." Mrs. Wallace thought the world of Chris. "Mind you though," she added, "it will cost you a dollar extra a day."

"Yes ma'am," said Frank. "Thank you."

She nodded. "That will entitle you to dining room privileges also. Now, for God's sake, get up in that tub! You're just a bit gamy, you know!"

Frank's face reddened. He grinned and said, "Yes ma'am."

Frank came out of the hot, soothing, delightful bath to discover he was without clothing. Everything from his pockets lay on Chris' dressar. His duffelbag lay crumpled and empty in the corner. If not for the robe Chris lent him, he would have been forced to sit around stark naked.

"Mrs. Wallace took them," said Chris.

"Why?"

"Well," explained Chris, "I would bet they are immersed in boiling water and lye soap right now."

"That's awful nice of her," said Frank sincerely.

"Oh don't worry," said Chris, rolling his eyes, "you'll get charged for it. But it won't be much."

"Great," said Frank. He was relieved that his laundry problem was taken care of.

"What are you going to do now?" asked Chris.

Frank shrugged. "I don't know...go home I guess. But I can't stay there long."

"Why not?"

"I have to find work. My folks are going through some rough times."

"What happened?"

Frank started to tell him about the drought. At first he chose his words carefully, not the type to burden someone with his own problems. But soon, in a burst of unintentional but uncontrollable emotion, the words just tumbled out of him. He talked of the drought, the fire, Whiley's death. It was the first time he had mentioned his brother's death to *anyone.*

Chris listened attentively and when Frank was finished he asked, "Christ, you mean the fire bankrupted the entire community?"

"Sure, between that and the drought," said Frank sullenly.

Chris sat back. How small his own problems seemed now. Frank had never talked so much to anyone, and no one had ever talked so much to Chris, assuming that - from his outgoing nature - that he was shallow and unconcerned. But he wasn't.

"So you've been sending most of the money you've made home and now you're out of work?" Chris asked.

Frank nodded and said nothing.

Chris thought for a moment, then said, "You know anything about carpentry?"

Frank answered, "I can swing a hammer, and I've done small jobs around the farm, that's all. Why?"

"St. Claire, that's my boss, told me that some people with money are going to build a resort on Eagle Lake."

"Where's that?'

"About four miles west of here."

"A resort?" said Frank.

"Sure!" Chris answered. "They figure they can get people from the cities to come up here and pay good money to live in the wild for a couple of weeks at a time."

"The hell!" said Frank, astonished.

"That's what they think," said Chris, shrugging. "Anyway, they got the road in already and they're going to start building in a couple of weeks. They're going to need carpenters and laborers. That's us!"

"Us? Are you going to work there too?"

"Sure, why not! It's good experience."

"What about your job at the office?"

"Not much work in the office when the camps are closed," said Chris.

And so it was agreed they would seek work in the future resort. That night Frank slept soundly in the first comfortable bed he had known in many months.

A bit crowded, but comfortable.

Chapter Fifty-two

The next day Frank wrote home to explain his reasons for staying on in Blackwing. He wrote the letter in a particularly encouraging tone. *"Do not worry about me,"* he wrote at the end. *"I'm doing just fine."* He gave Chris' address for return mail, sealed the envelope and left to post the letter.

The scene on the streets of Blackwing was the same as the day before. The Boomtown appearance had not diminished, in fact Frank thought the main street seemed even more congested.

The men themselves looked different now, however. The streets were crowded, but they were not *bustling* as they had been earlier. Men walked slowly, stiffly. Many had black eyes or downright ugly gashes on their faces from brawling.

Hard men and hard liquor, Frank thought, passing an enormous lumberjack whose left eye was completely swollen shut. *It's bound to get rough.*

He thought about his not-so-tough friends Curly Bill and Pumphandle, and figured a quick check of the saloons couldn't hurt, to make sure they were all right.

They were not in any of the saloons. Heading back down the street, Frank noticed a crowd at the train depot. Sitting there with their suitcases were his two friends; Curly Bill with his head bowed, elbows on his knees, his big hands covering his face, and Pumphandle curled up beside him in the fetal position, groaning at intervals. Frank chuckled.

"You two look like you did the town up *real* good," he said.

"Mornin'," said Curly Bill quietly, lifting his head from his hands when he heard Frank's voice. "We're leaving as soon as we can."

"Leaving?" said Frank with a mock smile. "Why, I thought you two were going to keep the town alive for a solid week!"

Curly Bill shook his head and closed his bleary eyes. Pumphandle, who had not moved, groaned.

"Did you two drink just a little too much last night?"

Curly Bill nodded. Pumphandle groaned.

"Did you visit the ladies again?"

Pumphandle sat up with great effort, and in unison the two men shook their heads.

"Why not?"

Curly Bill wet his lips and said, "Truth is, I guess me and this old fool are just getting too old for this kind of thing." Frank noticed a hint of melancholy in the man's voice. "I don't know if we'll even be able to catch on with another camp, come fall."

"Oh, you'll do just fine," said Frank, not sure if they actually would. Because of their youthful enthusiasm, and simply because they had been kind to Frank at the beginning, Frank had always seen them in a light of youth. But now, in the harsh sunlight, at the end of another logging season, he realized that neither were young men. In fact, they were both old, in their late fifties...too old - at least - to log, drink and brawl as they used to. Frank wondered if they knew anything else. Probably not, and this made him sad.

Nevertheless, he said, "You two know more about logging than any man in town!"

Both men looked at him with a tired nod of appreciation. A shrill whistle blew and everyone suddenly jumped up all at once around the depot.

"Well, that's it for us," said Curly Bill. Frank helped him to his feet. Curly Bill turned and helped Pumphandle up. Frank looked into their faces and then shook their hands with regret. He watched them board the train. After a while the whistle blasted again, and the train pulled away with long, laborious chugs.

Frank waved, though he could not see them in any of the windows. He knew that the chances of him seeing Curly Bill and Pumphandle ever again were slim, and he walked away from the train depot that morning with a sense of loss.

Moving along the main street, Frank noticed two young women ahead of him. Could it be? He looked more closely, and caught a glimpse of the golden hair. Sure, it was the girls from the boarding house. *Angela,* he thought. *Her name is Angela!*

His pulse quickened. His stomach seemed to fold over on itself. It was a tickling sensation, not all-together unpleasant. Then the two girls turned a corner and disappeared. Frank searched, but could not find them.

Chris Huntington sat at his desk for an hour, unable to concentrate. Finally, he closed the ledger in front of him and approached St. Claire's desk.

"I have to speak with you," he said.

St. Claire looked up and pointed to a vacant chair. Chris sat down and explained his plans, what he and Frank had discussed the night before. St. Claire listened without any interruption. When Chris finished, the objections he had been expecting did not come.

Instead, St. Claire said, "Well, if that's what you want, then the man to see if Mr. Bagely. He's staying over at the King Hotel. He doing the hiring for the Eagle Lake project. They're buying the lumber from us, so mention my name. You knock off early this afternoon and go see him."

Chris, surprised by the ease of St. Claire's reaction, couldn't think of anything else to say. He thanked St. Claire and returned to his desk.

Tom Reynolds worked diligently at his desk, pretending he had heard nothing.

St. Claire was expecting something like this. He had watched Chris slowly but surely master the different jobs in the office. *Hell, he really could run the office,* he often thought, *if I needed him to.* There was no question that Chris was quickly outgrowing the office job, and St. Claire had been expecting him to want to strike out on his own.

St. Claire waited until his two clerks left for lunch, then put on his coat and hurried to the King Hotel. Ten minutes of discussion with Donald Bagely assured that both Chris and Frank would be hired.

Works out well, actually, St. Claire thought, walking back to the offices. *Eagle Lake's only four miles out...I can still keep an eye on the kid and make reports to the old man.*

Later in the afternoon, Frank and Chris visited Bagely and were promptly hired. Both men were surprised by how quick and easy it went, but merely deemed themselves fortunate. Bagely told them that work would start in about a week and a half. Chris returned to the office and told St. Claire. They both agreed he should finish out the week. That would give Chris Huntington a full week of freedom, before starting a new job. *Perfect,* he thought.

Walking back to the boarding house (keeping an eye out for Angela and her friend), Frank thought of a problem his new job presented. He would need a permanent place to stay. Rooming with Chris indefinitely was out of the question. He wanted his own space. *Mrs. Wallace would never stand for that, anyway,* he thought. *But maybe I can ask her if she can recommend a place.*

He found her in the kitchen of the boarding house making bread. The aroma was warm and tantalizing, much like his kitchen at home when his mother cooked. This aroused a sharp, bittersweet homesickness in him.

"Thinking about home?" she asked him, with softer eyes than normal.

"Yes ma'am," said Frank.

"Would you like some coffee?" she asked.

"Yes, please," said Frank, sitting down at the kitchen table. Mrs. Wallace poured two cups and joined him. For a moment, neither spoke. Then Frank told her about the job and that he would be staying on in Blackwing. He asked if she could recommend a place for him to stay.

Mrs. Wallace hesitated when Frank finished speaking, watching him closely, as if making a decision about something, then she rose off her chair and said, "Come with me."

He followed her up the stairs and down the hallway, past Chris' room to the very end. In front of a doorway, she reached under her apron and produced a ring of keys. By now Frank had a good idea of what was going on, and it filled him with relief.

She unlocked the door and swung it open.

"Tell me what you think," she said. Frank walked in and looked around. The room was large, much larger than Chris'. Light shone brightly through two large windows on the opposite side. Furniture was piled helter-skelter about the room. Old bed springs leaned against the wall. On the floor lay carpets rolled and tied. There was even a birdcage in a corner this makeshift storage room, its stand flaked and pitted.

"Well?" asked Mrs. Wallace.

Frank nodded his head and said, "Nice."

"Not the junk," she said, "the room. If we clear it out and clean it up. Do you want it?"

"Yes, ma'am."

"Okay, we'll start in on it this afternoon."

Sure enough, that afternoon a man with a horse and buggy arrived. Together he and Frank carried everything but the best furnishings down and loaded them into the wagon. Mrs. Wallace set to work with soap and water, scrubbing every last inch of the room, top to bottom, left to right.

The following afternoon Frank eagerly moved into his new home, his *first* real home. It was a great feeling to be nineteen. It was a great feeling to be writing to his parents that everything was just fine and not be lying about it.

In order to get to and from work every day, Chris and Frank would have to have reliable transportation. That meant using Chris' Ford. Stripped of her tires, the car sat in the lot behind the boarding house. All winter long she had faced the bitter elements. She was still an object of beauty to Frank, but she needed some work. Armed with tools one morning, the restoration began.

Two days later, bright and shiny black, the Ford was putting its way down the main street of Blackwing. Chris and Frank rode with the air of British Gentry, inspecting their manor from the royal coach. Cigar smoke swirled above their heads and out the windows as Chris puffed away, delighted to be behind the wheel again after so many months. For a few hours they made their way up and down Blackwing's limited streets.

No longer did those streets teem with men. The special passenger train had been discontinued and even the imported ladies had moved on. Blackwing was returning quickly to its normal self, at least as normal as it ever got. It was never dull (too restless and full of transients to be dull). The saloons still did a great business, and the permanent whores made a living. Decadence was still the catch of the day in Blackwing, but the spring boom was over for another year.

"Say Bucko," said Chris, "let's take a ride out to Eagle Lake."

"Sure," said Frank, shrugging. "Think we can find it?"

"I got directions," said Chris. He turned the Ford around and took the main road out of town. During the ride Frank thought of the folly of a project such as Eagle Lake. Who would spend money to stay at a resort? It seemed foolish to him, but *someone's* bad idea had given him a job that summer, and that's all that mattered to him then.

Chris slowed the Ford and turned off the main road. The new smaller road twisted and curved for twenty minutes. The ground was rutted severely, and Chris had to drive slow. They began a decline, then saw it straight ahead; the lake. Proceeding another quarter of a mile, the road ended abruptly They stopped the Ford and climbed out.

Nailed to a tree was a premature, but optimistic, sign that read, "EAGLE NEST RESORT". Behind it, lush green grass stretched for about 200 yards down the hill to a sandy beach.

White birch and maple trees dotted the area around them. The beach extended on both sides as far as they could see, hugging the shoreline like an old friend. They walked down to it. Stirred by a moderate breeze, the water slapped softly against the shore. Frank stared out over the water. It was the largest inland lake he had ever seen. In the middle was an island, shrouded mysteriously in thick pine. It was absolutely beautiful. He reevaluated his thoughts of what men were planning to build here.

"Maybe a resort is not such an odd idea," he said.

"Bucko, I was just thinking that," said Chris.

Frank felt an inner peace swell in him, standing next to the man he could truly call a friend.

Chapter Fifty-three

Tyler sat at his desk, his eyes focused on the storm of dust particles floating in the bright rays of sunshine through his office window. His face was beginning to look haggard from lack of sleep. His eyes were puffy, and small lines were beginning to form around them. He had not slept in a long time, not since his meeting with P.K. Calender.

He was holding the Last Will and Testament of Peter Christian in front of him. He had read it several times over that morning in an effort to find any small mistake, *something* that could and would render it a non-legal document. Much to his chagrin, he found none. It was flawless; carefully worded, duly signed and witnessed. Tyler knew Peter Christian had taken his own life, but there could be no question as to the old man's state of mind at the time of the will being drafted two years before.

Tyler read it one last time, and then accepted the fact that all he could do was seek a hearing in probate court at the Cumberland County seat sometime in June. All that remained after that was to find Frank Burns, son of John and Agnes Burns, who resided on a farm four miles west of Fairchild. All of this information had been recorded by the old man. Tyler had started a letter to the Burns family, advising them of the will, but eventually tore it up, opting, instead, to meet these people face to face.

With a sigh he rose and put the old man's will in his briefcase. He locked his office, sent his secretary home for the day, and made his way down the main street of Benson for the train depot.

"Four-thirty in the morning," said the agent behind the wheel, "that puts you in Fairchild at ten the same morning."

Tyler frowned and said, "Don't you have anything going to Fairchild a little later in the day?"

The agent shook his head and said, "No sir. Only expresses run that route after the first, and they blow right through."

Tyler sighed and said, "All right, fine then." He paid for his ticket and left. That night he rehearsed many times what he would say to Frank Burns and early the next morning he rose, cleaned himself up, dressed and got down to the train depot just as light was forming in the east.

During the trip, Tyler dozed periodically, but heavy rest (the kind he really needed) eluded him again, as it had for two weeks. True to the agent's word, it was just about ten when the train chugged into Fairchild.

Viewed from the train platform, Fairchild looked like a hundred other small towns which Tyler had traveled to throughout the years. He made his way along Main Street to the general store, where he inquired about the Burns family.

"I'll take you," came a voice from behind. "For a dollar."

Tyler turned. There stood a small man whom Tyler judged to be a farmer, a dirt-poor farmer aged beyond his years.

He seemed friendly enough though. Tyler nodded and said, "Okay. A dollar."

Outside they climbed into a very dilapidated buggy and set off. The day was bright and warm. The buggy creaked and bounced along, threatening to break in half at the next rut in the road. The horse pulling the buggy was equally as tired and droopy looking. The ride was slow and long, but Tyler enjoyed it. He would never dream of living in such an isolated small town (Benson was bad enough!), but he had an appreciation for nature and loved spending time in the country. The only thing that marred the trip for Tyler was the old man's attempt at conversation.

"So you got business with the Burns family then, eh?" he inquired.

"Yes," said Tyler.

"What kind of business might that be?"

"It's of a personal nature," he answered, surprised (and annoyed) by the man's effrontery. The farmer turned his attention to the horse.

After a moment Tyler looked at him and said, "You know the Burns family well?"

"Yup."

"What kind of people are they?"

"Well that's a question that borders on the personal nature," the farmer said, grinning and exposing bad teeth. "You're not telling me nothing. I'm not telling you nothing."

Tyler rolled his eyes and looked at the countryside as it passed slowly. They passed a small, tarpaper shack, which looked rundown. Tyler studied it, never imagining that it was where Peter Christian had lived and died.

The driver pulled the carriage off onto a thinner road, which shot off the main road diagonally. He stopped the carriage.

"The Burns farm is right down there," said the old man. "In fact, you can see the house and barn through that stand of trees, eh?"

Tyler nodded. "You going to wait for me?" he asked.

"No need to. John Burns will bring you back in."

Tyler jumped down off the buggy and looked around hesitantly.

The old man laughed out loud and said, "Burns don't have no dogs. Never has!"

He began walking down the road. The buggy driver watched for a few minutes, then turned his carriage around and headed back toward Fairchild. The narrow road ran through the stand of trees and ended in front of the house. Tyler walked up on the porch steps and knocked. The door opened and a surprisingly beautiful face answered.

"Hello ma'am," he said. "My name is Michael Tyler. I'm an attorney from Benson. I'm looking for Mr. Frank Burns."

An attorney, Agnes thought, *what in the world?*

"Won't you come in Mr. Tyler?" she said. Tyler walked into the front hall. "I'm Frank's mother. Frank is not here, I'm afraid. He's in Blackwing. But my husband is out in the barn. If you'll make yourself comfortable in the parlor, I'll go fetch him."

"Thank you, ma'am," said Tyler. He sat down on a chair in the parlor and waited. Like the farm itself, the furnishings were old, but neat and well-maintained. The Burns appeared to be clean, decent people, and this surprised him. Tyler didn't harbor the usual arrogant contempt for farm folk that many people in his circle did, but it had been his experience that most of the farmers he'd met *were* the slovenly, simple-minded *hicks* they were made out to be. That didn't appear to be true of the Burns family.

Tyler heard the back door open and shut. He rose. Agnes came into the parlor. Behind her came Mr. Burns. Tyler blinked. The size of John Burns stopped him cold.

"I'm John Burns," he said, advancing his hand out. It was all Tyler could do to keep from closing his eyes in fear as his hand disappeared in the grip of the other. John Burns had a firm grip, but there was a gentleness to his motions which Tyler would not have expected, and which eventually put him at ease.

They all sat down, Tyler in his original chair, Mr. and Mrs. Burns across from him on a sofa. Tyler watched the big man labor down onto the sofa and he almost laughed. *I'd like to see Calender try to brow-beat this man,* he thought.

He stifled the laughter, suppressed the grin, and began. "As I explained to your wife, Mr. Burns, my name is Michael Tyler. I'm an attorney from Benson. I represent the estate of Peter Christian. I drew up this will for him two years ago, and your son Frank is the sole heir to all his moneys and properties. Although there is very little money, there *is* some property."

John and Agnes both sat, hand in hand, listening with no look of surprise, just interest.

"There are two parcels of land. The first is that on which his cabin still stands, which I understand is near here. The second is a section of land in Alamde County."

This brought surprise to the big farmer's face.

"I was not aware that Hemlock owned any land other than what he lived on," John said.

"Oh yes," said Tyler, "he owned it for quite some time, since he was a young man."

"Farmland?"

"No, mostly wooded, from what I understand."

"Oh," said Burns, his hopes visibly dampened.

"However," Tyler continued, "it is a *full* section of land, and it is worth something." He wiped a bead of perspiration from his brow. "First, let me ask you a few questions. Why is your son in Blackwing?"

"He worked all winter in a logging camp and now - according to his most recent letter - he's staying there and working a different job for the summer," said John.

"I see, I see," said Tyler. "How old is he now?"

Burns looked at his wife. "Nineteen?" he asked. She nodded.

"Okay," said Tyler. "Well, according to the law he's still a minor until he's twenty-one, so you are still his legal guardian. Although he will legally inherit the land, if he were to sell it, it would require your permission." Burns nodded. "Also, if anything should happen to him, the property would then revert back to you and your wife entirely. Now I don't have a specific date set yet, but sometime in July we'll all meet in probate court at the county seat and everything will be finished." He dug into his briefcase and produced a copy of the will. He handed it to Burns and said, "You look it over and I'll answer any questions you have."

He waited silently while Mr. Burns read. He felt terrible. *There's a fortune in the ground,* he thought. *I really should be telling them this!*

Fifteen minutes later, John looked up from the will and said, "I have no questions."

"Fine then," said Tyler. "Now if I may impose upon you to take me back to Fairchild, I have a train to catch this afternoon."

"My goodness!" said Agnes, jumping up. "Where are my manners? It's already noon. You'll stay for dinner, of course, Mr. Tyler."

"No, no," the lawyer protested, rising.

"Of course you will," said Burns. "Then I'll take you in." There was finality in the big man's voice, which prompted Tyler to sit down again.

"You men can chat while I get dinner," said Agnes, hurrying for the kitchen.

Oh God! Tyler thought, squirming in his seat. He already felt bad enough, he didn't need to "chat" with anyone.

He looked at Burns. Burns looked at him and smiled. His smile was even big.

"So," said Tyler, "the farmers don't prosper around here, do they?"

"No, we've fallen on hard times," said John. In a very quiet voice, he told Tyler of the years of struggle for all the small farmers, most recently the drought and fire. His words bore no hint of remorse or self-pity. Only when he spoke of Whiley did his voice crack slightly. Tyler listened quietly to the story, his shame rising.

During dinner, both John and Agnes sensed that the lawyer was deeply troubled about something, and although the reason was a mystery to them, they did their best to cheer him up with lively conversation. This only made matters worse for Tyler, who was coming to realize that he liked and respected these people.

The mare shook her head as they left the farmyard. Agnes stood in the yard and waved goodbye. Tyler waved back to her. He looked around at the land, the very livelihood of this family. He knew that if they lost it, they would lose more than just a piece of themselves. Add that to the struggles they'd already endured...Christ!

In town John Burns stopped his buggy near the platform at the train depot. Tyler's train was fired and stood ready, hissing steam in anticipation of the long trip.

"Well, thank you Mr. Burns," he said, jumping down. "You'll be hearing from me soon as to the exact date of the probate."

Burns nodded. "Thank you, Mr. Tyler."

Tyler turned his back and started toward the platform. Then he froze, grimaced in frustration, looked back at Burns (who was watching him), and muttered, "Son of a bitch, it's now or never."

He took a deep breath, and walked back around to Burns' side of the buggy. Burns watched him the whole way, with surprise.

He stopped, looked up at the hulking farmer and blurted out (before he could change his mind), "Mr. Burns, I know somebody who is going to try and buy or lease that section of land in Alamde County for a considerable amount of money. Would you allow me to act as your counsel in the matter and negotiate a deal? My fee would be on a percentage basis."

John looked down at him with surprise, then puzzlement, but never suspicion. "Yes," he said.

Tyler jumped up and grabbed his hand from the reins, shaking it. "You *won't* be sorry Mr. Burns, I can guarantee you that! You *won't* be sorry!"

"All aboard!" the conductor yelled.

Tyler headed for the platform. When he was on it he turned and yelled to Burns, "Remember, do nothing until you hear from me! Do nothing!"

"I won't!" Burns called back.

Tyler boarded the train and took his seat. *I haven't even got a contract with the man,* he thought. But it really didn't matter. He didn't have a contract with *P.K. Calender* either, and he was confident that John Burns' word was his bond.

Michael Tyler leaned back in his seat as the train began to sway. Before it was far out of Fairchild, he was slouched down, sleeping like a baby.

Chapter Fifty-four

Two days later, Tyler was poring over a desk full of proposals, satisfied that he was ready for *any* eventuality, when the telephone rang. He answered it and recognized the gruff voice immediately. It was P.K. Calender.

"Tyler," the voice said, "Calender. You ready to probate?"

Tyler smiled. "I haven't a definite date yet, but it will be in late July."

"Jesus Christ!" Calender said. "Can't you move it up further than that!"

"I could try."

"You'd better," said Calender.

"Why?"

"A major competitor is starting to show interest in the land," Calender said.

"Well, you have *everything* tied up in that area, don't you?" Tyler asked.

Calender paused, then said, "Not quite. We have everything *east* of Section 14. But they could come in from the west."

"I see," said Tyler. "Section 14 is critical then, eh?"

"Are you *joking?* That's where the heavy concentration of copper is! Without it, it wouldn't even be worth going in for!"

Tyler's heart leapt excitedly. He could envision the bidding war. He could envision a new way of life for the Burns family *and* himself.

"But we're going to get it," said Calender. "We'll have this deal cut and dried before anyone knows what happened. That's why we've got you, Tyler." Calender made no attempt to hide the disrespect in his voice.

"Well, that's something I've been meaning to tell you," said Tyler. "I'm representing the heir in the sale of this land."

There was silence on the other end, then Calender's voice came back dry and harsh. "You son of a bitch, you dirty S.O.B. We had a deal."

"No," Tyler corrected, "I agreed to nothing. You tried to force me into an agreement that I found - and still find - to be wholly unethical."

"I'll get you," Calender said, his voice raising sharply. "Do you understand, bastard? I'll RUIN YOU! I'll FIND THE HEIR AND TELL HIM EVERYTHING! I'LL TELL HIM HOW YOU WERE GOING TO *SELL HIM OUT!"*

P.K. Calender was totally out of control. Tyler took the earpiece from his ear and waited. When at last the screaming had stopped and he could hear only Calender's labored breathing, he said, "When you have calmed down and are ready to discuss terms and money, get back to me. And Mr. Calender, when I say money, I mean a *lot* of money."

"I'll have to talk to my partners," said Calender, in a subdued voice.

"Fine," said Tyler. Then he hung up, feeling stronger and more confident than he ever had, not just in anticipation of a bidding war, but because he had done the right thing *and* stood up to the likes P.K. Calender.

Chapter Fifty-five

Twenty-eight men labored diligently beside the blue waters of Eagle Lake. The prints called for eight well-spaced cottages nestled beneath the swaying, whispering branches of the largest trees. The main lodge was to stand close to the water, overlooking the lake like a guardian angel. Below it, a large dock was to point like a finger straight out in the direction of the island. When the project was in full swing, an estimated forty-five to fifty men would be employed.

For now, the twenty-eight toiled, building forms and attending to the preliminary work. The work was hard. *Harder than in the camp,* Frank thought. But he reveled in it. After a winter working in the camps, this was like working in Paradise. Each morning after a hearty breakfast (hearty indeed…Frank ate better his first day at Mrs. Wallace's than he had all winter in the logging camp), the two men - with lunch buckets under their arms, courtesy of Mrs. Wallace - left the boarding house, climbed into the Ford, and headed for Eagle Lake. During those days, the conversation during the ride was always lively and full of enthusiasm. The bond between Chris and Frank grew stronger. For the first time since Chris had met him, Frank was quick to laugh and find humor in things.

In their spare time they frequented the saloons. This held no particular allure for Frank, but Chris liked it and it was something to do.

Blackwing had a pool hall called *Hull's Billiards.* It was a wooden building, of average length, but very, very narrow. The boards of the hardwood floor tended to rise independently in the cold of winter, making it nearly impossible to keep a pool table level. In the spring, the boards receded to an only slightly different version of their original position, and no one complained. Five green felt-lined tables took up most of the walking space. There were benches against the walls and cue racks attached to the wall beside each table. In the front of the room, just to the right of the door, stood a large wooden counter with glass panels and a heavy glass top. It housed chewing tobacco and confectioneries.

One night Chris and Frank entered the pool hall. They sat down on a long bench that lined the back wall, and watched. The players spoke only in hushed tones as they played. Frank instantly became fascinated. Fairchild had never had a pool hall.

He turned to Chris and asked, "Do you know how to play?"

Chris shrugged. "I've shot a game or two."

"Show me how."

Chris looked at him with surprise. He would not have thought Frank would be interested in pool, as he eschewed the other things which were normally associated with it: excessive drinking, cards, gambling, smoking, et cetera.

The rack "boy" (he was at least sixty) hurried down to them when signaled, complaining that they had chosen the table farthest away from where he had been seated. They selected cues from racks hanging on the wall. Chris chose carefully, lifting one and then another, examining the length, straightness and weight of each before make a selection. Frank did the same, although he had no idea what he was looking for. When Chris was finally satisfied, Frank decided he was too, although he had chosen one with a slight bend in the middle.

Chris explained the game. "We'll play rotation. The object of the game is to hit this one-ball in first, then the two-ball, and so on, all the way to the number fifteen ball. Now, the number on the ball is worth the same amount of points. For instance, the one-ball is worth one point, the two-ball two points, get it?" Frank nodded. "At the end of the game, the one with the most points wins. Now, you can shoot combinations too. For instance, if I'm shooting at the one-ball and I hit it and the one knocks the ten in, the ten counts for me and I keep shooting."

Frank nodded, eager to get started. Chris explained how to lag for the break. They lagged, and Chris won.

Chris sent the triangle of balls scattering in all directions. By the time they all stopped, the two-ball had dropped in. He chalked up and took aim at the one-ball.

Watching Chris shoot, Frank leaned on the cue in his right hand. After a while, he switched it to his left hand and leaned on it for what seemed an eternity. Chris kept shooting until the last ball had dropped into the pocket. Then he chalked his cue and said, "Wanna play another game?"

"Where did you learn to shoot like that?"

"Well, I'll tell you. In college, I found it was a lot easier to learn how to play pool than *work* for extra money."

"What, you gambled for pool games?" Frank asked.

"Yes, and made a hell of a lot more than I would have working in a café or a factory."

For the next three hours, Chris explained about scratching, the kitchen, choosing a proper cue stick, and other key rules to playing the game well. He showed Frank how to make a bridge with his finger and how to hold the cue steady. He explained about the diamonds and how to use them. It was a quick, thorough crash course in pool. Time after time, Chris complained about poor table position and deliberately missed shots to give Frank a fighting chance. When they finally quit, Frank had improved about as much as could be expected of a beginner.

The next night they went straight from work to the pool hall. Frank was determined to win. He didn't.

After that, night after night, they played pool on the last table of the pool hall. Frank played his heart out and he did improve, but soon it was clear to Chris he would never be more than adequate at the game.

Each day at exactly noon, Martin Hull would turn the key in the lock to open his place of business. He had owned Blackwing's pool hall for fifteen years. Every day he would unlock the door, walk in, stop, and stare wistfully at the tables, hoping this would be a busy day. It seldom was. People in Blackwing, in general, wanted to drink and brawl, not play pool.

Still, he managed, mostly because he was a man of few needs. He was a short, square man, fifty-five years old. He had sharp brown eyes, a solid chin, and slightly graying hair. He always wore a black suit, shiny with age. No one could remember Martin dressed in anything else.

His routine never varied. He walked behind the counter, removed his wide-brimmed hat with both hands, placed it gently on the glass countertop, climbed atop the high stool and waited for his rack boy, Freddy.

Freddy was fifteen years older than Martin, but was a very spry, able-bodied man. He lived with his daughter, and working for Martin gave him something to do. He kept the place clean and racked the balls for the players. In turn, Martin kept him supplied with tobacco and paid him a small wage.

Hull's Billiards had a small group of regulars who came in every day. During the spring boom, of course, he did a better business (though still not on the same level as the restaurants and bars), but this was the wrong time of year, the *worst* time of year. Today, like every day for the next, oh, ten months or so, it would be just the regulars. And the regulars were, slowly but surely, moving out of Blackwing, or dying off. That saddened Martin. As a whole he liked his regulars. Most were good friends and good customers, and that made the fact that there were not many of them worth staying on for.

The only one of his regulars he really didn't care for was Bob Allen. To be sure, Bob was a very good pool player and a good customer, but he was a braggart and a bully, and not above cheating if he thought he could get away with it. And he had walked up to Martin one night in an obnoxiously friendly way, reached over the counter, and flattened Martin's hat. This, above all else, was unforgivable. *He doesn't even drink,* Martin often thought when Bob was in the pool hall. *He's an obnoxious drunk and he doesn't even* drink!

One night after work, Chris had a message waiting for him when he arrived at the boarding house. It was an invitation to have dinner with St. Claire. Chris called him and accepted. They agreed to meet at the Grantland House, the only place to even approach sophisticated dining in Blackwing.

Left by himself (and not wanting to spend the evening in his room), Frank decided he would go to the pool hall alone and see if anything was happening. The warm breeze of the day had carried into evening. Frank strolled leisurely, watching as the glowing sun draped itself over the horizon for a moment, then sunk slowly.

As he approached the boarding house where Angela lived, the two girls were sitting on the porch swing. He kept his head straight but watched them through the corner of his eyes as he passed. He saw Angela look in his direction and watch. He knew she was following him.

On the other hand, he thought, *why would she be doing that? I haven't talked to her in months, and then only for a moment in the street. I haven't done* anything *that would leave a lasting impression.* He kept walking, hoping that Angela would call to him. She didn't.

When he arrived at the at the pool hall, two of the tables were occupied. The usual groups were each in their usual positions, cues in hand, watching quietly. Without Chris there Frank had time to study the group more closely, and he realized for the first time that most of the regulars were quite elderly.

Martin spotted the young man who had been coming in quite a bit lately. "Greetings!" he called. "Where's your partner tonight?"

"He couldn't make it," Frank answered with a smile. Martin nodded. Frank took a seat on the bench and watched.

The door opened and a big man came in. Frank had seen him there many times, recognizing him as one of the regulars. He sat down right next to Frank. After a few minutes he turned to him and said, "I'm Bob Allen." He extended his hand and Frank shook it. After that they made small talk and watched others play. Several times Allen muttered, "Nice shot," on a shot that Frank did not think was particularly impressive. At length, the players at the first table quit. Frank felt a nudge on his arm.

"Wanna play some?" Bob asked him.

"Okay," said Frank. He motioned to Freddy. Freddy darted like a sprite to the table and racked the balls in eight-ball formation.

"Eight ball?" Bob said, raising his eyebrows. Frank nodded. They lagged for the break and Bob Allen won.

After four games, they were dead even, two apiece.

"Oh hell," said Bob, "let's make it a little more challenging. Say fifty cents a game."

Frank considered this. "Play for money?"

"Hell, yes! You afraid?"

"No," said Frank.

"Well then?" said Bob. "Let's go!"

Frank won the first game and Bob Allen paid him. On Frank's second shot the following game, as he leaned over the table, Bob said, "Bet you a quarter you don't make it."

It was a long shot, but not particularly tough. "Okay," said Frank, shrugging. He promptly sunk the ball and was paid the quarter.

When Bob's turn came he had nearly the same shot as Frank. The same bet was made. Bob sunk the ball and Frank paid him the quarter. By the middle of that game Frank and Bob Allen were betting on every shot.

Game after game flew by that night, and money kept changing hands. At first evenly, but then, slowly and ruthlessly Bob Allen hustled Frank, starting to make shots that Frank would never have guessed he'd make. By the end of the night, and before Frank knew what hit him, Bob was making *every* shot he took.

"Well, that's it for me," said Frank. Before Bob could protest, Frank added, "Fun playing with you. Have a good night."

In his room, Frank dug deep into his pockets and pulled out his money. He counted it. He dug again for the money he was sure he had missed. Nothing was there. Quickly he counted his money again. He couldn't believe it. He had lost twelve dollars! It seemed impossible. Yet, there was the evidence. He'd walked into the pool hall with twenty-four dollars and now had twelve. In the heat of the game and the sport of competition he had obviously lost more money than he thought.

He swore to himself, a deep regret settling in. That was money he could have sent home. That was money he *should* have sent home, right away, instead of taking it to the pool hall.

"Son of a bitch," he said. "Fool!"

He went to bed with an empty feeling in his gut. Even sleep would not release him from the guilt. He dreamed of his sisters dressed in rags and sifting through other people's trash.

It was on the ride home from work the next evening, when Chris suggested going to the pool hall, that Frank told him what had happened. Chris listened, his jaw jutting out in determination.

"Well, stay away for a few nights," he said. "And for Christ's sake, *don't* play for money ever again! Bob Allen took you for a fool!"

"You don't have to tell me that," said Frank glumly.

At seven that evening Chris popped his head in Frank's door and said, "Gotta go out for a while. See you in the morning."

Frank was laying on his bed, staring at the ceiling. He waved goodbye silently.

At seven-thirty Chris walked into the pool hall with a swagger. He spotted Bob Allen and sat down next to him.

"Where's your friend tonight?" Bob asked with a sly smile.

"He said he didn't want to go out tonight. I don't think he feels too good."

"That's too bad," said Bob. "Wanna shoot some?"

The two had shot three mediocre games when Bob said, "Say, want to make it more interesting?"

Taking great pains to hide the smile that kept tugging at his mouth, Chris asked innocently, "How?"

As the evening wore on, Chris had to laugh at the repetition of Bob's hustle. And yet, he *was* good at it. What Bob didn't realize, however, was that for every one of his own hustles,

Chris (acting most innocently) responded in kind. At the end of four hours of straight playing, they were dead even.

"I *thought* I could win some money tonight," Chris said, sighing. "But I guess I can't. You're just too damn good, and I gotta quit. I have to be up early in the morning anyway."

"Aw, come on!" Bob Allen protested. "Just one more hour."

"Naw, I gotta get to bed," said Chris. Then his face suddenly lit up. "Tell you what, though," he said, pulling a wad of bills from his pocket, "I'll play you one more game, win lose or draw, for twenty bucks." He slapped a twenty down on the table.

A murmur shot through the pool hall. Everyone had watched Bob Allen hustle Frank the night before, and were very curious to see what would happen when Bob and Frank's *friend* started playing.

Bob hesitated. He was suspicious, but riveted by the twenty. He reached into his pocket and pulled out a handkerchief to wipe his mouth. He wanted to say no. This was no penguin he was dealing with, and he knew it. But twenty dollars was twenty dollars, the most that had *ever* been bet in Blackwing's only pool hall, at one time. He counted out twenty one-dollar bills, laid them on the table and said, "Okay." Everyone in the hall, including Martin and Freddy, moved over and surrounded the table with great interest.

They lagged for the break. Chris won. The cue ball shot down the table like a comet. Balls flew in every direction. When the last ball had stopped rolling, three balls had dropped into the pockets, two solids and a stripe.

Chris looked the table over carefully. The solids were in a better position. There was one tied up, but nothing he couldn't handle. "Solids," he called, and began to stroke. One, two, three balls went in. He had two left; a clear shot and the one that was tied up. He studied the table. The six-ball was clear, but the two-ball was surrounded by three stripes. Chris knew he could make the six in the end pocket easily, but the angle was all wrong for breaking that damn two-ball loose. He wanted to run the table. He would settle for no less. He was not only doing it for his friend, but for himself, because he had come to realize that he *really* didn't like Bob Allen.

To run the table, he really only had one choice. He had to cut the six-ball across three-quarters the width of the table into the opposite end pocket and come off the cushion hard. It was an extremely difficult shot, one that most players would not even attempt. He would have to run almost straight sideways, and the cut would have to be paper-thin.

He leaned over the table, aiming and using all the left-hand English that he could, and stroked hard. He clipped the six ball on the very edge, sending it rolling slowly sideways across the table. The cue ball came off the cushion and cracked into the group of stripes that surrounded his two-ball. Meanwhile, all eyes were on the six as it rolled slowly toward the pocket for what seemed an eternity. It started to slow down. It went to the very tip of the cup, stopped and hung there. Then, almost as if it willed itself, it dropped in. The small gallery let out their breaths in unison.

Bob Allen swore bitterly, breaking the hushed silence.

The two-ball, which had been broken free, was now an easy shot. With an easy stroke, it dropped. Chris concentrated on the eight-ball. That was *not* an easy shot. But damn it, Chris Huntington was going to run that table. His best bet was to cut the eight-ball into a side pocket, but it would have to travel between two other balls and there was not much room. Like the shot before, this would have to be a precise clip.

He called to the side and leaned across the table. *Click!* The eight ball passed between the two centaurs and dropped into the pocket. Chris straightened up and smiled broadly, reaching for the money.

As he touched it, strong fingers tightened around his wrist. "We don't allow hustlers around here, do we boys!" said Bob Allen. He looked around. Stony faces stared back at him without a hint of sympathy. He turned back to Chris.

Chris' eyes smoldered, and he said, "Hustler? You were the one who suggested we play! And you're the one who suggested we play for money. If there's a hustler in here, it's you!"

Bob Allen grunted and tightened his grip on Chris' wrist.

"And, might I say, not a very *good* hustler either," Chris added with a smile. Everyone in the pool hall laughed.

Bob Allen studied the young man's face. Chris' eyes were confident, determined. There wasn't a hint of fear to be found. It was a look that said without words, *"Do not treat* me *like you treat others. I will not back down."* Bob had seen that look in the past and had ignored it. It had been a mistake to ignore it, and he had suffered for it. He didn't want to make that mistake again.

He released Chris' wrist. "Hell with it!" he said, stomping out the door and slamming it.

Martin Hull came to his side as he pocketed the money. "Be careful, boy," he said. "You have made an enemy. He will not forget this."

"What can he do? I'm not afraid of him."

"There are many ways to hurt a man," Martin said quietly. "Violence is only one of them, and often the *least* gratifying."

Outside, Chris assumed a jaunty walk, feeling pleased with himself. The next morning when Frank rose and inspected himself in the mirror, his eyes fell upon the money lying on top of the dresser.

"What the hell?" he muttered. He counted it. There was exactly twelve dollars, and it prompted a knowing and grateful smile to unfold across Frank's face.

Chapter Fifty-six

Wilby Furman carried the pails toward the pump. A grizzled, wisp of a man with yellowed, broken teeth, he had spent his entire life working in the camps. At the pump, he glanced back at the cabin and his spirits fell even lower. He had a serious problem on his hands and did not know what to do. He cursed under his breath as he pumped the water. Should he go into the cabin - march right in there - and tell the son of a bitch to get the hell out? That could provoke an unpleasant reaction. But Wilby was just about to the point where he didn't care anymore. Weak of mind and body, the only thing that had kept him alive for fifty years was his ability to stop caring in unpleasant situations.

He shook his head and pumped water into the pails. He had worked all winter in camp with the man. When camp broke, they took to drinking heavily in the saloons. Wilby got drunk then, got drunk for about a week straight. Like many men, Wilby occasionally got himself in trouble when he drank. And like most men, it was his big mouth that did the damage.

"Why doncha come and stay out at my place?" he'd asked the big man, who had been complaining about having nowhere to go.

"Where's your cabin?"

"About a mile out of Blackwing."

And so the man had come. *Just a couple of days of company,* Wilby had thought. *Doing the boy a favor, cuz he ain't got nowhere to go! We'll do some drinkin', maybe fix the place up a little.*

But there had been no fixing up anything - only drinking - by the big man. It went on and on. And the son of a bitch got *mean!* Like no other man Wilby had ever known, even his own father, that bastard was mean as a snake.

Slowly but surely he turned Wilby into a slave in his own cabin. "Get this for me, Wilby!" was what he usually said, or, "Wilby, you better get into Blackwing and pick up some whiskey before we run out!" in that raspy, rattled voice of his. The man showed no sign that he was leaving anytime soon, and Wilby was at the end of his rope.

Worst of all were the nights. It was a small cabin - only one room - and Wilby was forced to listen to the man's ranting, raving and cursing in his slept. Wilby thought the man was insane. Not *just* mean, but crazy too.

But I'm the fool, he said angrily. *I asked for this, and I got it. Curse my drunken mouth!*

He stopped pumping the water and sat thinking, staring off. Suddenly the cabin door burst open with a crash. Wilby turned and looked at the big man filling the entryway.

"Goddamnit, Wilby!" he screamed. *"Get in here with that water! I'm so dry I can't even spit!"*

Hiding his feelings, Wilby filled the pails and tried to smile. He hustled back to the cabin, spilling one of the buckets down the leg of his trousers in his haste. Frenchy Dumont made him go back and fill it up again. Running back, poor Wilby spilled it *again.* Frenchy sent him back a second time. When Wilby returned with the bucket full, Frenchy took the bucket, drank most of the water, dumped the rest of over his head as a bath, then placed the bucket over Wilby's head and tapped it hard with his knuckles.

"Thanks Wilby!" he said.

William Furman's drunken magnanimity *also* got him a night beneath the stars that night. Frenchy locked the door to the cabin, passed out, and could not be woken up. Wilby spent the night at the edge of the woods by an abandoned plow, planning a course of action.

Chapter Fifty-seven

Tyler lifted the receiver to his ear and spoke, "This is Tyler."

"When can we close the deal?"

It was Calender. "You read the proposals I sent?" Tyler asked.

"Yes."

"They're acceptable?"

"Yes."

"Well, then, three weeks."

"That long?" Calender asked. "Come on Tyler, you can do better than that!"

"Well, you realize," Tyler said, "that the new heir will not have taken possession of the property, but by meeting we can have everything sewn up when he does."

"If that's the best you can do," Calender said impatiently. "Are you *positive* your man's going to get the land, and there *won't* be any problems?"

"None. The will is ironclad, the land is his. And then it will be yours for the agreed-upon price."

"All right," said Calender stonily, "when do we meet? And where?"

"Three weeks from today, in Benson."

"Will the heir to the land be there?"

"No. We'll travel from there to meet him."

"Why can't we just all meet together in Benson?"

"We'll do it my way," said Tyler.

Calender agreed grudgingly and hung up without saying goodbye. Tyler hung up the receiver and chuckled. He could afford to. His client was going to make a fortune and some of that was going to rub off on him.

He sat down and penned a letter to John Burns, advising him that he would be bringing important people with him to negotiate for the land that his son was about to inherit. He also advised Burns to contact his son, Frank, and make sure he was present when they arrived.

He signed his name, sealed the envelope, tossed it in his outgoing box, leaned back in his chair, and smiled, satisfied that everything was working out better than he could possibly have imagined.

Chapter Fifty-eight

The mild weather allowed the workers at Eagle Lake to work long, hard and in relative comfort. Thus, Eagle's Nest Resort began to take shape. Some of the cottages were just about finished and the foundation for the main lodge was completed. Optimism among the contractors was very high. The laborers reveled in the atmosphere of enthusiasm, giving more than their share of work every day. For this they each received a small (but much appreciated) cash bonus. It was the best work experience many of the seasoned men ever had and Frank actually looked *forward* to going to work every day. That had never been the case in the camp.

The night trips to the pool hall continued for Chris and Frank, but they took care to play only with each other and apart from everyone else. Each night they passed the boarding house where they had stayed their first night in Blackwing, and each night Frank hoped for a glimpse of the blonde-haired Angela. He was always disappointed. Even on the loveliest nights, when he was sure Angela and her friend would be sitting on the front porch, he saw nobody.

He had been thinking about Angela more and more, and decided he *must* see her again. He just didn't know how. Certainly he could not bring himself to walk up and knock on the door. He *wanted* to, but it just wasn't possible. He had to find someone who knew her. He had to learn more about her. He *had* to learn more about her. At first he merely dreamed about her.

Now he still thought about her at night, but he was *awake,* unable to sleep, unable to think about *anything* else.

For a week he turned the problem over and over in his mind, but couldn't think of anything to do. Then one night at the pool hall he got an idea. While Chris was shooting (Chris took forever to shoot, planning every one of his shots, falling short only of taking out a compass and measuring the precise angle), he walked over to Martin, seated behind his glass counter and said, "Martin, you know the rooming house just down the street?"

Martin thought for a moment and said, "Ya."

"There are two sisters that live there with their uncle. They work for him. One is a blonde girl. Her name is Angela. Do you know her?"

Martin's world revolved around (and did not extend beyond) his home and his pool hall. He shrugged and said, "No boy, I don't. Sorry."

"Oh," said Frank with disappointment, "thanks anyway."

"Your shot Bucko," said Chris, walking up.

"*I* know her," a voice said from behind. Frank turned. It was Bob Allen. A teasing smile played on his lips. Frank shook his head and walked past him, back to the pool table.

"Little sweet on her, are you?" Bob said. "Oh, I don't blame you! Would you like to meet her? I could introduce her to you! I know her good!"

Chris stirred uneasily.

Frank took his shot, sank his ball, stood up and said, "I don't need your help."

"Sure you do!" Bob insisted. "Why don't we go a-calling? I'll introduce you all proper like. You *do* want to meet her, don't you?"

Frank took a second shot and said nothing.

"Oh *sure* you do!" Bob pressed on, grinning cruelly. "And I can help you out! All you need is money!"

Frank looked at him. "Money?"

Shit, Chris thought. *I was afraid of that!*

"Sure! You see, her uncle ain't really her uncle and her sister ain't really her sister. That's just a story they tell. She ain't nobody's niece or sister, I know of."

Frank looked at him, still not comprehending.

"She's a whore, you dumb son of a bitch!" Bob said, exploding with laughter. "You've gotta be pretty *dumb* not to see that!"

Hurt and shame flooded Frank's heart. And Bob Allen was doing a damn good job of rubbing salt in the wound with his exaggerated, obnoxious laughter. He all-out roared, rocking back on his heels.

Frank lunged forward, grabbed the man by his head, and slammed him down on the pool table, face up. He then leaned over Bob Allen and pummeled his face repeatedly, lifting his fist high behind his head and bringing it down with devastating force. Chris hesitated, allowing Frank his moment, then pulled his friend back with much effort. Frank, in a rage, tossed off Chris easily and charged Bob again, grabbing him by his face and banging his head against the table. This time Chris and Martin conspired to control Frank, and it worked...barely.

"Frank! Frank!" Chris screamed in his face. "It's over! You showed him! Let's get out of here!"

Frank quit struggling, his arms hanging loosely at his sides, breathing heavily. He was dazed, but managed to calm down.

Martin inspected Bob and could not tell if he was unconscious or faking it. He decided the best place for the man was not on a pool table, but on the floor, which is where he deposited him when he was sure the man was breathing. He would come to in a matter of time.

"Boys," Martin said, turning to them, "what Allen said here tonight was stupid and inappropriate, but I cannot have this going on here. I'm going to have to ask you both to leave. And don't come back." His voice sounded regretful, but his look was determined.

"Yes sir," said Chris nodding. He took Frank's arm and led him to the door. Out on the street Frank could walk by himself, but the only sound he made all the way home was a shuddering sigh. As they passed the now notorious boarding house, Chris cast a nervous glance through the parlor window, and then at Frank. Chris cringed: Of course, Angela was there *now,* looking through the window right at them. Frank gave no reaction.

In fact, he said nothing until much later in the night, when he appeared in Chris' room unexpectedly. Chris had gone to sleep. When Frank appeared in his doorway, he looked up, startled, and said, "Everything all right Bucko?"

"You know," Frank said, "my father has always told me to control my anger. He said anger was normal, but controllable. It *had* to be controlled. He's told me that my whole life."

"Yes," said Chris.

"Tonight, what I did...it's something I've never done before. I've never lost my temper like that."

"I know," said Chris.

"And the strange thing is," said Frank, running his hands through his hair, "It didn't bother me to do it. Not to *him,* anyway. I..." He hesitated, a tear forming in his eye. "I enjoyed it."

"All the more reason why you must control it," said Chris, "just like your father said."

Frank nodded, began to speak again but stopped, and went back to his own room.

"All the more reason why you must control it," Chris had said. And those words made a lot of sense to Frank, as he lay in bed, deep in thought.

They just didn't make doing so any easier.

Chapter Fifty-nine

Mrs. Wallace had a look of grim determination on her face as she scrubbed the shelves of the pantry. She paused a moment to brush back a wisp of silver hair from her forehead. How she *hated* this chore, and to make matters worse she was running behind time. She swore softly (then quickly crossed herself) when she splashed dirty water on her apron.

This was just not her day. She couldn't seem to concentrate on her work. Mother hen that she was, she was always quick to notice any change in the mind or heart of one of her brood at the boarding house, and change there had been, to say the least. For the past week Frank Burns seemed to be preoccupied with some deep, dark secret. The normally quiet but cheerful boy, always quick to smile if not to speak, was now sullen and uncommunicative. Whatever caused the change had to have happened the last time he and Chris went to the pool hall, she was sure of this. She also noted they had not gone since.

After she finished the pantry and disposed of the water, she hurried to the parlor to check the time on the grandfather clock that stood there. Thank goodness, she had more than enough time to get to the market and still start supper on schedule. Mary Wallace's success at what she did depended largely on keeping a tight schedule.

Through the parlor window she watched Ed Simon, the postman, stop at her box by the front gate, make a deposit and continue. Mrs. Wallace walked outside to the box and called, "Thank you Ed!"

Down the block Ed looked back and waved silently. Mrs. Wallace chuckled to herself and retrieved the mail. She walked back up on the porch, examining the three letters. The first, she knew, was a statement from the hardware store. The second was addressed to *Mr. Frank Burns.* It was from his family. *Maybe that will cheer the boy up,* she thought hopefully.

The third letter brought a flutter to her heart. It was from Francine. Dear Francine, her beloved sister. It had been four months since their last correspondence. She slipped the other two envelopes into her apron pocket, sat down on the porch swing with trembling, expectant fingers, and opened the letter. Slowly she read it, savoring each word, then reread it. A moist, faraway look came into her eyes, as she traveled back through the years. She loved and looked after her boarders, but they were not people she could relate to...mostly young people, and the old ones were even older than she. Mary Wallace did not have an intimate relationship with anyone in Blackwing, and her sister Francine (the last surviving of eleven brothers and sisters) was two hundred miles away. Old Francine was getting up in years herself. Had developed arthritis and poor eyesight, so it was difficult for her to write. When she did, it was a treat which Mary Wallace looked forward to and dropped everything else for. She sat on the porch swing for a long time, memories of her childhood twirling over and over in her mind like a kaleidoscope.

The long sound of the grandfather clock brought her back to reality with a start.

"Oh dear," she said. *Now* she was late. She hurried into the house, grabbed her coat, checked the clock and gasped. She didn't have as much time to get to the market as she once had. She untied the apron and pitched it in the corner of a closet. She hurried for the door, putting on her coat as she moved and fluffing her hair with her fingers.

And so, in the closet the apron sat, the two other letters tucked away in its pocket and forgotten.

A week was all Chris could endure; a week of Frank's moping around, hardly speaking, staying in his room. Sure, he had been hurt and - Chris could imagine - hurt badly. But enough was enough.

As they rode home from work one night, he decided to take the bull by the horns. Settling back on the seat of the Ford, he said, "All right, what's this all about. Where did you meet her?"

Frank looked surprised. "Don't you remember? She was one of the girls at the boarding house where we stayed our first night in Blackwing. Remember that noisy place?"

Chris shrugged and shook his head slowly. "I remember the place, but I don't remember her. You never mentioned anything to me about it."

"Well," said Frank, "the other times I happened to meet her you weren't around." He proceeded to explain the two chance meetings on the streets of Blackwing to Chris, going so far as to describe the strange feeling in his gut whenever he saw her.

"Are you talking about the two girls sitting in the *parlor* of that place, when we first walked in? One blonde hair, the other dark?" Chris asked.

Frank nodded.

"Which one was your fancy?"

"The blonde girl," said Frank. "Her name is Angela."

Chris flinched and smiled broadly. "Oh boy, I could have *told* you what they were," he said, laughing. "Two sisters living with their uncle? Come on!"

"I must be the biggest damn fool in the world!" Frank said.

Chris stopped laughing and sighed. "Not any more of a fool than the rest of us," he said. "She's a pretty girl, Bucko, as I recall. There's no denying that. Pretty girls make men do damn fool things."

"And you know," Frank continued, "right now, knowing everything that I know, I *still* get that feeling when I think about her."

"Well," said Chris, assuming a fatherly posture, "I can tell you two things. One, you're not the first man to feel that way.

And two, the sooner you forget about it, the better." Then he brightened and said, "And we'll start tonight, at the Silver Dollar!"

It took a moment, but eventually a slow smile played on Frank's lips, and he nodded.

Chapter Sixty

Sunday was a melancholy day in the saloons of Blackwing. One might assume that it was a day of repentance for the Saturday night sinners, or perhaps a day of reflection or remorse for the previous night's behavior. In truth, the remorse was not in their souls, but in their depleted money belts. And so it was that a group of subdued men sat around the table where the king of stud held court. Quietly they played poker, each hoping to recoup part or all of the money they had squandered the night before, and nursing painful hangovers.

Chris sat among them. The late afternoon sunlight stretched through the window across the sawdust floor of the Silver Dollar Saloon, laying orange across his feet.

"A funny day," Mrs. Wallace had proclaimed at breakfast. "Mark my words, there's a storm a-brewing."

And indeed it was a funny day. The land seemed to be splashed in a sickly, yellow tint, and the smell of rain was strong in the restless air.

All day the sun shone, however, and the sunset now was glorious. It was a warm, wonderful night in mid-summer, 1916.

Chris sat at the poker table, Frank stood at the bar, leaning on his elbows. The game held no allure for him. *Anything* having to do with gambling now repelled him, after his experience with Bob Allen at the pool hall.

He stared at his beer. A letter from home, normally something he could count on every two weeks, was overdue. This caused him only mild concern, but it was strange.

They're busy, he thought. *Summertime is a busy time on the farm.*

He changed his thoughts to Angela, for the hundredth time that day. He didn't understand why, and he certainly couldn't control it, but he could not get Angela out of his head. Whore or not, that was *her* business. Frank only knew how *he* felt.

He studied her in his mind, nursing his beer, only vaguely aware of the severely injured man sitting two stools down from him at the bar.

"Jesus Christ, Wilby!" the bartender said to this man. "What the hell happened to you!"

The shock in the bartender's voice made Frank look up and study *Wilby.* He was a runt of a man, his head coming up only to Frank's midriff. The right side of his face was a swollen mass of bruises, which had caused his right eye to shut tight. Frank stared and muttered, "Jesus," under his breath.

"Whiskey," said Wilby, through terribly swollen and split lips. The bartender poured his drink. Wilby lifted the glass and in obvious pain he drank it all at once. He slammed the glass down angrily.

"He *did* it to me," he said, his voice laced with bitterness, "the son of a bitch!"

"Who?" said the bartender.

"That bastard that I was good enough to let stay with me!"

"Why?"

"Cause he's a crazy bastard, that's why!" Wilby cried. *"Pure out of his goddamn head!"*

Frank and the bartender exchanged bothered glances. They shrugged to each other. Finally the bartender said, "Tell me about it."

Wilby let out a deep snort of disgust at the bartender's ignorance, but he sure as hell had a story to tell and he wanted to tell it. He told of the drunken invitation he had given the man to spend just a FEW days with him when they broke camp.

"Just 'til he could get transportation out of Blackwing, that was all!

"Well, the son of a bitch started drinking and took my place right over, like he *owned it!"* Wilby's volume rose sharply and hysterically. "The more he drank, MY booze, the meaner he got! Oh, Lord, I can still hear him! All night, swearing and screaming in his sleep! I can't tell you when he was nastier, awake or asleep! He kept vowing revenge, you know! At first he just talked in his sleep, but then he started telling me stories during the day and I could see he was cracking up!" Wilby glanced at both the bartender and Frank. "I mean *really* cracking you know? I've met some crazy bastards, but not like this. No sir! Not like this. This man is insane. *I swear it!"*

"Where is he now?" the bartender asked.

Wilby motioned for another shot. The bartender brought it and he took it quickly, again with pain. "Wait 'til I tell you boys *this!"* His voice was low now, barely a whisper, and his one good eye was open wide.

"Last night," he started, "he told me he killed a man once, and I believe him. Oh, yes, I believe him! He wasn't drunk now, mind you. Last night he was stone cold sober. And *that's* why I say he's crazy, because mostly that kind of talk comes outta the bottle, you know? But no, last night he's just sittin' there, sober, and he tells me he's plannin' to kill another man. I don't think much about it, right? I just stay the hell away from him, right? Well, this morning he gets up, and again he don't take a drink. He's been at my place for four months and I ain't *seen* the bastard sober until last night and this morning! He rousts me out of my bed, out in the goddamn yard, and says he's gotta go, gotta go today! Has to set things straight. I asks him what the hell he's talking about, and he says, like it was one of the most natural things in the world, he says, *'I've got to kill him. Won't be able to rest until I do. You can see to that!'*

"I tell you, boys, my blood ran cold. *'I'll catch the 3 o'clock freight out today!',* he says."

Frank cast a glance at the table across the room. Chris and the others were quietly playing poker, not listening to Wilby's story at all.

"So what happened then?" asked the bartender.

"Well, what do you *think* happened then?"

The bartender shrugged.

"He goes back into my cabin and takes my rifle down off the rack. I follow him in and he says, *'Where's the shells?'* I told him he wasn't taking my gun with him. That gun cost me good money...and *whack!* He swings it around and blows me across the face with it. *'Where are the shells!'* he screams again. He's standing over me and he hits me again with the gun."

Now tears were streaming down Wilby's face as he recounted the beating.

"Hell," he said, sobbing, "I was afraid to tell him, for fear he'd shoot me! But after a while, I knew he'd beat me to death if I didn't tell him, so I told him. He walks over, finds the shells, puts them in his pocket, and smiles at me! The bastard smiles at me like nothing ever happened. *'I'll be going now,'* he says. And he left."

Wilby fell to crying outright, and this grabbed the momentary attention of some of the poker players, including Chris.

"I'll be damned," said the bartender, scratching his head. "You think he'll really use it...the gun, that is?"

Wilby took a deep breath of air and winced as he attempted to dry his face. "Oh you bet," he said. "I feel sorry for anyone who tries to kick him off the freight. He'll probably shoot them on the spot."

"Where *is* the guy he's gonna shoot?"

Wilby took a painful sip of his beer and said, "Says the guy lives in Fairchild."

"Fairchild!" Frank nearly jumped off his stool. "Christ, Fairchild! I'm from Fairchild! Who's he gonna shoot?"

Wilby shrugged. "Never said. Never told me nothing about it, except that he was going to get his revenge in Fairchild."

"What was the guy's name? The guy who did this to you?" Frank asked.

"Dumont," said Wilby, "Frenchy Dumont. Son of a bitch!"

The name cut through Frank like a cold razor. "Dumont?" he said, his voice faint. "Dumont was here?"

Wilby and the bartender both stared at him, noting the change that had come over him when he found out the man's name.

Frank fought to stay calm. He couldn't panic. If Dumont was going to Fairchild, if Dumont was seeking some kind of crazy revenge against a man, that man was his father, Frank was sure of it. That meant Frank would have to stay calm.

He recalled the words Hemlock had said a year before. *'I never thought it would end there.'*

Apparently it hadn't. He pulled his gold watch from his pocket. It was exactly six-thirty. When he spoke, his voice was calm. "What time does the freight get into Fairchild?"

The bartender ran a hand through his hair and said, "Hell, let's see, it cuts back on the spur to Hanley, and then, well, shit, it makes every little stop between here and Fairchild. Must be a five, maybe five and a half hour run."

Hope swelled in Frank. That would put the train in Fairchild around eight-thirty. There *was* a chance.

"Chris," he said, "I have to go to Fairchild, right now."

Chris looked up, puzzled. When he saw Frank's face, he said nothing. He threw in his hand and scooped up his hat.

The wind had switched and the air now had a definite chill to it, as they walked quickly to the boarding house. On the way, Frank explained to Chris what Wilby had told him, and his own fears. Chris was confused, but very aware of the danger. The Ford sat waiting on the street in front of the house.

"Gas," said Frank. "What about gas?"

"Full, and there's a full can on the floor in back," said Chris. "But I need a coat. It's getting cold!" He started up the walkway to the house.

"Chris," Frank called after him, "bring your rifle and shells."

Chris stopped in mid-stride and turned back to him slowly. "Now wait a minute, Frank."

"Bring them!" Frank snapped.

"Oh God!" Chris mumbled. He turned back to the house and went inside. A few minutes later he reappeared, a jacket strung over one arm and the rifle in another.

Chapter Sixty-one

John Burns sat at the kitchen table. He brought a steaming mug of coffee to his lips, winced from the heat, blew on it, and then took a slow drink. In the parlor, Agnes sat mending socks that were hardly worth the bother, striving to keep busy.

The day was at once exciting and fretful. Even in church that morning, they were unable to concentrate. The letter from the lawyer commanded their thoughts. It had actually said very little, but *hinted* (quite affirmatively) that some very good things were about to happen. What did it all mean? In a few days they would know, and the wait was sure to be agonizing.

John thought about Frank. He wondered why they had not heard from him. John had written a week ago, telling him he should be present on the appointed day (set up by the lawyer). John had thought this would provoke an immediate, excited response from Frank, yet there had been no reply.

Frank's always been responsible, he thought, running a fidgeting finger around the rim of his coffee mug. *I'm sure everything's all right. He'll be here when he needs to be.*

He took another sip of coffee and sighed. It was a contented sigh, the likes of which he had not known for a long time. Had he been aware of the desperate race to Fairchild taking place at that very moment, the impending inheritance business would have been the furthest thing from his mind.

Chapter Sixty-two

Frank shifted hysterically in his seat as Chris drove the Ford at a prudent speed. As though he could read Frank's thoughts, Chris said, "Frank, I don't dare go any faster. If we hit a ditch we'll *never* get out, and that's not going to be good for anyone."

Frank merely nodded and watched the sky grow dark slowly. The pleasant evening had been squashed by a thick, low canopy of clouds. Occasionally, flashes of lightning foretold the coming of a storm. Between the darkness and the rain to come, the hazards of the road were bound to be doubled in strength and number.

The desperation and fear Frank was feeling brought out an uncharacteristic urge to talk, just to break the silence, just to keep from thinking. He told Chris the whole story of Dumont, going back to the very beginning.

When he finished, Chris shook his head, muttered an obscenity and resisted the temptation to push even harder on the accelerator.

A sudden gust of wind buffeted the Ford and Chris swore out loud, fighting the wheel. He gained control, but a few minutes later they were hit by a second blast, and then a third, each one stronger than the one before it.

"Storm's blowing in," said Chris, bending down and looking up at the sky through the windshield.

"Oh God," said Frank, frantically.

Indeed, the wind kept battering the car. Flashes of lightning became more numerous. Then it hit with a fury; steady sheets of wind-driven rain, taking to obliterating the very road they were traveling on.

Chris stopped the Ford. Frank looked at him and cried, "What the hell are you doing!"

"I can't see anything!" Chris said.

They waited for a minute or two. Suddenly it was over as quickly as it had begun, the sound of the beating rain dropping off abruptly. Sweat poured down Chris' face as he started driving again.

"Thank God the rain stopped!" said Frank.

"Well, be prepared for more," said Chris. "That might just be a prelude to something bigger." They both watched the sky, still filled with lightning, the Ford still being battered by the wind.

"It's gotta hold off!" Frank said, "Christ! It's gotta hold off!"

Almost mockingly, Frank's mind refused to clear itself as the Ford raced and Chris concentrated. He could not help but think about his father. Watery memories of his childhood burned inside his head with the strange clarity of a dream. In one memory, he could see his father lead a harnessed team of horses from the barn, into bright sunshine. The horses were monstrous in size, towering up to the sky. Frank and Whiley, two small boys at the time, were running at John's heels, and Frank could remember the deliberate half steps the man took, allowing the boys to catch up.

Down the length of the barn they went, to the field. Around the corner, out of sight of the house, their father stopped, peered back cautiously at the house, then picked up each boy and placed him on a horse's back. In a flash, their father was in front, his huge fingers locked into the bridles.

"Ready boys?" he said. Whiley and Frank nodded their heads. Slowly he led the horses on to the pasture, the boys smiling with excitement.

Riding atop the horse, Frank could feel the muscles rippling beneath him as the beast labored, his hands clinging tightly to the brass horn of the saddle. John whistled sharply as he led the horses, hoping Agnes would not see her two babies atop 700-pound horses.

But that's not how Frank and Whiley thought of it. Allowed the thrill of riding the work horses, they were now transformed into knights in shining armor, atop their fiery steeds, fighting dragons and rescuing princesses, riding the beast's of burden wherever their soaring imaginations chose to take them. Ahead of them, still whistling and casting nervous glances back at the house, was the gentle giant who allowed them this escape from reality, the gentle giant who was their father.

The sudden swerve of the Ford shook Frank from his daydream. Two deer had darted up on the road. Chris was lucky to avoid them.

"Shit," Chris muttered.

"We must be at least *half* of the way!" said Frank.

Chris shrugged and shook his head, his eyes locked on the road.

Frank looked up at the sky anxiously. There was lightning and thunder, and the wind was fierce (bumping the Ford in both directions), but as yet no rain. Both men knew that steady rain (not merely another shower, like the one that had blown by a few minutes earlier) could mean the end of their trip. If it came, and it was heavy, the road would be turned into a quagmire in no time at all. The little Ford would certainly meet its match, and they would never make it to Fairchild in time.

A few miles later, Frank's worst thoughts came into reality, turning his heart cold. When it came, it came quietly at first, like an assassin. The soft tempo of this rain had none of the fury of that which had lashed at them earlier, but it had an ominous permanency to it. Neither man spoke or even looked at each other, as both were useless gestures. Instead, they concentrated on the road.

With each passing mile the rain fell more heavily. Frank closed his eyes and groaned. There was little doubt they were driving right into the storm. Chris eased up on the accelerator. The rain began to pelt the windshield, obscuring his vision once again. Chris could feel the road becoming slick and soft under the wheels.

Then, like a giant hand swinging across the road, the wind slapped the right side of the car, nearly sending it into a sideways skid. Chris spun the wheel desperately. The Ford righted itself and plunged on like it had only one purpose in life. And on that night, at that moment, it did. Valiantly, with Chris' steady hand, it pressed on, a steady staccato of mud beating against the fenders. The rain fell even harder, and the soggy road began to pull and suck on the tires. Chris felt the Ford lugging a little, but thought it best not to mention it to Frank.

We must be close, he thought. *Just a little further, please!*

After a while, he could hardly see beyond the hood of the little automobile. Then he couldn't see anything. Absolutely nothing, but a blurred light. He had to stop the car. He eased up on the accelerator and braked gingerly. The Ford made a slow gurgling sound and lurched to a stop as the rain crashed down in full force. He sat back in the seat, his nerves raw.

"I'm sorry," said Chris. "I can't see *anything."*

Frank did not respond. He sat across from Chris in silent despair.

They sat for a long while (at least it seemed a long while), praying that the rain would eventually stop. It *couldn't* go on all night. This was a storm, a violent storm. And violent storms usually passed. The sound of the rain falling on the silent car was nerve-racking.

Then just as slowly and incrementally as it had come, the rain started to ease off. Soon it was a mere sprinkle, the storm pushing off to the east in an hysterical flurry of lightning.

"Let's go, let's go," said Frank. "The rain stopped!"

"Hold on," said Chris. "The rain stopped, but the car doesn't have to move, not through *this* mud."

Chris' first fear was squelched when the car actually started. He pressed on the accelerator and shuddered when he heard the tires spin.

"Come on, come on," said Frank.

Chris gunned the accelerator. The Ford protested with a high whine of its engine, then the tires caught and the Ford lurched forward, throwing their heads back.

"Thank you God," said Frank. "Thank you, thank..."

They drove for ten more minutes, at an agonizing crawl. The rain eventually stopped all together. Then Chris' eye caught something in the distance. He squinted and said, "What's that?"

Frank had been sitting with his head in his hands. He looked up in a snap, and pressed his face against the windshield. There was a large, dark shape approaching out of the darkness.

"It's the train depot!" he said, "It's the train station! We made it! We're in Fairchild!"

Moments later the Ford was dancing down the main street of town. "What now?" said Chris.

"Well," said Frank, "we have to get to my house. I have to tell my father, and we have to find Dumont!"

"Where?"

"I don't know, that's a problem. He could be anywhere. If he's come to kill, he won't let himself be seen, so I doubt he's right in town. Probably holed up in someone's vacant shed or cabin. There are sheds down at the lumberyard and the foundry...hell, he could even be in the depot!"

"Or he could be at your house," said Chris.

Frank nodded and said, "Yes he could. "That's where I gotta go first, before anything else!"

"You have to go?" Chris asked. "What do I do?"

"I want you to go to the first place you find open. More than likely it will be a saloon. Tell whoever you find there *everything!* Make sure they know how serious the matter is, make sure they know it's not a joke. Get someone to fetch Carmin Jones, he's the police chief." Frank looked intently at his friend. "You've *got* to make them understand," he said. Chris nodded. "I'm counting on you. Don't let me down."

"I won't," said Chris.

"I'm going home," said Frank, reaching for the rifle in the back seat. Quickly he loaded shells into it. He found an old rain coat in the back seat as well, and wrapped the gun in it. Chris watched with disapproval.

"Maybe I should go with you," he said.

"No," said Frank. "Just do what I told you. Besides, tough as this car is, she'd never make it a quarter mile on our old road after this rain, and then we'd both be walking." Grasping Chris' shoulder tightly, he said, "I will *never* forget what you have done for me this night." Then he got out and disappeared into the darkness.

The rain picked up again, soft but steady. Lightning streaked across the sky in all directions. In a few minutes, Frank was soaked through. The full fury of the storm had passed, but the wind was still strong and the thunder crashed as if the bottom was falling out of the world. Frank had trouble staying on the road out of town. If not for the bright flashes of lightning that helped him gain his bearing, he would not have been able to *see* the road. He would not have been able to see anything. Old familiar landmarks, which he had grown up with, now took on an odd, grotesque look in the gray flashes. Mud clung to his boots and this slowed him down.

Where was Dumont? That was the question first and foremost on his mind. He tried to imagine what Dumont's plan would be. Did a mad man *have* a plan?

I guess I should concentrate on getting home, he thought. He waited for the next flash of lightning to get his bearings. When it came, he recognized nothing. Another flash, still nothing. Good Christ, where was he? He had no idea. He was alone and lost in a world where nature was out of control and a very dangerous man could be lurking nearby.

Beside him, water ran deep and dirty in the ditch. He walked on, bending into the wind and rain. Lightning flashed again. There! Something ahead. He moved toward the object at a quickened pace.

He sensed what the object was before his eyes could confirm it. It was Hemlock's shack. That was good. His sense of direction was reinvigorated. He thought of the old man for a painful moment as he passed.

Then a thought struck him and he stopped dead. Turning slowly, he looked at the dark, deserted shack and he knew, he *damn well knew*, just as if a voice had shouted it from the furious heavens. It was the perfect ambush; the one place his father was sure to pass everyday, and the one place in which Dumont could stay out of sight.

A fear such as he had never known gripped him. He clenched his teeth, his lip trembling. This was no childhood fantasy atop a workhorse. This was no watery dream. This was real. His heart pounded louder than the thunder.

He moved toward the shack where he had spent so many nights visiting with Hemlock. Down through the ditch he waded in knee-high water. A bright bolt of lightning stretched from one side of the sky to the other, the entire countryside lit up in a dark gray for an instant, revealing Frank's presence vividly.

A surge of panic sent him running and diving up against the shack, flattening himself against it. He tore the raincoat away from the rifle and cocked it.

My God, he thought in a nervous humor, *Dumont is probably lying in some boxcar drunk, halfway across Cumberland County, and here I am hugging this wall like I'm in a war!*

He nearly laughed, but caught himself. On the other hand, it was quite possible Dumont was on the other side of the shack's wall, a mere six inches from him, waiting, listening.

Slowly, and as quietly as possible (the lightning and rain helped him in this respect, drowning out the noise he made), he moved along the length of the building. He peeked around the corner. Midway down that wall was the door. He moved. Halfway there he came to a window, and ducked down, hitting the ground with force. If Dumont had been at that window, it would have been over. He couldn't bring himself to pass it. Dumont would be able to look down and see him crawling under it. He knew his best bet was to retrace his steps around the shack, and come to the door from the *other* side, where there was no window.

Maybe, just maybe, he could surprise whoever was waiting on the other side of the wall.

He reversed his steps and made his way around the shack. The opposite windowless side also protected him from the rain. When the lightning flashed, he could see about 30 yards.

He came to the opposite corner and peeked around. Lightning flashed. All clear. Then it was black again, and he could see nothing. He felt the corner of the shack with his fingers and was about to step around to the front when a bright flash sent him ducking back. He waited a few seconds as the thunder exploded, then with only his fingers to guide him he made his way around the corner.

Once again the rain whipped into his face with a sting. He searched for the door, his fingers tracing the wall. They found it. Gently he fumbled for the latch. He found it, but he found something else as well. Further groping revealed it was a padlock. Someone had secured the cabin. He pulled at it, but it was locked tight. He felt relief flood his soul.

Once again the heavens sent forth frenetic light, turning the land gray and bright, and in this light Frank saw with horror that the hinges of the door swung free, torn from the door frame. There was another flash of lightning, then a loud explosion. But it wasn't thunder. The door frame splintered, showering Frank's cheeks with deep, painful slivers.

He froze.

There came a second shot, plowing into the door with sharp, destructive force. This time he jumped away from the door. He waited for the next flash of lightning, which this time would not only expose him to Dumont, but would expose Dumont to him, hopefully. He was watching.

Then it was daylight. His eyes searched, but he saw no one. A second later it was nighttime again. A branch torn away in the wind slapped against his leg and he jumped. His heart was pounding so hard he thought it would burst.

Christ! Don't stand there, move! MOVE!

He jumped back to the side of the shack, though it did not promise protection. At first he felt fear, then despair, now he was growing angry as he became accustomed to the current situation. His anger fed upon itself. He thought about hightailing to the farmhouse and alerting his parents, but now he stayed put. Dumont was a man who had viciously struck down his sister with a stone. A man who had nursed a twenty-year grudge against his father and now intended to kill him. A man who, if allowed to, would destroy his whole family. The rage he felt at the pool hall in Blackwing came to him in defense. *"All the more reason to control it,"* Chris had said, *"just like your father said."*

But Frank knew he father would not hesitate to kill Dumont. And neither would he. Not now. Not after so much had changed in his life.

He stood up and fired the rifle from the hip. This might send a message to the bastard that he was not playing games. Lightning flashed, and Frank caught his first glimpse of the hulking man over to his left. He turned and fired in one motion. It went black and the sound of Dumont's return shot told him he had missed. Fortunately, Dumont missed as well. After each shot he would have to move. He could not allow Dumont to pinpoint his position.

Crouched down behind the shack, he levered new shells into the chamber. What he needed were a couple of lightning bolts to flash across the sky all at once, holding the gray flash just a second longer. Just long enough to find Dumont and end him. Several more flashes came, but all were short. He did not move.

After what seemed an eternity, what he was waiting for came; several bolts of lightning spritzed across the sky. Light flooded the landscape, cutting through the rain. Frank's eyes searched. There, standing directly in front of him, not 30 yards away, was Frenchy Dumont. With his cheek resting on the butt of the gun he pulled the trigger. The rifle kicked back on his shoulder. A split second later he was hit with a terrible impact. It drove him off his feet. He crashed down, flat on his back. A strange, electric pain seared its way through his chest. He screamed out. A moment later, the pain lessened a bit, and he could not tell if he was conscious or not. He didn't know where he was hit. The pain had numbed, but spread throughout his entire body. A wave of nausea overtook him. He felt around for the wound, for the hot wetness of his own blood, but to no avail. With the next flash of lightning he examined his fingers. No blood.

Wherever he was hit, it would not matter at all if he didn't get up and defend himself. If Dumont caught him down like this, he didn't stand a chance. He clamored around the ground and finally found his rifle. It took all the strength in his body, but he managed to sit up and hoist the gun up with him. Grimacing from the pain, he managed to eject the spent cartridge and lever in a new one. Jamming the butt of the rifle into the mud, he pulled himself to his feet, and was rewarded with a sickening lightheadedness. His eyes swam dizzily. He tried to take in a deep breath, but that caused him to choke. There was a hot, salty taste in his mouth.

Leaning into the rain, he swayed. He gripped the rifle as tightly as he could (it was all that was left between him and certain death), but the feeling was leaving his fingers slowly, like water down a drain.

Another good flash of lightning came. His eyes searched the area. There was no one there. Dumont was gone. As far as Franklin J. Burns was concerned, anyway. How concerned *was* he now? *Very,* he thought.

I have to get to the house! I have to tell my family!

He was even more lost than before, but he walked in the direction he thought the farmhouse was. He could remember making a hundred lazy trips home from Hemlock's shack not even a year before. *I know where I am. I know where I am.* But did he know? *Yes I do. No, maybe not.*

He took a step forward. Then another. The third was a stagger, but he righted himself. The fourth one caused him to trip on something large. He fell forward, slamming his face into the muddy ground, the rifle tumbling from his grip.

In another flash of lightning he freed his tangled legs and looked at the object. It was Dumont, laying face down in the mud, his head partially submerged in a pool of muddy water, black strands of his beard floating up and encircling his head like a lion's mane. Frank closed his eyes and opened them. Another flash of lightning reaffirmed that it *was* Dumont. He reached out, grabbed the man by his hair and lifted his head up. His mouth hung open limply. Water collected together, ran down the end of his nose and chin, and dripped off in a steady stream. There was no doubt that Dumont was dead. *I'm pretty sure,* Frank thought. He dropped Dumont's head into the mud. *I'm pretty sure.* He reached across the terrible Frenchman to retrieve his gun, and that's when he saw that the other side of Dumont's head had been blown off, blood pooling around it. He jumped back and felt sick. He clamored to his feet and stood swaying in the storm. Then his knees buckled and he fell back to the ground. He lay on his back, staring up at the hysterical heavens.

Don't be hysterical, he thought very slowly, *I stopped him. Dumont is stopped.......dead.*

The rain beating down on his face hurt his eyes, so he closed them. And it felt *good* to close them. He could remember never wanting to go to bed as a child, and doing whatever he could to make his mother let him stay up just a little longer. That seemed absurd now.

Who, in their right mind.....would," he sighed deeply, his consciousness wandering, "ever *refuse sleep?*

His delirious mind thought back to the snow-covered field between his house and Hemlock's. A long time ago, he could remember barreling across that field in terrible cold with Whiley, in pursuit of a deer. He could remember having to stop every five minutes or so and call back to Whiley. *"Come on, Whiley! Come on! We'll lose him!"*

But now, in the dream Frank saw, lying in the mud on a warm, stormy summer night nearly two years later, there was something different. It was the same day, the same cold, the same deer, but *Whiley* was in front of the chase, calling back to *Frank.*

"Come on Frank! Come on, hurry up!"

"Whiley," Frank muttered aloud in the mud, "Whiley! The deer is *this* way!"

Fifteen minutes later the last of the storm blew out. The rain stopped, the wind died down, and the only lightning was silent lightning in the east. All was calm. Slowly, nature uncoiled itself and looked about. The crickets took up their nightly song. Birds peeked out carefully from their protective branches. Coated animals shook themselves dry and prepared to prowl the night.

Chapter Sixty-three

Wednesday morning Carmin Jones sat at his desk, looking very tired. He picked up the last pages of a four-page, handwritten report that he had prepared, and reread it for the hundredth time. Charley stood at the window, gazing out at the low, gray sky. In the west, it was beginning to show signs of clearing.

Turning, he glanced at the clock. "Nearly ten, Chief," he said.

Carmin acknowledged the comment with a silent nod of his head and read faster. When he finished, he took out his pen and signed the bottom, *'Carmin Jones, Chief of Police, Village of Fairchild, Cumberland County, Michigan.'*

Putting the report away, he rose and went to the door where Charley waited. They headed out and walked down the street in silence.

Everything's drying out, Charley thought to himself. The rain had stopped that Sunday night, but the sky had remained overcast. A closed sign hung in the window of the mercantile. Charley thought about the checkered wool jacket that hung in the store. He sure did admire that jacket.

Carmin Jones thought about retirement, seriously, for the first time. He wondered who would replace him. Charley? Perhaps. Then again, perhaps not. Charley was a good man, but Carmin thought he lacked the imagination for the job. In any case, he was too tired then to give it much thought.

They turned, passed the gate, and walked into the churchyard, stopping just midway between the gate and the front of the church. The long row of buggies indicated that the church was filled to capacity. Horses occasionally snorted and continuously swished their tails in silent, huffy impatience.

The road heading south out of Fairchild climbed a hill on its way out, and ran parallel to the church cemetery. Parked at the top of the hill, looking down at the church with Fairchild behind it, and the rest of Cumberland County stretching to the horizon beyond that, was a mud-splattered Ford. A young man dressed in a black suit stood beside it, hat in hand, tears in his eyes.

The grim, mournful peal of the bell sounded repeatedly, echoing over the landscape. The double doors of the church opened and Moses Clark stepped out to secure them. He was followed by the preacher. Six men labored behind him, carrying the solid oak coffin. John Burns appeared next, his arm wrapped around Agnes securely, not so much in affection, but as a tool to help the woman walk. Then the girls, Rachel and Caroline, emerged, their faces stained with tears.

Carmin and Charley waited until the last of the congregation was out and then fell in behind, respectfully. At the grave site, they stood back a bit from the others.

"Boy," Charley whispered, "they sure have had their share, losing two boys like that. I don't know how they can take it."

Carmin kept his eyes on the site and whispered back, "Charley, for some folks, it seems their burdens never end. But they'll survive. They got the faith."

To this, Charley nodded.

The preacher began reading from the book. When he had finished from the scripture, Carmin and Charley turned and headed back. Augie Johnson's wife walked by, crying softly into her handkerchief, flanked supportively by Augie on one side and Harry Medwick on the other. Neither man could say anything to console the woman.

As he walked, Harry felt the envelope in the breast pocket of his suit crinkle. He had just received it that day. It was a letter of acceptance from a school out east, his one way ticket to civilization. It was a letter he knew he would not respond to.

At the church gate Carmin and Charley met up with Doc Spencer, who had just emerged from the church. He had waited until the service moved outside before paying his own private respects.

"Good day, Doc," said Carmin.

"Gentlemen," he said, "I have in my office a bottle of very good Irish whiskey and after what has transpired the last couple of days, I think we all need a good drink."

Charley looked expectantly at Carmin. Carmin thought for a moment and said, "Charley and I would be honored."

The three men headed for Doc's office.

Chris Huntington was not a religious man, thus he had chosen not to attend the church service. But he was there, watching from atop Cemetery Hill as the procession left the church and made its way to the grave site. His eyes fell on the giant of a man, walking slowly. Chris knew that was Frank's father. It couldn't be anyone else. The resemblance was just too striking.

He thought about his own father and wondered if it wasn't too late. Maybe he would go home, let the bitterness go, and make peace *before* it was too late. Chris was aware, for the first time, how fragile life was. Yes, *"Too late"* could be twenty years in the future, but it could also be next week, tomorrow, that afternoon, in a few minutes...

...or right now.

He watched the service from his hilltop vantage point. Then it was over and the crowd began to disperse. Behind him came the shrill whistle of an approaching train. He turned in the direction of the sound, but could not see it through the woods. He turned back toward the town. He could see the depot about 500 yards beyond the church, and sure enough the train he heard appeared there after a minute or so, pulling up to the platform. Chris watched as three men alighted, three grim-faced men dressed in very expensive suits. He knew these kind of men, which is why they stuck out of the otherwise ordinary crowd coming off the train. All his life he had watched them pass in and out of his father's bank. Then a fourth man appeared and moved to catch up with the first three. His clothes were not as expensive, but he did not look so grim. He walked with a confident swagger, his red hair mussing in the breeze.

That was enough of that. Chris slipped a cigar from his pocket and clenched it between his teeth. He did not light it, but looked down at the cemetery one last time.

"So long, Bucko," he said with a melancholy shudder. He opened the door to the Ford, threw his hat in the front seat and got into the car. Sitting there with his fingers wrapped around the steering wheel, he sighed deeply. Ahead, the road would lead to Blackwing. Behind, the road would take him home. There was nothing left in Blackwing. At home there was his father, and a lot of healing to do. He decided he'd better get to it. It was going to be a long trip, but he was going home, for the first time in many years.

He whipped the Ford around and drove down the opposite side of Cemetery Hill. As the car gathered speed, bright sunshine burst through the clouds, sending zebra stripes across the land before him. This cheered Chris a little. Ahead he saw the backs of two small boys walking. Straw hats crowned their heads. On their shoulders they carried cane poles. They turned as Chris approached, smiles unfolding on the mouths. They waved excitedly as the flivver blew by them. Chris waved back. He scratched a lucifer and lit the cigar, blowing a puff of pale, blue smoke against the windshield.

A little while later, he saw the boys' destination, nestled in a small valley alongside the road. It was a lake, the now bright sunshine enhancing its deep blue.

God it's beautiful, thought Chris. *Life is beautiful. Fragile, but beautiful. Worth the ride, come what may.*

His attention was divided between the road and the lake. He was going in the wrong direction to notice the weathered signpost and the peeling black letters, which proclaimed to all who passed that this was Cumberland County.

About the Author

John P. Schroeder was born on January 4th, 1935 in Ashland, Wisconsin, where he attended school. He sailed on the Great Lakes for three years, in addition to working as a retail grocery clerk.

He was an easy-going man, who strived to make the best out of any situation. He had an appreciation for nature, which shines through vividly in his writing. John was an avid fisherman and outdoorsman, often referring to Fish Creek in Northern Wisconsin as his "second home". After becoming disabled from illness, John "retired" and took up writing.

Married, with three children and four grandchildren, John P. Schroeder was a writer in the purest sense of the word. He never let his increasingly debilitating illness keep him from his work. Though started late in life, writing remained a deep passion for him, right up until his death on May 11, 1993.

Paradigm Press is proud to make the works of this very talented man available to the public.